T0060633

CARAVANS IN THE DARK

CARAVANS in the DARK

A NOVEL

B. K. OLDRE

She Writes Press

Copyright © 2023, B. K. Oldre

All rights reserved. No part of this publication may be reproduced, distributed, or transmitted in any form or by any means, including photocopying, recording, digital scanning, or other electronic or mechanical methods, without the prior written permission of the publisher, except in the case of brief quotations embodied in critical reviews and certain other noncommercial uses permitted by copyright law. For permission requests, please address She Writes Press.

Published 2023
Printed in the United States of America
Print ISBN: 978-1-64742-434-3
E-ISBN: 978-1-64742-435-0
Library of Congress Control Number: 2022919246

For information, address:
She Writes Press
1569 Solano Ave #546
Berkeley, CA 94707

Interior Design by Kiran Spees

She Writes Press is a division of SparkPoint Studio, LLC.

All company and/or product names may be trade names, logos, trademarks, and/or registered trademarks and are the property of their respective owners.

This is a work of fiction. Names, characters, places, and incidents either are the product of the author's imagination or are used fictitiously. Any resemblance to actual persons, living or dead, is entirely coincidental.

In Memory of Václav Ladislav Holý, 1886–1942

Václav Ladislav Holý is just one of the many little-known men and women who lost their lives fighting for freedom. He was a merchant, a Sokol worker, an army corporal in WWI, and a member of the anti-fascist resistance. He was executed by the Nazis in Pardubice, Czechoslovakia, on June 5, 1942.

I was inspired to dedicate this book to Václav Ladislav Holý because I like to think that he may have been a distant relative. Like him, my Holý ancestors came from Southern Bohemia.

CHAPTER 1

Jana tiptoed into the pond, trying to avoid stepping on sharp stones and branches. She shivered as goose bumps blossomed on her naked flesh. It was a hot day for the beginning of October, but cold nights had chilled the water. When she'd waded in, waist deep, the sand turned to mud that squished through her toes, and each footstep sank in ankle-deep, stirring up swirls of muck.

She took a deep breath, fell forward, and thrashed forward, then back. A dark tangle of hair enveloped her face every time she raised it for a breath. She took another gulp of air, then floated, facedown, and opened her eyes. The weeds disappeared into the shadowy depths beneath the shimmering, light-green water. She rolled over on her back, floated, and gazed up into the canopy of green and gold leaves that bent over the pond, sheltering it from the blazing autumn sun and clear blue sky.

What a relief to get out of those hot sticky clothes. Jana was fifteen years old, and she was considered a young woman, so she had to wear long skirts. Not long ago, whenever she could, she would run around with the rest of the children, without thinking about what she should wear. Now, she was expected to stay covered up no matter how hot it was.

She would be in trouble if her stepmother, Zofie, who thought she was collecting apples, found out she'd been wasting her time swimming, instead. She hoped her stupid little brother, Ion, age twelve, wouldn't find her. She had practically raised him. But lately, he seemed to enjoy annoying her by following her everywhere she went and threatening to tell on her.

Today she'd outsmarted him by staying around camp and helping Zofie with the smaller children until he got bored and wandered off. When she was sure he had gone, she'd told Zofie she knew where she could find an apple tree in the woods, took a bag, and left. As soon as she was out of sight of the camp, she tucked her skirt up between her legs, and into her waistband, and ran.

They'd camped in this spot many times before, and she knew the paths through the woods that led to the pond. She'd often explored this area when she could slip away. The rest of the family seldom came here. The stream near their campsite provided water for cooking, washing, and drinking, and few of the others knew how to swim.

Jana sometimes liked to be alone, which wasn't easy living in a large extended family. They thought it was odd, but they made allowances for the "poor orphan girl" who had helped raise her younger brother and sister after her mom had died giving birth to Lili. She didn't want their pity. She was glad her dad had remarried, and now she was determined to enjoy what remained of her childhood.

She wasn't in a hurry to get married. Most of the girls her age could talk of nothing else. It was this boy was so handsome. He could handle a horse so well. Or their wedding would be so big and elaborate. But Jana saw that married women had to stay close to camp, cook, clean, and tend babies, and she had done plenty of that already.

Jana pushed aside the painful memories of her mother's last days, the fever, her father's frantic efforts to get her to the doctor—all of it too late. That was followed by a dark time. Tiny little Lili crying weakly, Ion too young to understand why his mother was gone, her father gone too often, and too often drunk. The aunts and Grandma

Berta helped when they could, but Jana had been the one who was always there.

Her father was happier since he'd remarried four years ago, and Jana hoped that would last. Her stepmother, Zofie, was young—more like an older sister than a mother—and still counted on Jana's help. Now, he was becoming annoyed with her refusal to consider any of the matches he suggested, and it was becoming embarrassing for him. She hated to cause him any bother, but perhaps she could postpone the inevitable a while longer.

Jana considered all this as she floated on her back; strands of her dark hair that had escaped the long braid down her back fanned out around her head like an exotic water lily. She wondered how much longer she could stay here and still have time to gather the apples, and then get back to camp before she was missed. A snapping branch startled her out of her reverie. She stood up to see what was there, but streams of water and tangles of hair obscured her sight.

"Who's there? Is that you, Ion? You idiot! I'll give you a thrashing when I catch you! How dare you spy on me!"

She heard a deep laugh and caught sight of a glint of metal behind some bushes. Her heart beat faster as she realized it wasn't Ion but a stranger. A *Gadjo*! She clamored toward her clothing piled on the shore and, while pulling on her clothes, swore and cursed, first in Romani then in Czech.

"Damn you and your mother! May you break out in boils, you devil! How dare you creep around in the bushes, you slimy worm!" she railed, replacing fear with anger.

He laughed again and then turned and strolled off. She noticed that he was wearing a gray uniform. The kind the German soldiers wore.

They'd seen a line of marching soldiers, just a few days ago. They'd slipped off the road and watched from a thicket of woods. It was never a good idea to be seen if you could avoid it. They'd also seen peasants, their belongings piled in horse-drawn carts or pickup trucks, heading away from the border. They looked tense and worried, and most of them spoke Czech. The soldiers followed the next day, striding along confidently and smiling.

Jana continued toward the apple tree, which was at the edge of a farmer's field and seldom picked. She'd never seen anyone around, and there were always apples covering the ground under the tree at this time of the year. She tucked her skirts up and hopped over the fence. She kept an eye out for the farm dog that she'd seen at other times, a medium-sized, black and white dog, as she quickly filled her bag.

The scent of ripe apples filled her nostrils as she bent to pick out the best ones from those strewn beneath the tree. Most of them were wormy, bruised, or green—those she left behind. A few were edible, though misshapen; a few were perfectly ripe and unblemished apples, and she stopped to admire them before adding them to her bag.

When her bag was almost full, she was interrupted by the dog who streaked across the open field, his teeth bared. She turned to face him, knowing that running would only encourage him to chase her. He came to a halt, a few yards away from her, haunches down as he barked and growled at her. She said, softly, "Good boy, nice boy," hoping he'd remember her voice from past times when she'd come with little treats for him in her pocket. Unfortunately, she didn't have anything for him today. She backed toward the fence, felt for a post, and when she touched one, whirled around and leaped over the fence. The dog raced toward her and caught the hem of her skirt, tearing it as she jumped. She ran down the path, shaking and laughing, at her narrow escape.

When she got back to camp, a couple of hours later, Jana was relieved, but also a little disappointed, that no one had missed her. Everyone stood together at the end of camp closest to the road to town. Jana's father, Josef, was in the center surrounded by the other men. The women, some carrying babies, formed the next circle, and the children ran in and out between the adults. Jana set the bag of apples on the table next to their wagon and joined the group.

"I don't know what it means, except trouble," Josef was saying. He looked worried. He was the oldest man of the family, and hence the leader of a group of twenty-three, which included his family, his mother, and his three brothers and their families. The role didn't suit him. He was never sure that he was making the right decisions.

"Trouble for the *Gadje*—but what has it got to do with us?" said Uncle Emil. A frown on his plump and usually cheerful face turned down the corners of his big mustache. Uncle Emil didn't like to stir things up. He always avoided trouble if possible.

Jana found her sister, Lili, age nine, with the women. Lili was quiet and responsible for her age. She preferred to stay close to home rather than to run with the other children.

"What's going on?" Jana asked.

"Daddy says there are lots of soldiers in town—Germans. He says it means trouble, and we should pack up and go, but some of the uncles say it has nothing to do with us and that they want to stay for the harvest festival," Lili said.

They came to Teplice every year for the Harvest Festival. The women told fortunes and sold herbs while the men traded horses. It was considered a prosperous stop, and they'd been looking forward to it. They counted on earning much-needed income before heading for their winter campsite.

Zofie pushed her way through the crowd. "Where were you all

afternoon, Jana? And why is your hair wet?" she asked, trying to look angry, but succeeding only in looking frazzled. She had baby Eduard on one hip, and Jana's little stepsister, Anna, was hanging on to her skirt, whimpering for attention. Without waiting for an answer, she continued, "I need you to help me so I can gather some wood and get dinner started." She handed the baby to Jana and, picking up Anna, headed back toward their wagon. "Go get some water, Lili. Come on, girls! Let the men talk. We have work to do."

Jana sighed and hung back to see if she could catch more of the conversation.

"From the looks of things, I doubt if the town will have a festival this year," Josef said.

Jana turned and followed her sister and stepmother. That evening, after they ate, the men sat together at Grandma Berta's campfire and talked in low voices until late into the night. Jana could still hear the low rumble of their voices as she drifted off to sleep between the two feather quilts she shared with Lili and little Anna.

The next day dawned bright and cold. Jana let the morning unfold slowly around her, listening to the familiar sounds. The birds were singing, the horses stomped and snorted, the women were building fires and filling kettles with water, the small children and babies whimpered for food, and their mothers soothed them in low voices, trying not to disturb those who were still sleeping. Jana could smell the coffee beans Zofie was roasting on a shallow metal pan over the campfire.

The daylight danced through her closed eyelids, and soon Anna started squirming and kicking. Jana's eyes flew open as she remembered the events of the previous day. Would they be staying for the festival or moving on? She reached out to where she had dropped her clothes into a pile next to their bed the night before and pulled them on while still under the covers. She nudged Lili who was still snoring.

"Wake up, Lili, it's morning." Lili sat up and rubbed her eyes.

Jana walked behind the wagon to the washing-stand, poured cold stream water into the washbasin, and washed vigorously. She cleaned her teeth with salt applied with one finger, combed her hair and rebraided it. After she'd finished, she joined the family sitting by the campfire on the other side of the wagon. Coffee was boiling, and stew left over from last night was heating up. The family ate the stew with bread and some of the apples Jana had gathered yesterday and washed it down with sweetened black coffee.

Zofie ate—mostly standing—bringing more coffee to Josef, blowing on little Anna's food to cool it, and feeding baby Eduard. She hovered nervously—looking even more tired and worried than usual.

"Are we going to stay or move on?" she asked Josef.

"We've decided to stay for a few days and see if there will be a festival," Josef said.

"In that case, I'd like to go into town today," Zofie said. "I need to do some shopping, and I can tell fortunes and make a little money. Perhaps I can also find out if there will be a festival this year or not."

"I don't know if it's safe. I haven't registered us with the police yet. I didn't know if we were going to stay."

"When is it ever safe? If I run out of milk for the baby, and we have to get it from a farmer, that might not be safe either."

Josef sighed. "Well, if you're going, take Jana with you. She can help keep watch and earn a little something, too."

"But, Papa . . ."

"Don't 'but Papa' me. You're not a child anymore, and it's time you stopped acting like one. No more sneaking off by yourself! Who knows what people will start to think—and then how will I find you a husband?"

Jana felt her face flush with anger and clenched her jaw. She knew that arguing with him wouldn't change his mind, and wouldn't end well. Papa would get angry and take it out not just on her, but on the rest of the family, too. She turned and walked away, without another word.

Jana helped Zofie wash the dishes and hang the sleeping quilts up to air and dry, and then they left the baby with Grandma Berta. Anna begged to go with them, so they took her along and walked to town. Ion and Lili had already run off to play with the other children.

The town looked very different than it had when they had been here last year. Then there was a bustling marketplace. Now there wasn't any sign of a market. Instead, soldiers marched through the streets and hung around in small groups on corners and in the marketplace.

Most of the village people didn't seem angry with the soldiers. They smiled and nodded at them as they passed. But some stared angrily at them when they weren't looking. Jana wondered why. She noticed, as she walked through the crowd and listened to their conversations, that the smiling villagers spoke German, and the angry ones spoke Czech. It was clear that the residents of German ethnicity were in the majority in this village, and they were happy with the occupation.

Zofie ignored the soldiers and approached the villagers, asking if they wanted their fortunes told or begging for coins. After approaching several women, one finally agreed to have her fortune told. Zofie held her hand, palm up, bent over it, and seemed to examine it intently.

Jana watched with little interest. She had seen this many times before. While seeming to focus on the palm, Zofie was watching closely for a reaction as she made some general pronouncements about health, money, and relationships—the things people usually wanted to know. Jana also kept an eye on Anna as she strayed away from her mother.

From behind her, a deep voice, speaking in German, asked, "Will you tell me my fortune?"

She turned and looked up into the smiling blue eyes of a soldier. "If you cross my palm with a coin," she responded in German.

As he dug into his pocket, she examined him. There was something familiar about this tall *Gadjo* with the blond hair and blue eyes. But what? And why were his two friends smiling and nudging each other so idiotically? She shrugged. Who could understand the *Gadje*?

"Here are two coins so that you will tell me about a lucky future," he said.

Jana slipped them quickly into her pocket and took his right hand, palm up, in both of hers. The hand was firm and hard. A workingman's hand. Probably a farmer.

"What is your name?" she asked

"Won't the Spirits tell you?" he replied.

"I can see nothing if you are not open." She dropped his hand.

"I'm Franz, and I certainly want you to see . . . and be seen," he said with a smirk.

"You are very far from home." She started with something very likely. She watched him out of the corner of her eyes. His grin widened.

"Those you have left behind miss you very much. You've left someone special." Why was he grinning and casting those sidelong looks at his buddies? What was it that they found so damn funny?

"But she is not the one for you," she continued.

"She is sleeping with your brother," she said, in Romani, annoyed by his grin.

“What?”

“There will be another. She will be your true love,” she said in German.

“Ask her if she’ll have her clothes on when you meet her,” called out one of his friends.

He laughed, and she realized who he was. He was the man in the woods!

She cast his hand aside and said coldly, “That’s all I see.”

“I saw a good deal more.” He laughed, playing to his friends. They were all laughing at her now.

Jana flushed with anger and spat at his feet. “And both of you will die violent deaths. You will curse the day you met her.” Then she whirled around and stalked away, with their laughter ringing in her ears.

Zofie looked up from her palm reading. “Jana! Where is Anna?”

Jana caught sight of her running around a corner, chasing a small brown dog. “I’ll get her,” Jana called back.

She ran around the corner in time to see Anna round another corner. She chased after her, calling, “Come back here, you little brat.”

She caught up with her in front of a gate of a fenced yard. Inside the fence, a couple of dogs were barking wildly at Anna as she tried to pick up the small brown dog, its front legs in the air and the rear ones trying desperately to regain a foothold on the ground. Its eyes were wide in terror.

“Hold still. Hold still,” Anna was telling the dog.

“Come on now. Put that dog down,” Jana said.

“No! I want to keep it!”

“You can’t keep it. It belongs to someone in the village. We have plenty of dogs.”

“No! It’s mine!” Anna wailed.

"Get out of here, you thieving Gypsies!" a gruff voice said in German.

The startled girls whirled around. Anna dropped the dog, which lost no time in making his getaway. They saw a disheveled old man glaring at them over the fence.

"You heard me! I said beat it!"

"We were just leaving," Jana said.

She grabbed her little sister's hand and pulled her back toward the town square, ignoring the plaintive cries that she wanted "her" little dog. When they arrived, Zofie was nowhere in sight. Jana wandered across the square, wondering where she had gone. Franz called out to her as she walked past him. "She's left town. She got kicked out," he said.

"Kicked out? By who?"

"The SS. They're in charge now. She went that way." He pointed in the direction from which they had come into town.

His smile seemed friendly enough, but she wondered if he was telling the truth.

A tall, unpleasant-looking man, dressed in black, approached them.

"I thought I told your kind to get out of here! There will be no begging or stealing in this town!" he barked.

Jana picked up Anna and ran as fast as she could in the direction the friendly soldier had indicated. She caught up with Zofie, who was waiting for her at the crossroad, and they walked back to camp.

Jana's father and Uncle Emil were sitting smoking by the smoldering remains of their morning fire. They looked up curiously at their unexpectedly early return.

"How did it go?" Josef asked.

Jana excitedly related the events of the morning. Zofie sank down next to Josef and rested her chin on both hands, just nodding from time to time in confirmation. Anna ran off to find the other children.

"It's as I thought," Josef said to Emil. "I think we'd better act fast now that they know we're here. I've heard strange things about these German soldiers, and the ones they call the SS."

Papa and Uncle Emil started toward Grandma Berta's wagon. Jana tagged along hoping to hear what they would decide.

"Stay with Zofie," Papa commanded.

"I'm just going to get the baby," Jana said.

"Never mind, I'll bring him when I return." He glared at her until she retreated to their campsite.

CHAPTER 2

Franz stayed on the corner after Jana and Anna had left town. His friends went to get a beer, but he wasn't ready to go inside yet. He wanted to stay outside and enjoy the good weather a little longer. He told them he'd catch up with them later, and then leaned against a lamppost and lit a cigarette.

As he smoked, he noticed a small brown dog as it wandered around the square. Its slightly crooked tail never stopped wagging as it sniffed the benches and lampposts. It wandered over to him and sniffed his boots. It reminded him of the little stray dog that was always begging for scraps in his home village. It made the rounds daily and seemed to do pretty well. It had grown fat and glossy.

"Aren't you the dog that the little Gypsy girl was chasing?" he asked it, as he scratched it behind its ears. It wagged its tail even faster.

After a few minutes, the dog wandered on, over to the black-clad SS officers, and began sniffing around them. One of them looked down as it sniffed his boots. Then the little dog lifted one leg and started to pee on the boot he'd been sniffing. "Stupid Jew mutt!" he shrieked, and viciously kicked the dog, sending it flying. It howled in pain and ran away yelping. The SS men laughed heartily and strolled away.

Franz watched, frozen in place, the cigarette suspended in midair. His face grew hot, and he choked back a curse.

"You swine!" he wanted to cry out. But his mother had taught him, "It's better to say one word too few than one word too many."

He took one last angry drag on the cigarette, threw it down, and ground it out with his boot. Now he was ready for a beer. He headed in the direction of the tavern where his friends had gone.

Along the way, he thought he heard whimpering from a narrow alley that ran between two buildings in the square. Peering down the alley, he saw the little dog, partially hidden in a pile of trash. He approached it slowly and crouched down to pet it. When his hand touched the dog's side, it yelped in pain.

"You poor little thing!" he said. *It must have a broken rib*, he thought.

He picked it up gently, trying not to cause any more pain, a little worried that it might bite him. Its eyes were wide with terror, but it did not struggle. He carried it out of the alley and down a street, wondering what he should do with it. He certainly couldn't keep it. He wondered if he should shoot it and put it out of its misery. But a shot would attract attention, and then he would have to explain. He was starting to regret trying to help the little dog. *Maybe I should leave it. Perhaps it will find its way home*, he thought.

As he walked along, wondering what to do, he passed a fenced yard, and several dogs in the yard started barking and jumping at the fence. An elderly man struggled out of an old, rusty lawn chair and poked his head over the fence.

"Who's there?" he snarled. When he saw the soldier, his expression changed suddenly to an ingratiating smile.

"Oh, pardon, sir. I thought it was those thieving Gypsies again."

"What? You saw them?"

"The little one had a dog. Is that the same dog?"

He seems to be trying to ingratiate himself to me. Perhaps I can leave the dog with him, Franz thought.

"Yes. It's my dog. That is, I found it. I think it's a stray. I asked the

Gypsy children to take care of it for me, but it got away from them, and then it got hurt," he improvised, hoping his story was plausible. "I think it might have a broken rib."

The old man shuffled to the gate, his bedroom slippers scuffing over the beaten-down dirt of his front yard, leaving little puffs of dust behind him. He yelled at his dogs to lie down, and swung his cane at them, his ancient sweater flapping like the wings of a tattered old bird until they retreated to the shade under the porch. He cracked the gate open and peered at the dog, and then at Franz. His face reflected a mix of obsequiousness, concern, and craftiness.

"Well, you can't expect much from Gypsies," he said. "I hope you didn't pay them yet," he said, emphasizing the last part of the sentence.

"No, not yet." Franz picked up the hint. "But I would be willing to pay you if you could take care of the little mutt. I think its ribs need to be taped, and just a little food and water. If you are willing to take it in, I can pay you something now, and more when I come back to see how he's doing."

"Come in, come in," he cajoled. "I'm sure we can come to an arrangement. Just shut the gate behind you."

He shuffled toward the door. The dogs ran out, barking, from under the porch, but he banished them with more cane swinging and cursing.

The shades were drawn and, at first, Franz couldn't see anything as they entered the house. It smelled of dust and dogs. As his eyes adjusted to the dim light, Franz saw a living room, filled to overflowing with worn and faded furniture, and piled on top of it, newspapers, magazines, papers, and books. The old man moved several piles of newspapers off the sofa and onto the floor. He gestured toward it.

"Won't you have a seat, Private . . . ?"

"Private Schmidt. And you are?"

"Mr. Pavlik. Can I offer you something to drink, Private Schmidt?"

"Thank you. That would be very nice." He sat down, holding the dog on his lap. The dusty smell billowed up from the upholstery as he sank into it.

After an interminable shuffling and clanging, Mr. Pavlik reappeared with two somewhat smudged glasses filled with warm beer, gave one to Franz, and sat on the opposite end of the sofa.

Franz took a sip and noticed, with surprise, that it was pretty good. "A good beer," he commented.

"Thank you. It's a Pilsner. One of the things Czechs do well. One of the few, I'm sure. No doubt your German beers are superior, but still, as you say, a good beer. Are you a beer drinker, Private?"

"I enjoy a glass from time to time, but I'm more accustomed to wine. My family owns a small vineyard."

"Indeed? What part of Germany are you from?"

"A small village in the southwest, not far from France."

"So, you are a long way from home."

The comment made him think of the Gypsy fortune-teller. She'd said the same thing.

Franz's father had often hired Roma people to help harvest the grapes in their vineyard. The grapes grew on steep hillsides and had to be tended and picked by hand. At harvest time, it was crucial to get the crops in as quickly as possible, while they were at their peak of ripeness, and before the weather turned rainy and caused the grapes to rot.

Before he was old enough to help with the harvest, he'd played with the Gypsy children whenever he got a chance. His parents tried to discourage him, but they were too busy at harvest time to keep an eye on him, and he would slip away.

"I can't tell you how glad I am that you Germans are here in the

Sudetenland. We ethnic Germans have put up with too much from these Czechs."

"You don't say."

"You saw how the crowds greeted you. They were delirious."

"Yes, very nice."

Franz had been pleased to be welcomed, just as they had been when they marched into Austria, but he felt uncomfortable with the old man's attempts to ingratiate himself and changed the topic to the unusually mild weather. They sipped their beers, shared a few observations about the weather, and haggled a bit over the price before agreeing.

When they'd struck a deal, Franz handed over the little dog. The old man handled him gently, crooning to him, as he laid him down next to him.

"I will take good care of him; you can be sure of that. What's his name?" Mr. Pavlik asked.

Franz paused and thought for a moment. "Rikono," he said, remembering that he'd heard Gypsy children using that word for "dog."

"Rikono, Rikono," Mr. Pavlik repeated, stroking the dog.

They finished their beer. Franz gave Mr. Pavlik the amount they had agreed on and promised to come back when he could. With a handshake, he was on his way. Mr. Pavlik walked him to the gate. This time the dogs seemed to know that he was not a threat and they merely lifted their heads and growled a little.

"Don't worry, I'll take good care of him," Mr. Pavlik assured him once again.

Franz brushed the brown fur off his gray jacket as he walked to the tavern. He decided not to mention the incident to his friends Paul and Rolf. They would tease him unmercifully about it.

They had known each other their whole lives. They were from the same village, they had gone to school together, and drafted together. Rolf was excited about being in the army, and thought of it as a big adventure, as playing soldiers had been when they were kids. He had liked being in the Hitler Youth and had swallowed the whole program.

Paul and Franz, on the other hand, had tried not to have anything more to do with the Hitler Youth than they had to. All that marching and the endless yammering on about the master race and racial hygiene seemed like a silly waste of time. He knew plenty of Germans who weren't so great, and some non-Germans who were just fine.

Like his parents, Franz wasn't convinced that Hitler was what Germany needed. They had listened to a few of his radio broadcasts and had been put off by them. His family was too busy to pay much attention to politics, but they were not opposed to Hitler, either.

"Let him have his chance," they'd said.

After the years of unemployment, and news about strikes, riots, and government chaos, if people were working, and law and order maintained, that was the main thing. The rest was just politics, according to his parents. Nothing but a lot of talk to get people stirred up.

Paul and Franz felt that their lives were interrupted when drafted, and just wanted to put in their two years and get out. Rolf was thinking about making the army his career.

"Where have you been?" Rolf and Paul cried as he joined them at their table.

"I just lost track of time," Franz said.

"Daydreaming as usual," Paul said.

"Or were you chasing after the Zigeuner girl?" Rolf said with a smirk.

"Never mind all that. Just buy me a beer," Franz said.

CHAPTER 3

When Josef came back from talking it over with his mother and brothers, he announced they would leave that night. They'd all agreed that it was dangerous to stay, though they hated to give up the profit from the sale of the horses, which they'd been counting on. They had a dozen horses that they had hoped to sell, in addition to the four they kept to pull the caravans.

"We'll head away from the border and find a safe place to camp for the winter. Perhaps things will be back to normal by next spring. We should pack up this afternoon and leave after supper. We'll head south—staying away from the main roads—then head into the woods to find a spot to camp overnight," Josef said.

"I need to get milk for the baby," Zofie said.

"Why didn't you get it while you were in town?"

"I told you, the soldiers kicked us out. I didn't have a chance."

"Well, we'll have to make do. Perhaps Antonie or Marianna will let you have some," Josef said. Antonie was Uncle Emil's wife, and Marianna was married to Uncle Tony.

"I don't want to ask them." Zofie flushed, thinking of how they smirked and gave each other sidelong glances because she wasn't able to breastfeed her baby. "I think I'll go to the farmer's house to buy some milk. We've bought milk from them before."

"Well, go quickly, then. We need to eat and get the wagon packed up before dark. I want to get a few miles down the road before we camp tonight."

Zofie got the gallon-sized milk can, tied the baby on her hip with a large scarf, and called to Jana to come along to help her.

It was about a mile down the road to the farmer's house. The sun slanted across the peaceful fields. The wind had turned chilly. Jana swung the milk can by her side, and Zofie crooned softly to baby Eduard as they walked briskly along.

The black and white dog barked as it ran to meet them. They strode forward, ignoring it while it circled them barking and baring its teeth. The farmer's wife poked her graying head out the door of the house to see what was causing all the commotion. She stood, squinting at them, with crossed arms and a suspicious look on her face. She wore a kerchief on her head, an apron over a flowered housedress, a shapeless gray sweater, and a pair of rubber boots. As they came closer, she seemed to recognize them from previous years. She had occasionally sold them milk, eggs, and butter, at two or three times more than the price she could usually get for it. She called to the dog.

"That's enough, Scruffy! Go lie down! Go lie down!" she commanded. The dog slowly sidled away, continuing to keep an eye on them.

"Beg your pardon, ma'am," Zofie said in her most ingratiating manner, "but we need some milk for the baby. If you can spare us a little, I would be very grateful, and would pay you well."

"I don't know if I have much to sell," she said, eyeing the size of the milk can.

"We'd be glad for whatever you can spare."

Then the farmer came around from the back of the house, clad in bib overalls and knee-high rubber boots. He had a big stomach and a belligerent look on his round, red face.

"What's this all about?" he asked his wife.

"They've come to buy milk," she replied.

"Come thieving, more likely," he said.

"No, sir," Zofie replied, in a supplicating tone. "We want to buy some milk for the little one." She thrust the baby toward him.

"Get that brat away from me! I saw her"—he pointed toward Jana—"stealing apples off my tree!"

"They were lying on the ground!" Jana retorted.

"That's it! Get going or I'll set the dog on you!" he shouted back.

"Oh, please, please!" Zofie begged.

"Scruffy, Scruffy, sic!" the farmer shouted.

The dog raced around the house, barking, with its teeth bared.

Zofie and Jana took off running at full speed, with little Eduard bobbling along on his mother's hip. The dog soon caught up with them and started nipping at their heels. Jana swung hard with the milk can and bonked him on the side of the head. He let out a yelp, turned around, and headed home.

Zofie scolded her all the way back to camp for being so careless and being seen while collecting the apples.

Josef was equally dismayed. He was also angry with Zofie.

"If you had just gone to Antonie or Marianna, as I told you to do, you would have been better off! Now we still have no milk and have wasted time. Now hurry and start supper, then pack up the wagon."

Zofie dashed around, barking orders at Jana and Lili.

"Gather some wood and get some water. Quickly!" She stayed in a bad mood all evening, making dire threats if the girls didn't work quickly enough. Josef glowered, his mustache tips pointing down and his face set in a frown. Ion had been sent to see to the horses; to be sure they were fed and watered before the journey began.

It was getting dark by the time they had extinguished the

campfires, packed the wagons, and gotten underway. The girls rode in the caravan with Zofie and the baby. Josef drove the wagon. His caravan was first, followed by Grandma's, and then the two younger brothers' caravans, followed by the extra horses.

As the wagon creaked and rumbled along, Zofie ignored Jana and talked to the other children.

After a time, Jana got bored. When Zofie was busy with the baby, she said, "I'm going to see what Ion is doing." She hopped out the back door of the slowly moving caravan before Zofie had a chance to stop her.

Jana waited until the wagons had passed and found Ion with the other older boys at the back, riding the horses. They each held the reins of another riderless horse.

"Ion, Ion, give me the reins!" Jana ran alongside him and called out.

"Forget it! Go back to the wagon where you belong."

"I can ride as well as you can. Please!" she implored. When he laughed at her, she yelled, "Just give it to me, or I'll pound you."

"Okay, okay. Suit yourself!" he said and flung the reins to her. She grabbed hold of the horse's neck and leaped onto his back.

"Ion," she said quietly, "I have an idea. Are you ready for some fun?"

"What kind of fun?" he asked.

"You know the farmers who wouldn't sell us some milk?"

"Yeah."

"What if we sneak over there and get some?"

"How? We'll get in trouble."

"Come on, don't be such a baby. We'll just ride over there. I'll sneak in the barn, while you hold the horses. I'll get the milk, and we'll be back before anyone knows we're missing."

"What about the dog? You said there was a dog that chased you."

"Don't worry about the dog." She pulled a wrapped-up chicken leg out of her pocket.

"And what are we going to say when Zofie wants to know where the milk came from?"

"Leave that to me. I'll think of something," she said.

"Okay, but if we get in trouble, I'm going to say you made me."

"I don't care. I'll get the milk can, and then I'll be back. Hang on to my horse."

She threw the reins to him and nimbly jumped off the horse. She ran up to her wagon. The uncles paid no attention to her when she ran past them. Kids always ran back and forth while the caravan moved along.

She managed to untie the milk can from the side of the wagon. She'd taken the precaution of not tying it on too tightly while packing up, in case she had a chance to go through with her plan. She wrapped the folds of her skirt around it, hoping nobody would look too closely, and ran back to Ion.

"Here," she said, handing it up to him.

She leaped back on her horse and took the reins.

"Let's fall back," she whispered. They slowed their horses and let the others pass them. Nicu, Emil's oldest son, rode along with them for a while, chattering away. But they both ignored him, and finally he gave up and rode ahead to find more interesting company.

When they went around a bend, they let the others disappear. Then Jana said, "Let's go!"

They wheeled their horses around and walked in the other direction. When they thought they were out of earshot, they kicked the horses and galloped off toward the farm.

The speed was exhilarating. The fresh wind washed over Jana's face, arms, and legs. As they neared the farm, they slowed the horses to a walk. They turned on a path into the woods that Jana knew led to the apple tree. She had planned that they would ride across the field and approach the barn from the back. Now that it was dark, they could do that without being seen.

They jumped their horses across the fence and made their way slowly across the field. Jana strained to hear any indication that the farmer, his wife, or the dog had spotted them. All was quiet as they got to the barn and dismounted.

"Hang on to my horse," Jana whispered as she took the milk can from her brother. "Take some of this chicken"—she gave him some, and kept some—"in case you see the dog."

She crept toward the back door of the barn. She waded through a pile of manure as she snuck toward the door in the dark and stifled a yelp of disgust. She slid the door to the side, and it groaned a little on its hinges. She stopped, listening for any reaction. But all she heard was her breath, which sounded like a roaring wind, and the restless movement of the cow in the barn.

She crept through the small opening in the door. The cow was facing away from her in the narrow stall. It craned its neck around, eyes wide with fear, and stamped its back feet.

"Hurry up!" Ion hissed through the door.

"Shut up!" she whispered.

She wedged her way in beside the cow and patted it on its side, murmuring to calm it, as she did with horses. Then, after removing the cover of the milk can, which she hooked on a nail, she leaned under the cow and milked into the can. The stream of milk made a pinging sound, and a cat startled her as it came meowing around the corner to see if it could get some milk. Jana ignored it, and working quickly, filled the can, replaced the cover, and slipped back out the door.

"I'll hold the horses—get on," she whispered. When Ion was on his horse, she handed him the milk can and jumped up on her horse.

"We have what we came for—let's ride straight to the road," she said. As they rode past the farmer's house, the dog came tearing out from under the porch, barking. They both tossed their chicken toward him and kicked their horses into a run. They laughed as they tore back down the road, gravel spraying out from under the horses' hooves.

After a half hour or so of fast riding, they caught back up with the others.

"Where were you?" the other boys asked.

"Oh, nowhere. Just for a ride." And though the boys begged, Jana and Ion wouldn't tell them.

Jana rode along with the boys until the caravan turned off on a path into the woods where they stopped for the night. She took the milk can and retied it to the side of the wagon. Then she went to the stream and washed her feet and legs, just downstream from where the boys were watering the horses. The water was icy cold. With her teeth chattering, she ran back to the wagon and nestled between the feather quilts with her sisters, who were nearly asleep. Lili asked sleepily, "Where were you?"

"Never mind. Go to sleep," Jana said, then rolled over and fell asleep, dreaming about the day's events.

The next day dawned bright and cold. Jana woke up to the odor of pine trees and coffee brewing, and the sound of wind in the pine trees. She jumped out of bed, smiling to herself over the adventures of the previous night. She watched as Zofie bustled around the campfire. After a while, Zofie went to get the milk can. She seemed resigned to having to appeal to one of her sisters-in-law for some milk for the baby, after all. When she unhooked it from the side of the wagon, her eyes opened wide with surprise, and then narrowed with suspicion.

"Oh, did I tell you? Somebody—Nicu, I think—brought that. I'm not sure where he got it," Jana said.

"I know you're lying. Don't think I don't," Zofie hissed. She glanced over at Papa, not wanting to get him stirred up.

Jana laughed, while Zofie glared at her.

They traveled several more days before settling in at a campsite. They'd camped here before. It was an abandoned farm, off a deserted logging road. The property, owned by a friendly farmer, couldn't be seen from the road. Water was available from an old well, and from a nearby stream.

They could get food and firewood from the woods. The boys could catch fish in the stream, and fashion snares to trap birds, squirrels, rabbits, and other small game. Papa knew a shop owner in the nearby village who was willing to sell them any supplies they needed, without asking too many questions. If they kept a low profile, they might be able to stay here through the winter.

The men constructed a shelter for the horses from saplings and canvas, for the cold months ahead. They would rather have had the money from selling the horses than extra horses to feed. But perhaps they would be able to do some horse-trading later. The days passed peacefully, and they settled into a quiet rhythm.

CHAPTER 4

A few days later, after everyone was asleep, the sound of horses and the murmur of low voices awakened Jana. She opened her eyes and peered around in the dark. Everyone else inside the caravan seemed to be sound asleep. She crept over to her parents' bed.

"Papa," she whispered. But then she saw that he was not there.

"Go back to sleep, Jana," Zofie whispered, then rolled over, pulling the blankets up around her.

Jana crept over to the window and peered out into the dark, trying to see anything moving. But the night was too dark. She decided that Papa must have gone out to check on the horses, went back to bed, and fell asleep again.

A few nights later, she was awakened again by the same sounds. This time, after checking her parents' bed and seeing that Papa was again missing, she pulled on her clothes as quietly as possible and crept outside. The cold night air made her teeth chatter, and goose bumps popped up on her arms. She clenched her teeth to stop the chattering and stood, frozen in place, her head cocked to one side, listening. Finally, she heard sounds again coming from the direction of the road. She ran quickly and quietly toward the sounds. She went around the bend in the path that led to their campsite and, there on the road, were the shadowy figures of three men and two horses.

Jana shrank into the edge of the forest, crouched down, watching intently.

One man was holding the reins of the horses as the others untied four large, heavy bags from the saddles. She listened intently; she couldn't make out what they were saying, but she recognized one of the voices as Papa's.

What's he doing out here in the middle of the night? she wondered.

Papa and the two strangers turned and walked down the path toward the camp. "We'll be back for this stuff tomorrow. We've bribed the man who will be on guard duty," one of them said as they passed.

She followed from a safe distance and watched as they put the bags into an old shed where they stored horse feed and then walked back toward the road.

Jana stole silently over to the shed and peered inside. It was pitch black. She wouldn't be able to see anything tonight. She decided she'd take a look tomorrow if she got a chance.

The next day she waited for an opportunity, and then slipped away and snuck into the storage shed. Inside it was dark and dusty and smelled of hay. She stifled a sneeze as she waited for her eyes to adjust to the dim light. Behind some bales of hay, and covered with a horse blanket, she found the four large burlap bags, tied shut with twine. She struggled with the knots and finally got one bag open. Inside there were a couple rolled-up blankets, cans of food, and loaves of bread.

That's odd, she thought. *It looks like camping supplies. But why would men sneak around in the middle of the night to hide camping supplies?*

She carefully retied the bag and replaced the horse blanket. She opened the door to the shed and Papa was standing there—hands on his hips and scowling. He grabbed her by the arm and shook her.

"What are you doing sneaking around? I suppose that was you I heard yesterday rustling in the bushes! Why are you always looking for trouble?"

"You're hurting me!"

"You don't know hurting! I ought to thrash you."

Jana was frightened. She had never seen her father this angry.

"Stop it or I'll yell, and then everyone will know your secret!"

He dropped her arm and paced back and forth, muttering to himself.

"All right, I'll explain, but I don't want any questions from you, and you have to promise not to tell anyone."

"I promise."

"Okay. Those men you saw me with last night are my cousin Vaclav's boys. They're trying to help some people stranded between the Czech and German lines. I don't want to go into any details."

"Why are they stranded?"

"I said no questions! The less you know, the better. Now go back where you belong and keep your mouth shut!"

Jana could tell he meant it. "I will," she promised.

Huddled over the small, smoky fire, a thin man, Alois, shivered in the cold, damp night air. He blew on the fire, trying to keep the feeble flame going as he fed another damp twig into the fire. It gave off a cloud of thick smoke, causing him to cough and his eyes to water.

His wife, Heda, sat nearby, silently rocking back and forth, holding their whimpering baby. Alois watched as Heda tried to make the baby more comfortable by stuffing grass around him, since they had no more dry diapers, but it didn't seem to help, and the poor thing cried all the time, except when he was sleeping. His cry had become a weak hiccup. Alois hoped the baby would drift off to sleep soon. Fortunately, Heda was breastfeeding the baby, so he'd not gone hungry, yet. But he knew if Heda didn't get more to eat than a few of the potatoes left behind by the harvesters, which they'd dug out of the field with their bare hands—the only thing they'd had to eat in the past few days—her milk would soon dry up.

Alois tried to ignore his chattering teeth and growling stomach. If he could get a decent fire going, they could roast the potatoes. He couldn't help but think about what they would be having for dinner if they were still at home—perhaps a beef roast, with carrots and onions, along with potatoes? Well, there was no use thinking about that, he told himself. It was all gone now.

Bitterness rose up inside him as he remembered how the Henleinists, ethnic Germans who supported the Nazis, had woken them up, pounding on their door in the middle of the night. There'd been about a half dozen of them—drunk, swaggering, and waving their guns around. They'd knocked him down and kicked him, while Heda screamed. Then they told them they had five minutes to collect their things and get out.

Heda had frantically packed a suitcase with clothes for the three of them and diapers for the baby. Meanwhile, Alois had stuffed his pockets with watches, jewelry, and anything of value he could grab. Heda'd filled a bag with food while he ripped a blanket off of their bed and rolled it up to take along. Then they had been forced out of their house and into the back of a truck.

He'd watched as their small stucco cottage, which they'd moved into only last year while expecting their first child, receded from view as they were taken for a wild ride through the sleeping town and out into the country. A few miles outside of town, German soldiers stopped the truck, ordered them out, and forced them to walk down the road, away from their home.

Since then, they wandered the no-man's-land between the German and the Czech armies. They'd tried, several times, to sneak back home, but they were always caught and turned back at gunpoint by

German soldiers guarding the new border. Then they tried going the other way but were turned back by the Czech soldiers, who guarded their side of the border. The Czechs had apologized, but explained that their government feared an influx of refugees. They had been ordered to turn everyone back for the time being.

Finally, dazed and exhausted, they'd settled down here, in a small wooded area on the edge of a potato field. He'd managed to construct a small tent-shaped shelter out of fallen branches by sticking the ends into the ground, crisscrossing the branches at the top and interweaving other branches horizontally. Each day he passed some time repairing and improving it. It wasn't much, but it kept off some of the rain.

Now their only hope was that the Czech soldier he'd talked to would get a message to his cousin Albert. The soldier had promised to do so, in exchange for a watch. And, that Albert would somehow manage to help them. Otherwise, they were doomed. The late October nights were growing colder and colder as they huddled together under their only blanket. Without help, they would either freeze or starve. As the cold mist turned into a steady drizzle, Heda crawled into the little shelter they had constructed. He stayed outside and kept watch. In the darkness, he heard Heda's stifled sobs.

Alois gradually became aware of the sound of footsteps approaching. His eyes strained against the darkness, waiting tensely to see who was coming. Hope struggled with fear. Had help come at last, or was it more trouble?

Two shadowy figures stepped into the small circle of flickering light cast by the campfire.

"Are you Albert's cousin?" the taller one asked.

A wave of relief swept over him. Heda stepped out of the shelter.

"Yes, I'm Alois, and this is my wife, Heda."

"You can call me Josef, and my friend is Antonin," he replied. "Gather up your things and come with us. We have to move quickly so that we can get to a safe place, behind the Czech army line, before dawn."

"How can we get across?" Heda asked.

"Just follow us. We know the best way. We've bribed a soldier to look the other way. Have you eaten?" Josef asked, looking at the potatoes by the edge of the fire.

"No. We haven't had anything except potatoes for days, and not even that tonight," Alois said.

"Here, this will tide you over. We'll have a decent meal once we get you to a safe place," Josef said, handing them each a chocolate bar.

Alois's hands shook as he opened it. He bit off a corner. The taste was an explosion of flavor. He closed his eyes for a moment to savor it, and then quickly gobbled the rest of it up.

Heda quickly nibbled half of her bar, then wrapped the other half and put it in her pocket. After they gathered their child and their few belongings, she scooped up the half-baked potatoes and dropped them into the can that they'd found and had been using to collect water, and took those along, too.

A few moments later, they had extinguished the campfire and disappeared into the night.

CHAPTER 5

The late afternoon sun slanted through the trees when the dogs began to bark furiously. Jana heard several people approaching on horseback. The little children stopped playing and ran to their mothers. Papa and the uncles were sitting by their campfires; they looked at each other and then got up and strolled toward the road. Soon, friendly greetings rang out, and everyone rushed out to greet the visitors.

"Look, it's my cousin's sons, Otto and Max, and their friend Albert!" Papa exclaimed, giving Jana a quick warning look. Three young men—two Gypsies and one Czech—smiled and greeted everyone.

Jana had played with Otto and Max when they were all small children, but she hadn't seen them in years. She was astonished by how handsome Otto had become. He was slender, and athletic, with thick black hair that he wore combed back, big brown eyes, and white teeth that flashed when he smiled. When he smiled, she felt suddenly happy and returned his smile. *So, these were the mysterious night visitors,* she thought.

She tried not to look at Otto, afraid that he would see something in her eyes that she wanted to conceal, but she found it hard to take her eyes off of him. He noticed her looking at him and smiled at her. She blushed, looked down, and smoothed her skirt, fingering it nervously and feeling very confused.

The adults were happy to have a reason for a celebration, so they decided to have a party to welcome the visitors. The children were sent to forage for wood, some of the boys went out to catch fish and game, and the women dug through their provisions to see what kind of feast they could put together.

The men constructed a shelter—like the one they'd built to shelter the horses, where everyone would be able to get together out of the cold. They built a firepit in the center, with a hole in the roof above it, placed rugs and chairs around the firepit, and stacked bales of hay around the walls for additional seating. To make a long table for the feast, they stacked hay in one corner, placed planks across several bales, and threw tablecloths over them. Then they dug out their tobacco, wine, and musical instruments.

The shelter was soon hot, smoky, and fragrant with the odors of cooking food. The women bustled around the fire preparing the feast. Meat and fish roasted on spits over the fire. Big pots simmered, full of sweet and savory dishes. They cooked cabbage rolls; a stew made with chicken, pork, rice, and cabbage, and flavored with vinegar and paprika; and sweet dumplings cooked in milk. Flatbreads and cornmeal cakes, flavored with caraway and coriander, were baked on griddles.

Jana and the other older girls served as cook's assistants. They crushed spices, tended the fire, drew water, and kneaded the dough while keeping the little kids out of the way.

Grandma Berta sat in a chair close to the fire, supervising everything. She would sample dishes and decide what needed a little more of this or that. From time to time, she would rise, stir something, and declare that it was almost done or needed more time.

Shortly after nightfall, all was ready, and the party was underway. One toast followed another, and, when everyone had eaten their fill, the music began. The men and Grandma Berta sat nearest the fire; the women and children formed a ring around them.

Jana sat in the shadows, on one of the bales of straw, where she could see without being seen. She was hardly aware of the others around her, the cold penetrating the canvas behind her, or the hypnotic rhythms of the guitar and violin music. All of her attention was focused on Otto—the way he tossed his head when he laughed, the way the firelight played across his face.

After a time Papa noticed Jana sitting in the shadows. "Come, dance for us, Jana!" he called. "Come on, come on. She's shy, but an excellent dancer," he said to the visitors.

She knew he wouldn't stop until she gave in so, reluctantly, Jana stepped forward. The chairs were shifted around to make room for her, and she began to dance. At first, she danced slowly and self-consciously. Never had her arms and legs seemed so heavy and awkward! But soon the music possessed her. She floated and twirled. Eyes half-closed, hands clapping, fingers snapping, feet stomping, she danced faster and faster, as the music sped up.

When the music stopped, she stopped, too, and opened her eyes, flushed, panting for breath. She'd stopped in front of Otto. She stood for a moment, looking straight into his eyes. Time stood still.

"Bravo!" Papa cried, clapping loudly. "Who wants another drink?"

The spell was broken. Otto looked away. Jana felt her face grow hot. To hide her embarrassment, she walked quickly to the buffet table, drank some water, and examined the leftovers. Although she wasn't hungry, she spent as long as she could selecting a few morsels and arranging them on a plate. Then she returned to her seat in the shadows to eat. After she'd finished, she kept busy by helping Zofie with Anna and baby Eduard. Zofie looked at her in surprise but was grateful for the help. In spite of herself, Jana kept noticing Otto: his voice, his laughter, and his smile.

Oh, this is stupid! she thought.

"Zofie, I'm tired," she said suddenly. "I'm going to bed. I'll take Anna with me."

From their bed in the caravan, she listened to the sounds of music, laughing, and talking, and watched the patterns from the fire on the windows of the caravan. Sleep eluded her as she strained to pick Otto's voice out from the others. A little while later, Lili crawled into bed with them.

"You like him, don't you?" Lili whispered.

"I do not!" she said, but she found that she was still listening for his voice.

After the women and children had left for the night, and they put aside their musical instruments, the seven men—Jana's father, Josef; his brothers, Emil, Tony, and Martin; and the visitors Otto, Max, and Albert—drew their chairs in closer. Martin put another log on the fire. Josef opened another bottle of raspberry brandy and passed it around, and then he passed around a bag of tobacco. When everyone had refilled their pipes and cups, they settled in to talk.

They caught up on old times and exchanged pleasantries, with many effusive offers to "stay as long as you like," and equally effusive thanks for the hospitality extended.

Otto addressed Jana's father and his three brothers. "My father sends his greeting and invites you to come to Prague to stay with us for the winter. His woodworking business is doing well, and he has lots of work waiting to be done. He said he would welcome help in the shop if you are interested, and he will pay you well."

"That's a very generous offer. Tell your father that I thank him," Josef said. "I will discuss it with my brothers, and I will let you know what we decide."

The mood became serious as the discussion turned to recent events.

Albert stared gloomily into the fire for a few moments and then said, “This has been a disastrous time for Czechoslovakia. As I’m sure you know, President Beneš resigned in protest and fled the country after Hitler stole a huge chunk of our nation, the so-called Sudetenland. I’m afraid that he got what he wanted so easily that he won’t stop until he has the rest of it.

“The British and French cowards, who were pledged to protect us, deserted us and conspired with Italy and Germany to give away a large part of our country. Only the Soviet Union was willing to fulfill its treaty obligations. I guess we should not have expected anything better from capitalists.

“October 28 will be the thirtieth anniversary of the republic. I wonder if it will be the last one.” His face, which had been filled with good humor all evening, hardened into a mask of outrage.

“Are the Russians any better than the Germans?” Emil asked. “Aren’t they all the same, all the—” A warning look from Josef cut him off. He stopped short of saying “All the *Gadje*”—which is the word for non-Gypsies—clearly forgetting for a moment that Albert was also a *Gadjo*.

At this Albert began to speak excitedly about the Communists, how they stood for universal brotherhood and equality, and how they alone were willing to honor their pledge to stand up for Czechoslovakia. Martin, the youngest of Jana’s uncles, who was about the same age as Albert, Otto, and Max, listened intently to this analysis.

Tony, the third oldest brother, was small, lean, and muscular. He was usually the most practical of the four brothers. He said, “I don’t know about all that. I’ve heard politicians make promises and have seen them broken. I believe what I see. But I can tell you this—these Nazis are no good. We all know what happened in Burgenland," he continued. "The Gypsies from that part of Austria were rounded up after the Germans took over. Men, women, and children—they were supposedly all spies. They were just rounded up and taken away. Who knows what will become of them?"

Otto and Max looked at each other. "It's funny you should bring that up," Otto said, laughing a little. "Not that we're asking you to spy . . ."

"What my brother means," interrupted Max, Otto's younger brother, in low, conspiratorial tones, slightly slurred now from an evening of drinking, "is that we could use a little help finding our way around."

"We don't want to involve you in any way. That is, we don't want to put you in any danger," Albert said, as he hitched himself upright in his chair. He was starting to feel the effects of a long day and the brandy. "Otto and Max told me that you might be willing to share some of your knowledge of the back roads and out-of-the-way camping spots and, perhaps, names of some contacts. They also said that you might have some horses that I could buy. If you are not interested, I completely understand. I know you have your families to think about."

"I don't think we will want to get involved," Tony said. "After all, this is not our fight."

"This is our country, too!" Otto said. He stared into the fire with a stony expression on his face. "Most of our people have settled, as my father has. We no longer travel the open road. The future of this country is also our future. I've gone to school with the others, and have started college this year, at the university. I want to finish and have a career. If we do nothing, the Nazis will arrest us and send us all away, as they did in Austria. We need to fight! I believe it is our fight whether we like it or not.

"In fact, right now, some of our people, as well as others, are stranded between the Czech and German armies. Albert's cousin and his family were among them. These are people who fled their homes when the Germans arrived or were evicted by the Henleinists. Now they're not being allowed into what remains of Czechoslovakia. Whole families are living in the open between army lines—Jews, Gypsies, Communists, and Democrats—anyone who is afraid to stay, or was forced to leave."

"Why can't they get into Czechoslovakia?" Martin asked.

"The Czech government is afraid to do anything that would give Hitler an excuse to take the rest of their country, such as sheltering his enemies," Otto said. "Food and other supplies are available to help them, and there are others, besides us, who are willing to help, but the army will not allow anyone through to deliver it. We need places to stockpile goods and information about the best way to get past army lines without being seen. Then, perhaps we could help more of these people."

"What happened to your cousin and his family, Albert?" Tony asked.

"They found help, and got out," Albert replied, with a nearly imperceptible glance at Otto.

"I see," Tony said.

The discussion went on late into the night until the fire had burned down to embers and the first traces of dawn light streaked the sky, but they hadn't reached a decision. In the end, they decided that Otto, Max, and Albert should stay for a few days. They would stay with Martin and Grandma Berta.

Josef, Emil, and Tony went to their wagons for the night, leaving the younger men still passionately discussing politics.

The three older brothers met early in the morning outside the horse shelter, while the younger men were still sleeping.

"What do you think?" Josef asked his brothers.

"I think we would be foolish to give away too much information. If people know our routes, campsites, and contacts, it will be hard to slip away quietly when the time comes. Getting involved in this sounds risky," Tony said.

"But surely these boys pose no danger for us. It sounds like Albert's cousin was desperately in need of help," Emil said. "After all, we also need friends. We wouldn't get very far without friends we can count on."

"I hate to turn away Vaclav's sons, or a friend of theirs," Josef said. "Vaclav has been very kind to me in the past, and his offer to let us stay with him this winter certainly is tempting. If we stay here, with our horses, we'll have to feed them, as well as ourselves, all winter long, without any money coming in."

"But do we want to be in the city if the Germans come, as Albert seems sure they will? Wouldn't it be better for us to be hidden away?" Tony asked.

"Maybe they won't take the whole country," Emil said, wrinkling his large forehead. "The Allies have guaranteed the new borders."

"Guaranteed!" Tony scoffed, cutting him off. "What good are such guarantees? It does seem likely to me, though, that if they do come, they will not be here for long. How can one country control such a large area? It would probably be only a matter of a few months."

Josef stroked his mustache nervously. "I think we should help them. But let's try to keep this as quiet as possible. They will be the only contacts between their friends and us. The fewer people we involve, the better. Our wives may suspect something, of course, but don't answer any of their questions," he said. "As far as moving, let's stay here a couple of weeks and see if things settle down, and then move into Prague before winter sets in, if it seems safe."

After more discussion, they all agreed.

The next several days found the men huddled together in intense conversations, looking at the horses and hunched over maps. Jana stayed close to their caravan and campfire, trying to avoid Otto. She was in torment, having decided to stay away from him, but always aware of him.

One day, as she was gathering firewood, she came face-to-face with him in the woods. She turned to flee.

"Don't be afraid."

"Afraid?" She stopped and turned around. She looked at him haughtily though her heart beat loudly against her breast. "I'm not afraid."

"Then why have you been avoiding me?"

His eyes penetrated deep into hers. She blushed and looked down.

"What makes you think I've been avoiding you?" she said.

He ignored the question and watched her for a moment. She looked up questioningly.

"I wanted to tell you how much I enjoyed your dancing the other night," he said. "You are a wonderful dancer."

"Thank you." She felt awkward and struggled to think of something else she could say. "Are you going to be staying much longer?" she finally asked.

"No, not long. Jana?"

"Yes?"

“It’s just that . . .” He paused, and then said, “I wish things were different!”

He took a step toward her, reaching out with his right hand. She felt frozen in place. Suddenly, he dropped his hand to his side.

“I have to go now,” he said, brushing past her, continuing down the trail.

She turned her head toward him and caught his scent as he passed, a compelling combination of smoke and sweat and something else.

She had a hard time sleeping that night. When she awoke the next morning, the visitors were gone.

CHAPTER 6

Crash! The sound of shattering glass, and the wild barking of his dogs, jolted Mr. Pavlik awake. He fumbled on the nightstand for his glasses and shuffled his feet into his slippers as the little dog, Rikono, dove under his bed.

"What did you do?" he asked the dog.

Just then, another crash and the sound of shattering glass came from the living room, and his dogs barked and howled even more wildly.

"What the devil is going on?" He shuffled to the bedroom door and peered out. Both of the living room windows were broken. The curtains and a pile of newspapers next to one of the windows were starting to burn.

"Oh my God! It must be those Henleinist bastards!" he cried. His hands shook as he grabbed a kitchen towel and started beating at the flames.

Young Nazis, who were followers of the Sudeten German Nazi leader, Henlein, loved to march around in groups by day and cause trouble by night. They'd taunted him for years for patronizing a nearby butcher shop owned by a man who belonged to the Social Democratic Party, which was hated by the Henleinists. They called him a race traitor, tried to trip him, and threw rocks at him every chance they got, even though he was as German as they were.

As far as Mr. Pavlik was concerned, he didn't give a damn about politics. It was the closest butcher shop, and the butcher always threw in extra bones for his dogs, for free. He wasn't about to let a group of punk kids tell him where he could do business. Eventually, they'd driven the butcher out of business. He'd lost customers, thanks to Henleinist harassment, and he couldn't afford to keep replacing broken windows. He'd packed up his family and moved. Now Mr. Pavlik had to go miles farther to buy his meat, and there were no more free bones for the dogs.

He continued to beat at the flames, but the fire was spreading, and the smoke was growing thicker. He started to cough and choke.

"Help! Help!" he shouted.

He felt a tugging at his robe. He looked down and saw the little dog tugging at him.

"We'd better get out of here," he said to Rikono. He picked up the little dog and shuffled out into the yard. His other dogs came running to meet him.

"Come on. Come on," he called to the other dogs, as he shuffled out of the gate and down the street. The lights were going on in the house next door. A woman poked her head out.

"What's going on?" she asked.

"My house is burning!"

"Oh no! I'll send my husband to get help," she said.

Several motorcycles came whizzing past. The young men riding them were laughing and yelled out, "That's what you get, you old bastard!"

Their harassment had stopped for a while, after the Czech government had declared martial law in September. But now that the German army was in charge, the Henleinists had a free hand to start their harassment again, but the German army was starting to crack down on them and trying to restore order.

The neighbor lady invited Mr. Pavlik in, but she didn't want the dogs in her house, and he didn't want to leave them, so finally she brought a kitchen chair out into her yard. He sat down, hunched over in his bathrobe, surrounded by his dogs, and watched as the fire department battled the blaze. By the time they put out the fire, much of his house had burned.

A couple of German soldiers drove up and got out of their truck. "Hello, Mr. Pavlik," one of them said.

"Private Schmidt, is that you? What are you doing here?"

"We've been sent to round up the arsonists and turn them over to the police. Did you recognize them?"

"I can't say for sure," Mr. Pavlik said.

He knew very well who they were. They were the same bunch that had been harassing him for years, but now he was scared. If they were capable of this, what would they do next?

"Well, did you see which way they went?"

"They went that way." He pointed.

"Do you have a place to stay?"

"I guess I'll just put the dogs back in the yard, after the fire is out, and spend the night here with the neighbors."

"What about after that?"

"I don't know." He felt suddenly very old and tired.

"Well, I'll try to check in on you, if I get a chance," Franz said.

"Don't bother. I'll manage," Mr. Pavlik said.

Franz and the other private jumped back in the truck and took off in the direction Mr. Pavlik had indicated.

Several days had passed before Franz got a chance to come back to check on Mr. Pavlik. His house was an empty charred ruin. There was no sign of anyone around. He went next door, knocked on the door, and a woman opened it.

"Good morning. I'm Private Schmidt. Can you tell me if Mr. Pavlik is staying here?" he asked.

"Not anymore. His son came to get him."

"Oh, I see. Well, that's good, I guess. I didn't know he had a son." Franz felt a little disappointed. "Well, I guess I'll be going then. Thank you." He started to turn away.

"Just a minute. I almost forgot, he left his son's address—something about your dog that he's taking care of."

She returned shortly with a note and gave it to him.

"Thank you," he said, and she closed the door.

He read the note as he walked away. Written in an uneven hand, with badly formed letters, as though he was unaccustomed to writing, it said, "No more money needed for the care of your dog. It's a good dog and is no trouble. Pick him up when you are able." Below that, he'd written his son's address.

Franz smiled, folded the note neatly, and inserted it into his billfold.

CHAPTER 7

When Otto and Max got home, Otto returned to his classes at the university. Otto was the first in his family to go to the university. In fact, most of his relatives couldn't read or write. His parents were proud of him, but they didn't understand why he wanted a degree. After all, they'd done okay, and education wouldn't change the color of his skin. They worried that, with a university education, Otto would never really fit in, anywhere.

On one gray, drizzly Wednesday morning in early November, Otto sat in a lecture hall. He only half listened to the professor who paced in front of the class and droned on about the founding of the republic in 1918, and the founder, and first president, Tomas Masaryk.

Otto absentmindedly jotted down a few notes as he listened. Normally, he would be very interested in this topic, but today his mind was on other things. He wondered how Albert's cousin and family were doing, and what they would do next. Also, Jana's image kept intruding on his concentration. He remembered how beautiful she looked as she danced around the campfire, and how she watched him when she thought he wasn't looking. He wondered what she had been thinking. But what good would it do to think of her now? This was not the time to think of love.

He was awakened from his reverie by a growing commotion in the rear of the class. A group of German students and their teacher were sitting in on the lecture today. They were whispering loudly to one another.

The professor stopped his lecture and addressed them.

"Is there a problem?"

They looked at each other, and then at their teacher, who stood up to speak for the group. "We didn't come here to listen to this talk about Masaryk. As far as we're concerned, he was nothing but a liar and a cheat!" he said.

Several of the Czech students leaped to their feet, their fists clenched, and started shouting. The one closest to Otto shouted, "What are you talking about? Shut up, you ignorant lout!"

"Gentlemen, please! Let's discuss this like gentlemen," the professor pleaded, trying to regain order.

"Our university was closed in 1934. Just another stab in the back!" an ethnic German student yelled. "It won't be long before we return the favor and close this university. Herr Hitler will see to that!"

"We can't even learn in our own language, and we have to listen to Masaryk described as a philosopher! A crook is more like it! Herr Hitler will soon deal with the lot of you," another student shouted out.

This was more than Otto could bear. "Shut up, you bloody idiot!" he yelled.

"Oh, big talk from the Gypsy trash! He'll deal with your lot, too!"

Otto stood up and glared at him, silently. He wanted to lunge for his throat, but if he did, he knew he could be expelled, and then his hopes for the future would be dashed.

"I can see that we're not going to get any more work done today," the professor said. "Class dismissed."

The students poured out of the classroom and down the stairs. They broke up into small groups in the lobby of the building, and onto the stairs outside of the building, and continued to argue and shout at each other.

Suddenly, one of the German-speaking students noticed a bronze bust of Masaryk, sitting on a column in the lobby. "There he is!" he shouted, pointing. "There's the old fraud!"

Another German student produced a piece of rope and looped it around the head of the bust. To the laughter and encouragement of his friends, the boy pulled the bust off the column, and it landed, with a crash, on the marble floor. He dragged it out the door. It fell out of the noose and bounced down the stairs outside of the building.

Then groups of young men jumped at each other and started trading punches.

Otto searched for the boy who had called him Gypsy trash. He found him in the middle of the melee, shouting and waving his arms around, his eyes wild with excitement. Otto walked up to him and punched him in the face. Blood spurted from his cut lip. The boy took a swing at Otto, missed, and they fell to the ground, together, kicking and punching.

"The police are coming!" someone yelled, and the crowd scattered, leaving the dented bust of Masaryk lying on the ground at the bottom of the stairs.

When Otto returned to his classes the following Monday, the Masaryk bust had disappeared. Otherwise, everything seemed to be back to normal. Otto was afraid that, at any moment, he would be summoned to the dean's office and expelled, or suspended, but nothing had happened, so he started to relax. Meanwhile, he kept a lookout for the German students, but they were nowhere to be seen.

On Wednesday, he went back to his history class. As soon as he sat down, the professor approached him and handed him a sealed envelope.

"It's from the dean," he said.

Otto opened the envelope with a sinking feeling. The news was as bad as he had feared. He was suspended for the remainder of the semester for violating the school's code of conduct. Angrily he crumpled the letter, shoved it into his knapsack, and stormed out of the room.

"I'm sorry," the history professor called after him.

"Well, that's that!" he muttered. How would he ever be able to finish college now? His heart was heavy with disappointment and anger.

Otto wandered the streets aimlessly for hours, as the sun sank and the gray day became a starless night. He was hardly aware of his surroundings as he pondered what he should do. He thought he had a plan for his life and now, in a moment, it had all changed. The job, the house, the car, the family—he had wanted to live like the others, not to wander endlessly or scrape a living day-to-day as so many of his people did. Poof! Vanished like the illusion it had probably always been. He struggled with anger, bitterness, and despair, but most of all, with indecision.

He found himself wandering across a bridge, and gazed down into the swirling water below. One quick jump and it would be over! He took out a cigarette, struck a match on the railing, and considered it.

One quick moment of agony, and then nothing. He took a drag on the cigarette. The harsh taste of the tobacco filled his lungs and seemed to clear his head, and he thought about nothing for a moment. He just stood there, leaning on the cement guardrail, and smoked while watching the dance of the streetlights on the swirling water below. As his thoughts drifted, Jana's face came to mind. He saw her little face in his mind's eye, always so animated, one moment smiling, and the next scowling. The thought of her made him smile. He took one last drag on the cigarette and flicked the butt away, watching as it dropped into the water below.

"To hell with that. It's just a suspension, an interruption, not the end!" he said, out loud to himself, then squared his shoulders and walked purposefully off. He'd decided to go see Albert.

When he arrived, he walked up the narrow staircase to Albert's apartment and knocked on the door.

"Who is it?" Albert asked.

"It's me, Otto."

There was the sound of a chair scraping against the floor, a murmur of voices, and then the sound of the door being unlocked and unchained.

"Hey, great to see you!" Albert grabbed his hand and pumped it.

A small group of young men sat in the one room apartment. The room was thick with smoke. Some sat on the bed, others on wooden chairs around the kitchen table. There was a bottle of brandy and some empty beer bottles on the table, and almost everyone had a glass or a bottle of beer in one hand and a cigarette in the other. The conversation had stopped when he came in. They all sat looking at him or trying not to. Otto recognized a couple of them as friends of Albert's that he'd met before.

"Hello." He nodded to them. They nodded back.

"This is my friend Otto, who I told you about. He and his brother helped my cousin," Albert said.

The faces all became friendly, and there was a chorus of greetings.

"Maybe this isn't a good time," Otto said.

"No, this is perfect. I was trying to contact you, but nobody seemed to know where you were. Come in. Want a drink?"

"Thanks." He took it and leaned against the sink.

"We were just talking about how the government has suspended the activities of the Communist Party," Albert said. "It seems they are willing to bend over backward to accommodate Hitler."

Otto was not surprised to learn that the subject was politics. It was a favorite topic of Albert and his friends. Some of them were Communists. All of them were nationalists and followers of Tomas Masaryk, the first president of Czechoslovakia who, together with Eduard Beneš, the second president, had established Czechoslovakia as an independent country after the Great War.

At first, Otto didn't try to follow the conversation, which seemed to be speculation about repressive measures being implemented by the government, apparently, in hopes of preventing further German demands. Instead, he kept ruminating about his future. After a while, he tuned back in.

"It's only a matter of time until the Germans march in and occupy what's left of our country," Albert said.

"No, no! The British and French would never allow it!" a chorus of voices protested.

"The British and French!" Albert said. "We can't count on them. They're the ones who sold us out! We need to be ready to defend ourselves. At least we can circulate the news from abroad. The newspapers are already being censored. The news I hear on the radio, from abroad, is not being printed in the newspapers, and German democrats and other refugees from the Sudetenland are being returned. We should find ways to get them out of the country if they wish to leave."

One young man got up and said, "I wish you all the luck in the world, but I can't get involved with any of this. I just want to finish school and lead my life. If you want to play the hero, go ahead." He stalked out.

"Anyone else who wants to go, go now. We won't think less of you," Albert said.

A couple more of the young men left, with mumbled apologies, and then there were only six who were left, including Albert and Otto. They looked at each other and smiled nervously.

"Now the question is, what to do?" Albert said.

The conversation raged back and forth, without any resolution, until one by one they said their goodbyes and left. Finally, only Otto and Albert were left sitting across the table from each other, bleary-eyed from smoke, drink, and lack of sleep.

"I got suspended for the semester today . . . I guess it's yesterday now," Otto said.

"You're kidding!"

"No. I was starting to think the whole thing would blow over, then bam! Out of the blue."

"I'm sorry. What are you going to do now?"

"I wish I knew, but I don't. Get a job, I guess."

"Maybe this is a bad time to ask this or, who knows, maybe this is perfect timing. Can I ask you to do a favor for me?" Albert said.

"Sure, what is it?"

"Tell me if it's too much. You've already done so much. My cousin and his family . . ."

"What about them?"

"As you know, they're staying at my parents' summer cottage."

"Yes?"

"Well, they're going to need supplies. I would go, but I'm known in that area. If they saw me, they would know where I was going and wonder why. We never go there in the winter. Besides, the roads are bad, so it would have to be on horseback."

"Sure, I'll do it." Otto shrugged.

"I'll pay you, of course."

"Don't be silly. We're friends. You'll do me a favor someday in return. I'll get my brother to help me out again. He's usually up for a little adventure," Otto said.

CHAPTER 8

Jana peered out the window of the caravan as it bumped along over the uneven cobblestones of the narrow streets that twisted and turned through Prague. She was happy to be sitting inside the caravan on a night like tonight. The weather had turned colder, and damp, icy winds blew off the river. Her father's shoulders hunched against the cold as he steered the horses.

They were approaching a large arch of blackened stone, topped with golden peaks that reflected the streetlights. They drove through this arch and onto the St. Charles Bridge. Statues of saints, blackened by decades of soot, were only dimly visible, as they stood guard on either side of the bridge. Ahead, at the top of the hill, was a magical sight—a great cathedral and a palace, bathed in light—but they did not climb the hill. Instead, they crossed the bridge, then turned left and followed the river. They bounced along for some time and, gradually, the houses lining the streets became shabbier, and the shadows between streetlights lengthened.

Jana was not in a hurry to arrive at their destination. They were going to her father's cousin Vaclav's house where they had been invited to spend the winter. It was all arranged, and they were expected. Jana had pretended to be indifferent when her father had announced the decision, but at that moment, she had felt both giddy and frightened, and had been able to think of little else since. To live under the same roof with Otto would be torment, but it would also be wonderful! She had decided that she would avoid him, and never let him know how he made her feel. Actually, she wasn't sure what she felt.

At last, they arrived. Jana had been here before, but not for years. The sprawling old house was set back from the road, on the outskirts of town. Lights shone from the windows, and smoke poured out of the chimney. The horse-drawn caravans clopped along, down the uneven dirt road, and passed the house. The backyard widened and, hidden now in the shadows, was a barn, which was also the workshop for Vaclav's furniture business.

Vaclav and several boys burst out of the back door with shouts of welcome as soon as they stopped. Before long, everyone was laughing and talking loudly while the boys unharnessed the horses and led them away.

Jana wondered where Otto was as Zofie handed her the baby and bustled her, and the other children, into the house. No sooner had she crossed the threshold than Vaclav's wife, Aunt Marie, enveloped her in a huge bear hug. Aunt Marie was almost as wide as she was tall.

"Come in! Come in! Oh, it's so good to see you!" she exclaimed, over and over, as she hugged each visitor, in turn.

Still, there was no sign of Otto.

Soon, everyone was crowded into the house, and platters of food were being passed around. After everyone had eaten, the children were assigned to their rooms, all the girls in one room, all the boys in another.

Otto's brother, Max, went out with Jana to help her carry in their quilts and pillows.

"Where's Otto?" she asked, trying to sound casual.

He shrugged. "Otto? I don't know. He comes and goes as he pleases. Sometimes he's gone for weeks at a time while staying with his friends from the university."

Jana's heart sank. She felt very crabby as she tried to claim a spot in the corner of the girls' room where she, Lili, and Anna could sleep. Vaclav's girls were not happy about sharing their bedroom with all the cousins, and loud arguments broke out as furniture was moved around to accommodate everyone. Only after several dire threats from their mothers did the girls settle their differences, and finally everyone was quiet. The adults continued to talk and laugh downstairs. As she tried to fall asleep, Jana felt tears running down her cheeks. This was going to be a long winter.

After she had spent several days moping around the house, hoping Otto would come home, she got bored and started hanging around the woodshop.

"Let me come along!" she begged every time someone went to drop off or deliver furniture. When there was room, they let her ride with them as the horse sauntered along, pulling the delivery wagon through the narrow, winding streets of Prague, across bridges, through squares, and up and down the hills.

Jana soon knew her way around the city. The castle on the top of a hill looked down on the city. The gentle curve of the Vltava River bisected it. She liked looking at all the old buildings, towers, statues, and churches—some well maintained, some tumbling down. Best of all, she liked to get a glimpse into the houses they stopped at—a momentary portal into other people's lives.

One day, after she returned from making deliveries with Max and Ion, she walked into the woodshop, and Otto was there, talking to her father and his father.

He turned and looked at her with a mixture of annoyance and relief. He had bruises that had faded into yellowish patches on his face.

"Hi. What happened to you?" she asked. She tried to sound casual, though she noticed that her heart was beating faster.

"Never mind. I just ran into a little trouble. What I want to know is why are you riding around town?" He frowned at her.

"Why not? I like it!" she retorted.

"Well, you're not going to do it anymore."

"What? Says who?" she said, her voice rising in anger. She looked at her father. He only smiled and shrugged.

"I say, and my father says. It's our business and our wagon. I won't have you riding around in it. Stay in the house with the women where you belong."

"You can't order me around! Papa, please . . ." she pleaded, turning to him.

"That's enough, Jana," he said. "We're guests here and will abide by their decision. Now go into the house."

She burst into tears and ran into the house.

Zofie looked up from feeding baby Eduard. "What's the matter?" she asked.

Jana ignored her and ran past her and up the stairs to the girls' room. She opened the door, but when she saw several girl cousins in there, she slammed it shut again, ran down the stairs, and out the front door.

"Where are you going?" Zofie called after her. Jana ignored her.

"I hate him! I hate him!" Jana muttered as she walked. Hot tears of anger poured from her eyes. "I can't believe that I ever thought I liked him. He's horrible! Just horrible!"

She walked on and on, hardly knowing where she was going. After a while, she came to the river. The water flowed by, the steam rising from the surface. She imagined getting in a boat and floating down the river. Where would it take her, she wondered, this rushing water? Away from here is all she cared about, away from the pressures and expectations of her family, away from the future with all its unknowns, with all the possibilities and perils. Away from Otto! First, he was gone when she wanted him near, and now he was here, and she wished he wasn't. It was all so confusing.

As she walked and pondered, she came to a bench, sat down, and watched the river flow by with the lights of the city gleaming on its surface.

"Hey, honey," a male voice said. "How'd you like some company?" She looked up to see a seedy middle-aged man wearing a too-tight suit and threadbare overcoat.

"No thanks," she said.

"Oh, come on. You look kind of lonely to me." He approached her. She could smell that he'd been drinking.

"I was just leaving," she said and turned to go.

"Not so fast, sweetheart." He lunged for her and grabbed her arm.

A bubble of fear rushed through her. She turned and bit down on his hand, hard. He let out a yelp and let her go. She turned and ran. When she stopped running, she was halfway home. The shadows grew deeper around her, and she hurried toward the light and warmth of home.

CHAPTER 9

Albert took a deep breath and then knocked on the door. His mother opened it and the familiar odors of baking bread and his favorite meal—roast pork, boiled dumplings, and sauerkraut—wafted out with her. She was wearing a print apron over a print dress that hung awkwardly on her thin frame. She stepped aside. He came in, reached down, and hugged her.

"I hope you're hungry," she said. "Go sit with your father; the food will be ready soon."

Albert went into the parlor. His father was sitting in the overstuffed green chair. He lowered the newspaper and looked up at Albert over his reading glasses.

"Albert, welcome! How are you?"

"I'm fine," he said.

"Are you sure? You look a little worried."

"Who's not worried, things being the way they are?" Albert said as he sat down on the edge of the sofa.

"True, true. How about a beer to get our minds off those things for the moment?" He folded the newspaper, set it aside, and then hoisted himself out of his chair. He had gotten portly over the years, and his vest strained at the buttons.

He returned with two large glasses of golden beer, each topped with a foamy cap. He handed one to Albert and settled back in his easy chair with his. Albert was trying to decide how to bring up the thing that he'd come to talk about.

"Father, I need to talk to you about the summer cottage . . ."

"What about the summer cottage?" his mother said, sticking her head out the door to the kitchen. "Come to the table—dinner is ready."

They picked up their glasses of beer and took their places at the dining room table. Further discussion was delayed while they passed the food, and his father said grace. Finally, his father said, "You were saying something about the summer cottage."

"It's a little complicated. It's about the occupation—you know that people were kicked out of their homes," Albert said.

Both of his parents stopped eating and looked at him intently.

"And what does this have to do with the summer cottage?" his mother asked.

"It has to do with Alois," Albert said.

"Who?" his father asked.

"My brother's boy," his mother said.

"Oh yes, Alois. What about him?" his father asked.

"He was kicked out of his home, along with his wife and baby," Albert said.

"Oh, for heaven's sake!" his mother said.

"They had nowhere to go. They were living out in the open and could have died, but they managed to get word to me," Albert said.

"I see," his father said, laying his knife and fork down on the edge of his plate. "And they are living in the summer cottage?"

"Yes," Albert said.

"How can you get yourself involved in such things?" his mother said. "How can you get *us* involved?"

"Please, dear, let's stay calm," his father said.

"How could I not!" Albert said. "Was I supposed to let them die?"

"Surely they would have managed, somehow. There must be something they could have done. People are not just thrown out of their houses with nowhere to go," she said.

"They most certainly are!" Albert said, his voice rising. "You don't understand what these people, these Nazis, are capable of, Mother."

"That will do!" his father said. "Don't raise your voice to your mother."

"I'm sorry," Albert said.

"Now, I suggest that we eat in peace. You and I will talk about this later," his father said.

After an uncomfortable meal, and stilted attempts at small talk, Albert and his father went into the parlor, while his mother cleared things away. After his father had resettled into his favorite chair and lit his pipe, he said, "Well, my boy, what do you propose?"

"I think that Alois and his family should be allowed to stay in the summer cottage until things get back to normal."

"We have no idea how long that will be, of course," his father said.

"No. But lots of people think the war will start soon and that it won't last long. They say the Germans are not prepared for a long war," Albert said.

"So they say, but we can't be sure. At any rate, staying for the winter is not practical. There's no work—how will they buy food? Even if they had the money, the roads are not well maintained. How will they get supplies?" his father said.

"I have friends who say they can bring things in on horseback," Albert said.

"People will know they are there. If they're hiding, they are not very well hidden," his father said.

"I thought of that. Most likely, they'll contact you. When asked, you could simply say you are letting some out-of-work relatives live there, temporarily," Albert said.

"And their papers? Do they have identity papers? Are they going to register?" his father asked.

"I don't know," Albert said.

His father fell silent as he puffed and gazed into the glowing bowl of his pipe. "There's a complication," he said. "You know your mother doesn't get along with her brother—Alois's father. Do you know why?"

"No. I've always wondered, but she never wanted to talk about it," Albert said.

"He married a Jew," his father said.

"My uncle?" Albert asked.

"Yes, he married against his parents' wishes. After his marriage, his parents refused to see him, and they never spoke of him. They never met his children. It was like he'd never existed. Your mother sided with her parents, and it drove a wedge between her and her brother. She couldn't give him up entirely. They kept in touch with occasional letters. It's a shame because they were so close while they were growing up. He was a nice fellow. I knew him when your mother and I were engaged and for a few years after we were married, before his marriage."

"It's terrible that his parents would turn their backs on him like that. I thought he must have done something dreadful, like commit a crime or something, but he just married the woman he loved!" Albert said.

"A Jew. Your grandparents were good people, but they had certain ideas. That's just the way they were. I'm afraid your mother is a bit the same. It's not her fault—she just doesn't understand. She's led a very sheltered life and still believes what she was taught as a child," his father said. "Because Alois is half-Jewish, he's a Jew as far as the Nazis are concerned, and his child probably is, too."

"So, if the Nazis took over the rest of the country, they would be in danger," Albert said.

"I'm afraid so. You know how the Germans treated their own Jews. It's not safe for them to stay at the summer cottage. I wonder—why did your cousin contact you? I didn't know that you even knew him," his father said.

"We met at a hockey match several years ago. I think I mentioned it at the time. We played against his team, and I was curious because his name was the same as Mother's maiden name, and there seemed to be a family resemblance," Albert said.

"Oh yes, yes. I remember that now," his father said.

"We met again, occasionally, over the past few years, but I didn't know him well. I was very surprised when I got his note. I suppose he didn't know who else to turn to. I felt I had to try to help. What will they do now? We can't just throw them out!" Albert said.

"No, of course not, but we have to get them safely out of the country. I have some business contacts that might be useful. Accountants meet all kinds of people. Let me work on it for a few days. Come for dinner next Sunday, and we'll see what I've been able to arrange. Meanwhile, find out what papers they are carrying, and try to get their pictures, in case we need to . . . improvise. They can stay where they are until everything is arranged," his father said.

Albert looked at his father as if he were seeing him for the first time. He had always seemed so stodgy and ordinary. Now there was a gleam in his eyes, a smile curled up around his pipe. He was positively enjoying this!

"Thank you, Father. I'm glad you're willing to help."

"Well, what are you going to do? After all, they're family," his father said.

* * *

Jana lay awake, trying to sleep. The stuffy bedroom seemed airless. She tiptoed over to the open window and knelt in front of it, hoping to find a cool breeze. She'd opened the window earlier to let some fresh air into the stuffy, overcrowded bedroom that she shared with her sisters and girl cousins. She knelt, leaning her head on her arms, crossed on the windowsill, and looked up at the sliver of the new moon. She closed her eyes and imagined riding a horse, under the stars, across a cool dark pasture.

Suddenly, she heard a low murmur of voices, and the sound of horses, below in the backyard, and opened her eyes to see Uncle Vaclav step out of the shed, carrying a lantern. Following him were two shadowy figures. As he raised the lamp, she recognized Otto and Max. They were each leading a horse.

"Be careful," Vaclav said to them and then turned toward the house.

Otto and Max silently led their horses off into the night. A few moments later, Jana heard the back door open and close.

The moon glinted off the snow as they followed the path through the woods.

"Hold on," Otto said.

"What for?" Max sounded cross. He'd been complaining about being cold and tired.

"I need to look at the map," Otto said. Albert had drawn them a small map to guide them to the summer cottage.

He pulled it out of his pocket and held it up, hoping to catch enough light from the moon to read it, but it was too dark. He pulled out a small box of matches, lit one, and held it up to the map, squinting at it.

"There should be a path off to our right coming up pretty soon."

"It's about time. Why are we doing this, and not Albert?" Max complained.

"We volunteered," Otto said.

"You mean *you* volunteered. Next time, you go without me. I barely know these people," Max said.

"Would you just shut up? We're almost there now," Otto said.

They rode silently through the night for another half hour before they came to a clearing in the woods and a small summer cottage, just as Albert had described it. Otto thought it was strange that there wasn't any smoke coming out of the chimney. They dismounted and went up to the door. Otto knocked lightly, then more loudly. There was no answer. He tried the door. It wasn't locked. They went in and had a look around. No one was there.

"What the . . ." Max said. "Are you sure we're in the right place?"

"Positive. There aren't that many summer cottages in this area. We couldn't have gone that far off course," Otto said.

"Well then, where are they?" Max asked.

"How should I know? Would you shut up and let me think? Let's see if we can find a light." Otto lit a match and held it up.

He found an oil lamp hanging on the wall. He took it down, lit it, and then held it up to look around. They were standing in the kitchen. It contained a wood-burning stove, a rocking chair next to the stove, a large enamel sink with a hand pump, some cupboards and shelves, and a kitchen table surrounded by four wooden chairs.

They checked the rest of the cottage. There were two other doors—one opened into a bedroom; the other was the door to the cellar. A steep staircase led up to a sleeping loft. It didn't take long to determine that no one was there. Dishes were stacked on the counter, and a towel hung on a hook next to them. The wood-burning stove was still warm.

"It looks like they were here. They must have left just a short time ago. Go outside and see if you can see anything. I'm going to start a fire in the stove," Otto said.

Max returned a couple of minutes later. “I didn’t see any trace of them. They must have left.”

Otto and Max decided to stay the night. By the time they’d taken care of the horses and stashed the supplies that they’d brought, the stove had warmed the little cottage. They unrolled their sleeping bags next to the stove and settled in for the night. The next morning, they were awakened by the sound of someone who was knocking loudly on the door.

Otto sat up silently and nudged his brother, who was still snoring.

“What?” Max said before he saw his brother put his finger up to his lip, motioning him to be silent.

Otto reached under his sleeping bag, pulled out a gun, and handed it to Max.

“Cover me,” he mouthed silently and gestured toward the bedroom with his head.

The pounding on the door started again.

“Just a minute!” Otto called out. He quickly grabbed his brother’s sleeping bag and clothes and threw them into the bedroom after his brother.

He opened the door, barefoot and shirtless, rubbing his eyes sleepily, and yawned to show that he had been sound asleep, though he felt wide awake and alert, now. Standing at the door was a short, plump police constable, his horse standing in the yard behind him.

“Who are you and what are you doing here?” the policeman demanded. He stuck his head into the cottage and looked around suspiciously.

“I’m a friend of the family. I was just passing by and thought I’d stop and make sure everything here was okay, and spend the night since it was getting late,” Otto said with a disarming smile.

"How did you get in?"

"It wasn't locked. Do you want to come in? It's cold standing here with the door open," Otto said.

The officer stepped inside, and Otto closed the door behind him.

"How about a cup of coffee?" Otto asked. He picked up the metal coffeepot and, going over to the sink, pumped water into it.

"Where's the other one?" the policeman asked.

"The other one?" Otto repeated, stalling for time. He put the coffeepot on the stove, opened the stove, stirred the embers with a poker, and put another log on.

"I saw two horses in the stable."

At that, Max stepped out of the other room. He'd gotten dressed, and was pointing the gun at the policeman.

The policeman started to reach for his gun.

"Uh-uh. Don't try anything," Otto warned. He stepped over and took the pistol out of his holster. Checking it, he saw that it was loaded.

"What did you do that for?" Otto asked Max, in Romani.

"Do what?"

"Barge in like that. I could have talked our way out of here. Now the situation is serious. We can't just say 'sorry' and let him go," Otto said.

"He knew I was here. I had to get a jump on him," Max said.

"What are you two talking about?" the policeman asked.

"The weather," Otto replied in Czech.

"Have a seat." He gestured with the gun toward one of the kitchen chairs.

The brothers continued talking in Romani.

"What are we going to do with him?" Otto asked.

"I don't know," Max said.

"I guess we should tie him up. See if you can find some rope. I'll keep an eye on him," Otto said.

Max rummaged around inside cupboards and drawers. "Damn it! There's no rope! Should I go look in the barn?"

"Sure, go. No, wait. Watch him for a minute while I get dressed. It's cold in here," Otto said. He finished getting dressed, then said, "Okay, you can go now."

Otto sat down across from the policeman and laid the gun on the table in front of him. They sat watching each other. Neither one said anything for several minutes. The little policeman looked nervous. Beads of perspiration stood on his forehead, despite the chill in the room. Otto drummed his fingers on the table next to the gun.

"Will someone come looking for you?" Otto asked.

"I suppose so. My deputy knows where I went. He'll come looking for me eventually," the policeman said.

After a few more minutes, Max returned with a short length of rope. "Is this long enough?" he asked.

"Is that all you could find? There's got to be more rope around here somewhere. Wasn't there any in the supplies we brought?" Otto said.

"No. I looked," Max said.

"Look again!" Otto said.

"I looked, I'm telling you. You can go look if you want to," Max said.

"Well, what else? Can we lock him in the bedroom?" Otto asked.

"It won't work. The door opens into the room, and it doesn't have a lock," Max said, examining the door.

"Watch him. I'll see if I can find some rope," Otto said.

As he started looking through cupboards and drawers, the coffee-pot started to boil. "I guess we won't have time for coffee this morning," he said. He picked up a pot holder, took the coffeepot off the stove, and started pouring the boiling water down the sink. As he did so, he glanced up through the kitchen window and noticed the outhouse.

"Let's lock him in the outhouse," Otto said.

"What?" Max laughed.

"Sure, why not? The door opens out. We'll just stick him in there and wedge a board against the door," Otto said.

"It won't hold him for long," Max said.

"It doesn't have to. Just long enough for us to make a run for it. Get our horses ready, and find something we can wedge against the door," Otto said.

When Max came back, Otto motioned for the policeman to get up. "Let's go," he said in Czech.

"Where are you taking me?" Clearly, he hadn't understood their conversation.

"Just on your morning trip to check on the horses," Otto said. The brothers looked at each other and laughed.

"What do you mean? You better not do anything crazy!"

"Just get going." Otto grabbed his arm and pulled him along, while Max followed behind with the gun. Max opened the door of the outhouse, and Otto shoved the policeman in. Then Max picked up the plank that he'd found and wedged it firmly against the door.

"Let's get going," Otto said.

"What about his horse?" Max asked as they jumped on their horses.

"We'll take it with us for a little way, and then let it go. That'll give us a head start," Otto said.

"Shouldn't we keep it?" Maxed asked.

"No, a horse is too hard to hide. It's too risky. I'll keep his gun, though," Otto said and stuck it in his saddlebag.

They got on their horses, grabbed the reins of the other horse, and rode off. They hadn't gone far before they heard banging and then the sound of splintering wood. After a mile or two, they released the policeman's horse.

CHAPTER 10

Helena stared out the kitchen window over the sink, the potato she was peeling momentarily forgotten in her hand as she thought about how she closed the door and turned away that morning. "I'm sorry, I wish we could help, but we just can't get involved. I'm sorry," she'd said. The look in their eyes as she'd closed the door haunted her. Had she done the right thing?

She glanced at the clock. A few minutes later, right on schedule, Karel walked through the door. He kissed Helena on the cheek, as usual. She murmured a greeting.

When they sat down to dinner, Helena fussed over arranging the serving dishes on the table, lost in thought. After a few moments, she sensed Karel was watching her, looked up, and smiled nervously.

"I was reading the paper on the way to work this morning," he said. "It's terrible what's happened in some of the Sudeten-area towns. I wonder what ever became of your nephew and his family."

"Albert was foolish to get involved with them," she said.

"Albert is a good boy. He has a good heart," he said.

Helena looked at Karel sharply. She felt her face flush and looked down at her plate. "Yes, he is a good boy," she said, "but sometimes overly impetuous, like his father."

"Impetuous? I'm an accountant!" He sawed at his ham with unnecessary vigor.

They ate in silence for a few moments.

"Anyway, we must look out for ourselves and our son first. God helps those who help themselves," she said.

"It could have been our son, you know," he said.

"But it wasn't. If my brother hadn't married a Jewess, none of this would have happened," she said.

"It might have. Just being Czech in the Sudeten area can be dangerous these days," he said.

"Then he shouldn't have gone there to live. All this moving around and mixing with all sorts! What for?" she said.

"These are new times. People mix more than they used to," he said.

Helena put down her fork and knife and grabbed her napkin, anxiously twisting it. "Look what that's brought—nothing but grief. If my brother had stayed home and married one of his own kind, this would never have happened."

"It's too late for 'if only.' The question is what to do next," he said.

Helena continued to twist her napkin. Karel rested his hands on the table, knife in one hand, fork in the other, resting them on the edge of his plate, and watched her for a moment. He looked like he was trying to think of something he could say that would make her feel better, but he couldn't.

"They came to me after you turned them away," he said.

"I see. I thought they might, but I hoped that they would find another way. What did you do?" she said.

"Nothing that should cause us any trouble. Don't worry," he said. "They just needed identification papers. We talked it over and agreed they should leave the country while they still can. They had to leave everything behind. I put them in touch with some people who can help them."

"How can they afford to go abroad?" she asked.

"I loaned them a little money," he said.

"You loaned them money? We can't afford that! How much money?" she asked.

"Not much. Don't worry about it! They'll pay us back as soon as they're able," he said.

She stopped twisting her napkin and sat, now limp armed, her shoulders slumped.

"Don't worry, Helena. Everything will work out. You'll see," Karel said. He started eating again and finished his meal with gusto.

Karel was just settling into his favorite chair with his pipe when the phone rang in the hall. Helena answered it and came to get him. The color had drained from her face.

"It's for you. It's a long-distance call from the police," she said.

He got up and walked to the phone, nervously rubbing his palms on his vest.

"Hello."

"Hello. This is Officer Kepka. I'm afraid I have some bad news about your summer cottage."

"Oh? What's that?"

"It seems there was a break-in. I went to investigate, due to reports of unexplained activity there, and found it occupied by two Gypsies. Were you aware of that?"

"No, I wasn't." Karel knew that Helena was listening from the kitchen, so he tried to keep his answers as neutral as possible.

"They claimed to know you, and had your permission to use the cottage."

"No, I'm afraid that's not true."

"What about your son? I believe you have a college-age son."

"That's true, but my son is busy with his studies. I'm sure he wasn't there."

"Perhaps these Gypsies were friends of your son."

"I doubt that. Probably just vagabonds looking for a warm place to spend the night."

"Smoke was noticed coming from the house for several days."

"I'm sorry. I don't know anything about it. Was there any damage to the place?"

Officer Kepka hesitated.

"I believe there was some damage to the outhouse door."

"The outhouse door?"

"Yes."

"How odd. Was that all?"

"As far as I can tell, but perhaps you should come up and look around."

"Yes, perhaps I'll do that. Thank you, Officer. Was there anything else?"

"Yes, well, there's the missing gun. There was a scuffle, there were two of them, and they took my gun."

"Oh my! You don't say!"

"So, if you hear of anything, please let me know. I will need to follow up on this."

"Of course, of course."

Karel jotted down the officer's name and phone number and promised to let him know if he heard anything.

CHAPTER 11

It had been days since Jana had last seen Otto. Since then she'd been stuck hanging around the house with the other women and girls. Oh, they kept her busy, all right—wash this, carry that, hold this baby—but it was all so boring!

She'd watched for her opportunity and, when no one was looking, slipped out the back door and headed toward the barn for a change of scenery. She took a deep breath of the cold, crisp air and then ran across the backyard through the thin layer of newly fallen snow. The smell of new wood greeted her as she entered the barn. It took her eyes a few moments to adjust to the dim sunlight that filtered through windows coated with years of dust. No one was around. They must be out picking up work or making deliveries. She shivered and hugged her sweater around her. The barn was cold. The dying embers in the potbellied stove, in the center of the room, provided the only warmth.

Glancing around, she saw the usual piles of wood of different sizes and shapes, stacked here and there, and the sawdust-covered floor. Half-finished chairs and a chest that was being repaired stood amidst the clutter. Then Jana noticed something new—a large, battered cardboard box near the entrance. She tried lifting one edge. It was heavy, but not heavy enough to be full of wood or tools.

She examined the box and noticed the word "puppets" written on the side of it. Now she was curious. She knelt in the sawdust and opened it. Inside she found yellow, crumpled newspapers, and nested in them, packages—each about two feet long, also wrapped in newspaper. She took one out and hefted it. It was heavy for its size. She laid it on the floor and gingerly unwrapped it.

It was a large wooden doll, dressed in red, wearing a pointed hat, with a bell at the end of the point. His expressive face had big eyes and ears, rosy cheeks, and a mischievous smile. The paint was chipped in spots, and the costume somewhat worn. Strings were attached to his arms legs, and head. The strings were all attached at the top to two crisscrossed pieces of wood.

Jana picked him up. The arms and legs swung loosely, and the bell on his cap tinkled, making her laugh. She laid him back on the newspaper, placed it back in the box, and pushed the box into the next room. Then she took out another bundle.

One by one she unwrapped the packages, so immersed that she forgot about the cold. She found a queen, a knight, a king, a fairy, and a devil. Each one ingeniously carved, painted, and dressed in cute little costumes, down to tiny leather boots or shoes. Soon, crumple newspapers and puppets surrounded her.

Otto went home to see his dad and hide the gun that he'd taken from the policeman. He went directly to the barn where he usually found his father working or sharing a smoke and a drink with some of the other men, but today there didn't seem to be anyone around. He was just about to leave the barn when he heard rustling sounds coming from the adjoining room, and went to investigate.

Otto found Jana unwrapping a package. She seemed not to notice him, and stared at what she had found, a skeleton puppet with empty eye sockets and an evil grin. It startled her, and she let out a little gasp.

"I see you've found the puppets," Otto said. Jana whirled around with a guilty look on her face, hiding the skeleton puppet behind her, to find Otto watching her with a look that was a mixture of annoyance and concealed amusement.

"I . . . I was just . . ." Jana stuttered and blushed.

"That's okay. Sometimes my dad works on them for the Sokol," he said.

"Sokol? Isn't that a gymnasium?" she asked.

"Yes, but it's also a meeting place. They have other events, such as puppet theater. They're probably going to put on a Christmas play and hired my dad to get the puppets ready for it. I'm looking for him. Have you seen him?" he asked.

"No, have you looked in the house?" she asked.

"Not yet." He turned and left.

Jana lingered over unwrapping the packages. Each one contained another surprise: a wolf, a bear, a tin soldier, and other figures. She was only dimly aware of the sound of horses and then the men's voices as they returned from their deliveries. She was admiring the ingenious hinged joints and clever costumes when Uncle Vaclav came into the room.

"How do you like the little playthings?" he boomed.

"They're great. Is it okay that I unwrapped them?" she asked.

"Of course. Why not? Would you like to help me fix them up? It's a job that needs to be done soon, and I have a lot of other projects I'm working on. It would be a great help," Uncle Vaclav said.

"I'd love to!" Jana said.

Otto went back to the house to wait for his father to return. His mother made a big fuss over him, as usual when he visited, bringing him food and drink and plying him with questions. His answers were evasive. After a while, they heard the horse-drawn cart pulling into the driveway. Otto kissed his mother goodbye and went back outside.

"Well, hello, stranger. Where have you been?" Vaclav asked.

"Oh, you know, staying with Albert, mostly," Otto said. He helped his dad unhitch the horse and put him in his stall.

"Do you have a few minutes? I want to talk to you, Dad."

They went into the barn. Vaclav poked at the fire in the potbellied stove and then threw another log on the fire. Meanwhile, Otto strolled casually over to the door to the next room.

"Jana, aren't you getting kind of cold out here?" he said.

"No, I'm fine," she said.

"My mom was looking for you. I think she needs help with dinner," he said.

Reluctantly she put down the puppet and left.

Otto and his dad pulled a couple of old wooden chairs up to the stove and made themselves comfortable. Vaclav pulled out his pipe and bag of tobacco and filled his pipe. Otto lit a cigarette.

Vaclav talked about the weather and how business was going for a few minutes, watching Otto out of the corner of his eye and waiting for him to tell him what was on his mind.

Finally, Otto just blurted it out. "I got suspended from school."

"Really? How did that happen?"

"I got into a fight. It's a long story."

"Take your time."

Otto told him how the German students had created a disturbance in history class, and about the fight that ensued.

His dad listened quietly, nodding occasionally. Then, after a few moments of silence, he said, "It sounds like it was a fight that was hard to avoid. Oh well, it's probably for the best. Why don't you move home and help me with the business?"

Otto looked at his father in frustration. He didn't know what kind of reaction he'd expected, but he hadn't expected this blasé acceptance. It seemed like his father felt relieved more than anything.

"I don't know, Dad."

"Maybe it's time to think about getting married. Jana is about the right age, and you two seem to like each other."

"Jana? She's just a child. I'm not interested in marrying her, or anyone else," Otto said.

Just then, he turned and saw Jana standing in the doorway. She'd obviously overheard what he'd just said.

"Your mother was not looking for me. You're a liar, and for your information, I wouldn't marry you if you were the last man on earth!" she said and slammed the door.

Vaclav laughed. "What a little spitfire!"

Otto just grunted angrily, opened the door of the stove, threw his cigarette butt in, and slammed it shut.

"You want me to marry her?" he asked.

Vaclav was still laughing. Finally, he said, "Well, I don't think she'd have you, now. But I'm sure she'll get over it. She wouldn't be so angry if she didn't like you."

"Maybe, but I'm not ready to marry anyone just yet. I want to finish college. I'm just suspended. I can go back next semester. Right now, I'm going to go and try to earn some money," Otto said. "I hear there are good-paying jobs in the Skoda Works armaments plant. Now that war is on the horizon, they're hiring extra help."

"But will they hire a Gypsy?"

"I don't necessarily have to be a Gypsy, as far as they're concerned. I can get identity papers with a good Czech-sounding last name. I'm light-skinned enough to pass," Otto said.

"That's all the way in Plzeň. I don't like the idea of you being so far away from home," his father said.

"I could save money. I could afford a place of my own. Then, maybe, I'll be ready to get married," Otto said, hoping this would influence his father.

"I guess that makes sense," his father said, "but I hate to have to tell your mother."

Jana cried herself to sleep that night, but then told herself she didn't care what Otto thought. After all, she didn't want to marry him, either. For the next few days, she sometimes wondered where he was, and what he was doing, but gradually she thought about him less and less often and, instead, spent hours absorbed in working on the puppets. She sanded and repainted their faces, took off their costumes and carefully washed them, and enlisted the help of her mother and aunts in showing her how to repair those that needed repair. They were happy to see her keeping busy, staying out of trouble, and taking an interest in washing and repairing clothes, if only those belonging to puppets. Soon it was time to pack them up and send them back to the Sokol.

The evening performance for adults was *Dr. Faust*, but there was also an afternoon matinee of fairy tales for children. In appreciation for Jana's work, the two front rows of the matinee performance were reserved for her and her family. Her brothers and sisters and younger cousins all wanted to go, and they filled all the reserved seats.

They saw two fairy tales, *The Devil's Mill* and *The Kids and the Wolf.* Jana was mesmerized as the puppets she'd worked on came to life and spoke.

In the story of *The Devil's Mill,* a veteran soldier outsmarts the devil. The story begins with a mill sitting in a remote spot. The mill turns and turns, but grinds no corn, because a devil inhabits it. The soldier has heard of this mill and goes there, lights his pipe, and waits. Jana jumped a little when the devil appeared in a puff of smoke, at the stroke of midnight.

The soldier petrifies the devil with a magic incantation he's learned, ties up the devil, and starts to beat him until the devil promises the soldier a reward if he releases him. The soldier unties the devil and is rewarded with a bag of gold. He uses the gold to build a new mill and takes his sister, who is a widow, and her six children there to live. They live happily ever after.

The second story was *The Kids and the Wolf.* In this story, three naughty little kids are left alone at home while their mother goes shopping. They are told to stay indoors, but soon are bored and go outside to play. There they are spotted by a wolf who tries to catch them. But they are too quick for him. Jana laughed at their antics as they ran circles around the wolf.

The wolf then devises a clever scheme to get close enough to the kids to grab them and eat them. He disguises himself as their mother. He covers himself with flour, so he appears white, and uses honey to sweeten his voice. His plan might have worked, except the bear comes along. The bear recognizes the wolf, beats him up, and puts him in the zoo.

In the shadows at the back of the auditorium, a short, balding man sat, sweating uncomfortably in his overly tight wool suit. It was Officer Kepka, and he was trying to get his two grandsons to pay attention to the puppet show, and stop kicking each other. He noticed with irritation the Gypsy children who filled the front rows of the auditorium.

Dirty Gypsies! he thought. *They shouldn't be allowed in here at all, much less be allowed to sit in front of everyone else.*

Ever since the Gypsies had made a fool of him by stealing his gun and locking him in the outhouse, he had tried to track them down. His contacts in Prague had told him that Albert, the son of the family that owned the cottage, had been seen at this branch of Sokol, and in the company of a couple of young Gypsy men. Bringing his grandsons to today's puppet show was another chance to come here, in hopes of spotting them.

Just then, a girl in front of him turned her head and he saw a glimpse of her face.

There's something familiar about that girl, he thought. Then he remembered—she was the one who'd bitten him! More Gypsy mischief. Why had she been hanging around that night, all alone, if she wasn't a prostitute? A man had certain natural urges, after all.

He grew angrier as he brooded about both incidents. He watched her throughout the show and as she got up to leave. He ignored his grandsons, who fidgeted and whined beside him.

After the girl had left the auditorium, he jumped out of his seat and dashed after her, pulling his hat down over his eyes so that she wouldn't recognize him.

"Come on, come on," he said as his grandsons hurriedly grabbed their hats and coats and ran to catch up to him. He stopped, abruptly, in the lobby, watching her from a distance.

He saw the Gypsy children as they ran around like a brightly colored whirlwind, laughing and jabbering in their language, their hair wild and uncombed, and their clothes untucked, too big, torn, or multicolored. The girl was in the middle of the commotion, talking, laughing, and running to grab one of the smaller ones who had strayed too far. He couldn't help but notice how lovely she was, slender and graceful, with big brown eyes and long dark hair. Somehow, that made him even angrier.

As he watched, a prosperous-appearing middle-aged Gypsy man and a Czech man walked up to the girl and talked to her. It looked like the Czech man was being introduced to her. *Jana*, the Gypsy man called her. The Czech man shook her hand and nodded and smiled.

"Let's go, Grandpa!" He looked down and saw one of his grandsons tugging on his arm.

"Just a minute," he snapped.

The Czech man who'd been talking to Jana circulated throughout the lobby, stopping to speak to several more people in the rapidly thinning crowd, and then went into an office.

Just then a young Gypsy man came through the door and said something in Romani to the group, and they all started to leave.

Officer Kepka looked at him with startled recognition. He was one of the men who'd attacked him and stolen his gun! So, his plan had paid off. He'd finally found them, and they were all connected, somehow. He looked around to see if there was a police officer who could help him arrest all of them.

"I'm hungry. I want to go home," whined his other grandson.

Of course, if he did turn them over to the Prague police, the girl might identify him as the drunk who tried to pick her up one night when he was supposedly working, and the details of how two Gypsies had jumped him and locked him into an outhouse would certainly make him a laughingstock, and might also mean his job, his pension. Worse, he could count on his grandsons to repeat every word they heard, and if his wife found out he'd been prowling for women when he was supposedly working, he would be better off dead!

"Okay, okay," he grumbled.

I'll have to wait for another opportunity to get even, he thought.

CHAPTER 12

The new year of 1939 settled into a humdrum routine for Jana. The excitement of Christmas and the puppet show was in the past. Otto had gone to Plzeň, to work in the Skoda Works, so there wasn't a chance of seeing him or exchanging a word with him. His absence made everyday life seem very dull.

The daily routines of cooking, cleaning, and childcare kept Jana busy but didn't keep her mind occupied, and she chafed at the boredom. Whenever possible, she would get away and find a place where she couldn't be drafted as a mother's helper.

One of her favorite hiding spots was in their wagon, which was parked in the back courtyard, next to the barn. Although it was cold, when the sun was shining, it was reasonably comfortable. She'd climb into her parents' sleeping compartment and draw the curtain that separated it from the rest of the interior, wrap up in a blanket, and daydream while looking at a few magazines that she'd managed to stash there.

Jana had only attended school sporadically, during the winter months, due to her family's travels during the warmer seasons, so she was a slow reader, but she liked the glossy pictures and read what she could, wondering what the other words meant. *Perhaps Otto will teach me when he comes back*, she thought

Max, Otto's brother, helped his father with his furniture repair business. He usually came and went several times a day, picking up and delivering furniture. Jana was peering out the window, through the crack between the curtains, idly watching Max unload furniture one day when she noticed an odd thing. He was unloading a chair that she was sure she'd seen before. In fact, when she thought about it, it seemed like she'd seen it on more than one occasion. She sat up straight, suddenly very alert.

What's going on? She wondered.

When he'd finished bringing in all the furniture, she jumped out of the wagon, ran around the back of the barn, and peeked into the window of the workroom. Max was standing by the potbelly stove, holding the chair she'd seen him unloading. He looked around. She ducked as he began to turn in her direction. Her heart beat wildly as she stood upright and peeked through the window again. Max was standing with his back to her now as he removed a leg from the chair. Then, after fumbling with it for a few moments, she saw him remove a rolled-up paper from the inside of the leg, quickly shove the paper inside his jacket, and replace the leg of the chair. He glanced around again, and Jana ducked down again. When she looked again, Max and the chair were gone.

Jana ran back around the barn, and as she was rounding the corner she ran into Max, who was waiting there for her. He grabbed her by her arm and shook her.

"What do you think you're doing?" he said.

"Nothing. Ouch, let me go! You're hurting me!"

"Nothing, huh? Let's see about that."

He dragged her back around to the window where she'd been standing moments before. Her footsteps stopped there.

"If you're going to sneak around, you could at least try to be a little cleverer about it. Didn't you think I would see your footprints in the snow? Now tell me what you saw!" he said as he shook her again.

"I didn't see anything!" she yelled as she kicked and hit him with her free arm.

He grabbed her other arm and held her at arm's length while she continued to try to kick him, but his arms were too long. She bent her head and bit down on his hand.

"Ouch!" he yelled, letting go for a moment.

She took off running as fast as she could. He ran after her and grabbed her around the waist with one arm, and pinned down her arms with the other arm. She wiggled and thrashed around, cursing at him.

"Listen to me! Listen to me!" he said.

They continued to struggle until they fell to the ground, and he had her pinned. She finally realized it was useless. He was much stronger than her.

"Now will you listen to me?" he panted.

"Okay, okay! But get off me! You're crushing me!"

He got up and stood with his hands on his hips, panting. Jana got up and straightened out her skirt, brushing off the snow.

"You're tough, for a girl," he said, and laughed after he caught his breath. "Now tell me what you saw, or I'll slap you silly!"

"You don't scare me," she said. "If you touch me again, I'll tell my dad, and he'll beat the crap out of you!"

"Okay, okay! Let's call a truce. This is important. I have to know what you saw," he said.

"I saw everything—the chair, the leg, the paper you took out of it and stuffed inside your jacket," she said.

His eyes widened in fear. "We have to talk. Come into the barn with me," he said.

She followed him into the barn and over to the potbellied stove. Jana stood close to it, suddenly aware that she was cold and damp from rolling in the snow. Max's face was very serious now. He sat on a stool and looked down at his hands for a few moments, evidently trying to decide what to say.

"Can you keep a secret?" he asked.

"Of course," Jana said.

"If anyone found out what I'm doing, I could be sent to prison, or worse. Do you understand?"

She could see by his expression that he meant it. "Yes, I understand."

"Someone, I can't tell you who, has access to information that they need to get out of the country. I'm helping. The government has already imposed censorship on the press, and certain information cannot be printed."

"But why? The Germans haven't taken over the whole country, just the Sudetenland," she said.

"That's true, but they're trying to please the Germans and do things their way so they won't take over the whole country. They want to hang on as long as they can."

"Why do you care? What does this have to do with us?" she asked.

"We can't stay isolated forever. Times are changing. The old traveling ways are dying out. We need to become part of the society we live in," he said. It sounded rehearsed as if he was repeating something he'd heard before or something he'd worked out beforehand.

"Will you keep it secret?" he asked. "It's very, very important. No one else knows—not even my father—only Otto, and now you."

"Don't worry. I won't tell anyone," Jana said.

"Why are you all wet?" her stepmother, Zofie, scolded when Jana went into the house. "You're soaking wet! What have you been doing?"

"Nothing. I was just playing in the snow," Jana said.

"Playing! You're not a child anymore, Jana. You should be helping me, not running around in the snow like you're touched!" She handed Jana baby Eduard who was howling. "Change his diaper. I have to start dinner," she said and stormed off into the kitchen.

During dinner, Jana's father listened with downcast eyes and wrinkled brow to Zofie's litany of complaints about Jana—she was always wandering off, she complained too much. and didn't help enough. It was all too familiar.

"Maybe she needs a change of scenery," he said, after Zofie at last wound down. "Vaclav said there was a job open, working in the kitchen at the castle. They're hiring a woman to help with preparing and serving food."

"That's right," Vaclav said. "I know the families of some of the women working there, and they tell me that they rarely see anyone outside of the other members of the staff. They'll keep an eye on her, so she'll be safe. It wouldn't pay much, of course, but it would be something, and keep her busy."

"Max could bring her in the morning and pick her up later, while he is out making his rounds," Josef added.

Max and Jana glanced at each other. He looked alarmed. She immediately looked down at her plate.

"No, no! I don't want her to come with me!" Max protested.

"Why not?" Josef asked.

"Well, because . . . She's a girl! I just don't."

"Max, that's no way to speak to my cousin," his father said. "I know Otto was against Jana riding along with you on your route, but this won't be riding around all day—just there in the morning and back at night. The girl is bored!" He smiled at her fondly. "What's the harm? Are you interested?" he asked Jana.

She nodded.

Max's face darkened with anger, but he didn't say anything more.

"Okay, then. It's settled. I'll arrange it, and she can start in a few days."

CHAPTER 13

Otto stubbed out his cigarette and then lingered for a while longer, leaning against the wall. Next to him was a pile of wooden pallets. He'd taken shelter behind it, shielded from the wind, for a quick smoke break. He shivered in the cold winter day, but he still wasn't in any hurry to go back to work, though he knew he would have to, soon. Lately, he'd noticed his foreman and another man meeting out here. He was curious to find out what they were up to.

A train whistle sounded as the train left the rail yards of Skoda Works after dropping off its load of coal, iron ore, or limestone. All day and night trains came and went, bringing supplies to the huge complex for the manufacture of iron and steel goods. The sound seemed to tug at his chest, and he yearned to just hop on a train and disappear from this place, but he knew he had to stay, for a while.

Otto was about to head back in when the sound of two men approaching stopped him.

They stopped on the opposite side of the pile of wooden pallets.

"This may be our only chance." Otto recognized the voice of his foreman, Mr. Jelinek. "They are starting to replace us with Germans."

"It's too risky. If we get caught, we'll be shot," the other man said.

They were speaking very softly. Otto strained to hear more.

"We knew that before we started this, but it won't come to that. All we have to do is get you to replace the quality inspector, at least for one day. Then you will look the other way during the second inspection after the alloys are added. I'll give you the word when we're ready. Don't worry. It's all been worked out. Just do what we agreed on. Chances are, they'll never put it together and figure out what happened. If they do, we'll already be transferred out of here before then."

"Is this going to work? How do you know what to add, or how much?"

The response was inaudible. Otto leaned toward them, trying to catch their words, and a little loose mortar crumbled to the ground. The voices stopped abruptly, followed by the sound of footsteps retreating. Otto stood frozen in place, peering through the stacks of pallets, but it was too dark to see anything. He tried to think of what to do next. Should he try to go around the other side of the building?

No, there's a fence along the back—that won't work, he thought.

He lit another cigarette and nonchalantly strolled back toward his workstation. Mr. Jelinek was waiting for him.

"Where were you?" he asked, eyeing him suspiciously.

"I had to answer nature's call."

"What took you so long?" He scrutinized Otto's face, clearly looking for signs of nervousness or evasion. Otto smiled back at him, with what he hoped was a disarming expression.

"Had to have a smoke, too. Sorry." He flicked the cigarette away.

"Wipe that stupid grin off our face and get back to work," Mr. Jelinek growled and stalked away.

He's suspicious, Otto thought, *so he'll watch me even more closely. Well, that's okay, because I'll be watching him, too. I wonder what he's up to. "Is this going to work? How do you know what to add, or how much?" What were they talking about?*

Several times he thought he caught Mr. Jelinek watching him, but when he looked up, he turned aside. That night, on the way home, it seemed that a man was following him, but he couldn't be sure. Maybe he was just going the same way.

Otto had been working at Skoda for several weeks now. He was staying with his cousin's family. They were expecting another child, their fifth, but they were happy to put all the kids together into one bedroom so they could free up a room for Otto, in exchange for a modest payment for room and board.

They lived on the far edge of town, so early every morning, before light, Otto picked up the lunch bucket his cousin's wife packed for him and walked the several miles across town to work. About halfway there, he crossed the town square and passed by the tower of St. Bartholomew.

Sometimes, when it was especially cold, he stopped in the church to warm up. He sat in the back row and watched a few elderly ladies saying their prayers, while the priest said Mass in front of the altar, with the statue of the Madonna watching him. The Madonna wore a gold crown and held a baby who appeared to be about two years old, who had a halo around his head and held a golden apple. They both looked off to the side, and not at each other, leaning away from each other, so their bodies formed sort of a Y-shape. Each time he looked at it, Otto wondered what they saw.

It was a long walk. Otto often thought about his family while he walked and was surprised to realize that he missed all of them. He especially missed Jana's animated little face. He smiled at the thought of her. He wouldn't have wanted to admit it, but sometimes he prayed for all of them when he stopped in the church. He didn't know any real prayers, so he just made them up, then crossed himself like he saw the old ladies doing, even though he felt kind of silly doing it.

About a week after the overheard conversation, as he left the church, he noticed a man walking toward him, a cap pulled down and collar turned up against the cold. As he approached, the man stopped, pulled out a cigarette, and patted his pockets. As Otto was about to pass, he said, "Excuse me, do you have a light?"

Otto stopped, pulled out a book of matches, and lit the man's cigarette. The man mumbled thanks, and then looked up from under his cap. Otto recognized him as the man he had seen talking to Mr. Jelinek. "Meet us tonight, at the pub over there"—he nodded north—"at the end of your shift. To talk about what you heard."

"Who are you?" Otto asked.

"Come tonight if you want to know," he said and walked on.

Otto stood inside the door of the pub for a moment while his eyes adjusted to the dim light of the smoke-filled room. Then, off at a corner table, he spotted Mr. Jelinek and the mysterious stranger. He made his way across the crowded room, pulled out one of the old wooden chairs, and joined them at their table.

"Hello, Josef—if that's your name," Mr. Jelinek said.

This caught Otto by surprise. He'd registered for work using falsified papers, under the name of Josef Tucek.

"What do you mean?" Otto asked.

"Skip it. We did a little checking, and we know that you're not who you say you are," Mr. Jelinek said.

Otto took out his pack of cigarettes and offered them to the other men. They waved them off, and he lit one. "Who's your friend?" he asked Mr. Jelinek.

"You can call him Petr. It's better if we don't get too well acquainted. Do you want a beer?"

"Sure. Do you mind telling me what this is all about?"

"We'll get to that, but first, let's relax and enjoy our beers."

They sat, drinking their beers and making a little small talk about the weather and the relative merits of dark versus light beers. Then Mr. Jelinek put down his beer and leaned back in his chair, his eyes narrowed as he looked at Otto.

"First, I'd just like to point out that you could get in a lot of trouble for using fake identification papers, and we know where you live. We had you followed, so don't think about repeating anything you hear tonight or it could be bad for you. Got it?" he said.

"Yeah, I got it," Otto said. He was starting to feel a little nervous. "What's this all about?"

"Are you a good friend of the Germans?" Petr asked.

"What? Not at all! I guess they'd be okay if they stayed where they belong and minded their own business but, obviously, that's not what they're doing," Otto said.

"Do you consider yourself a patriot, Mr. Tucek?" Mr. Jelinek asked.

"Sure I do," Otto said.

Mr. Jelinek took another drink of beer, then put his glass down and said in a low voice, "Pressure is being brought to bear on the management at Skoda to start selling guns to the German army. Soon, many of the managers and foremen will be transferred, or lose their jobs. We're going to be replaced by Germans."

"How do you know that?" Otto asked.

"That's not important. The important thing is that I do know. Before that happens, we want to strike a blow for our country. That's where you and Petr can help. Petr studied chemistry at the university. He tells me that certain small quantities of sulfur and zinc can cause the steel to become brittle so that, if made into guns, for example, the guns will explode after being used for a while."

Petr and Mr. Jelinek watched Otto, to see his reaction to this idea.

"How would we do it?" he asked.

"Well, since you're involved in moving around raw materials, we just need to get the materials to you and let you know when and where to deliver them. They will be added when the alloys are added. Petr will make sure that the steel passes its final inspection. Every heat of steel we can tamper with is around 240 tons. That makes a lot of guns, and they can be pretty well dispersed before the problem is detected."

"Can we get away with it?" Otto asked.

"Yes, I think so," Mr. Jelinek said. "You can, probably best of all, since you're working under an assumed name—as long as you disappear before the guns are found to be defective and traced back to the plant. Sorry, but it seems you're going to have a short career here at Skoda."

"Suits me fine," Otto said. "Just let me know what to do, and when. I've been looking for a chance to fight the enemy."

"Okay, great," Mr. Jelinek said and ordered another round of drinks.

CHAPTER 14

The morning of March 15, 1939, dawned. Snow fell steadily, and the cold wind swirled it around the German soldiers as they trudged along. Darkness started to fade, and the feeble light tried to shine through the gray, overcast sky. The faint light held no warmth.

Their packs seemed to be getting heavier as they tramped endlessly down the road, but Franz almost welcomed the extra weight. Without the extra exertion, he knew he would be even colder.

The company ground to a halt once more, and the cursing started again. Either another vehicle had broken down or more obstacles had to be cleared from the road.

"Oh crap, not again." Franz lifted the pack off his back and let it fall onto the snow-covered road. He sat down on it and got out a cigarette. Just as he lit it, his sergeant drove up.

"This isn't break time, Private. You, you, and you, come with me," he said, pointing to Franz and his friends Paul and Rolf.

They climbed into the back of the truck, and then they were driven to the front of the line, where a group of men was clearing sandbags and rubble off the road, a roadblock that had been left there by the Czech army as it had retreated.

"This is the pits!" Paul groused under his breath.

"Just another day of fun," Franz agreed. "Well, let's get it over with. The sooner we get to wherever it is we're going, the sooner we can get some rest."

"A warm bed, and maybe a warm little *fräulein*," Rolf said. "Bet I can carry more than you guys." He grabbed two sandbags in each hand and ran toward the side of the road.

"Dumb as an ox, but strong," Franz said to Paul.

They laughed, and both joined in the contest. Soon they'd worked up a sweat, and the roadblock was cleared. Then they jumped back into the truck and caught a few minutes of sleep while the company re-formed into marching order. It seemed like they'd just closed their eyes when they were rousted out of the truck, and they fell back into their positions, marching mechanically, half-asleep, one foot in front of the other.

The snow was still falling as they marched into Prague. Now wide awake, they marched down streets that were lined with people. Groups of German citizens waved swastika flags and cheered. Others cursed at them in Czech, shook their fists, and threw snowballs at the trucks and tanks. Most of the people just stood and watched silently, with looks of disbelief or anger on their faces. Some were crying.

The troops marched through the city for hours, their legs stiff from marching and the bitter cold, as the raw March wind whipped their faces. The uneven and slippery old cobblestones echoed with the sound of hobnailed boots, the roar of tanks, trucks, and other military vehicles.

Franz, Rolf, and Paul trudged along wearily with the others, through narrow, winding streets, across wide squares, over bridges and back again, past statues, fountains, and monuments. They began to wonder if the leaders were lost, or simply didn't have a destination.

The crowds thinned, and people hurried by, huddled against the cold wind, seeming to go about their business and ignoring the troops. Suddenly a man cried out in German, "Why don't you bastards march straight into the river?"

Rolf turned sharply to see who'd said that, tripped over an uneven cobblestone, lost his footing, and fell backward, landing on his backpack. At this, a few passersby stopped, pointed, and laughed uproariously. Franz felt his face grow hot as he reached down to help up his friend. The rest of the troops continued past them, as though they were a rock in a stream. Rolf struggled up without his pack and equipment, grabbed his rifle, and pointed it at the civilians on the sidewalk.

"Who said that?" he demanded. "Say it again, and I'll blow your head off!"

"Calm down! Come on, we'd better catch up or we'll be in trouble. They're going to have to let us stop soon or we'll be dropping like flies. Not exactly the impression they want to make," Franz said.

He helped Rolf get his backpack back on, and they jogged to catch up with Paul.

"What was all that commotion back there?" Paul asked.

"Just some jerk trying to show off," Franz said.

Eventually, the troops began to march off in separate directions. Franz's division was marched to an elementary school that had been cleared out for their use. They were told to go into one of the classrooms and move the furniture out of the way. Then they finally could rest.

As they unrolled their sleeping bags, Paul said, "You know, I couldn't help but notice that everything seems pretty peaceful."

"What do you mean?" Rolf asked.

"Everything we heard on the radio, and read in the papers, about how the Germans are being oppressed by the Czechs. The ones we saw today didn't look oppressed."

"We can't figure out what's going on just from what we can see in one day!" Rolf said. "We have to trust our leaders. They have the big picture."

"Yeah, I suppose you're right," Paul said, sleepily. He yawned and lay back on his sleeping bag. "I'm going to catch a little shut-eye. Wake me up if you guys decide to do anything." Then he rolled over and went to sleep.

Franz was too tired to say anything, but privately thought it best not to believe everything you hear, but there wasn't much he could do, anyway. If you're a soldier, you just do what you're told, so there really wasn't much point worrying about it. He closed his eyes, and all he saw with his eyes closed was snow, endless falling snow, and then he, too, fell asleep.

Albert had stayed up most of the night listening to the radio. Yesterday Slovakia had seceded. Rumors had been flying the last few days about German troops massing on the borders and President Hácha's sudden trip to Berlin. He had finally fallen asleep, exhausted, in the early hours of the morning, as the few flakes of snow had increased to an early spring snowstorm and gradually covered the city with a blanket of white. The alarm he'd set for six o'clock jolted him awake, and he groggily staggered to the radio, fiddling with the knob to get a station between the static. What he heard woke him completely, like a dose of cold water.

"Attention! Attention! German army infantry and aircraft are beginning occupation of the republic. The slightest resistance will bring utter brutality. All Czech commanders must obey German orders. Czech army units will be disarmed. Military and civil airplanes must remain in airports."

This command was repeated every five minutes. In between, classical music was played. This was the moment Albert had been expecting for months, ever since the Munich Agreement gave away the Sudetenland and Czechoslovakia's defenses along with it. While he'd expected it, he'd hoped that he was wrong, but he had not been. After listening to the same announcement several times, Albert searched for another station and found a station broadcasting martial music.

"*Fini* Czechoslovakia," the announcer said, and went on in heavily German-accented Czech to announce that German troops would occupy the whole of Bohemia and Moravia today, in order to secure peace and order and protect the German inhabitants of these provinces, whose lives and property had been threatened by the Czechs.

Albert switched off the radio in disgust. It was time to get ready to meet his friends at the Jan Hus monument in the Old Town Square. They'd agreed, months ago, when this time came, that they would meet there. This monument to a national hero, with the inscription "Truth Prevails" on its base, seemed like a most appropriate meeting place for such an occasion.

The morning light was feeble and gray. Snow swirled around the buildings and spires of the churches, settling on the cobblestone streets and the statues standing guard along the Charles Bridge. Albert made his way through the narrow, winding streets and across the bridge, to Old Town Square. When he arrived, he saw his friends standing on the steps that surrounded the huge black monument of Hus, portrayed as gazing off toward the horizon. Some looked dejected, some defiant, and they all looked cold—shifting from foot to foot and hunching into their coats—as they smoked nervously, standing in small groups of two or three, waiting for him. As he arrived, they gathered around him and looked at him expectantly, waiting for him to tell them what to do. Suddenly, he felt a little nervous as he realized he didn't really know what to do next, either.

A passerby on his way to work approached him and asked, "What's going on?"

"Haven't you heard the news on the radio?" Albert asked.

“No, I don’t have a radio,” he said.

“The Germans are invading,” Albert said. “They say that the troops will probably be in Prague by nine. We’ve been instructed to remain calm, go to work as usual, and offer no resistance.”

The man looked shocked. “They’re invading? Where’s our army?”

“They’ve been ordered to offer no resistance,” Albert said.

The man stared at him in disbelief, and a few others also gathered around Albert, asking each other what was going on. Albert went up a few steps and stood next to the pedestal of the monument, and loudly repeated the news so that they could all hear. They stood there, looking at him, and he felt he should say something more.

“This is a sad day for our country,” he said. “We’ve been abandoned and betrayed by those who said they were our friends. Czechoslovakia is no more. The Slovaks, persuaded by the Germans, have declared their independence. When we were sold out at Munich, we lost our fortifications, and now we stand alone and helpless before the brutality of the Nazis. Many of us knew this day was coming, but still, it is a shock.” He straightened his shoulders and gazed out at the small group gathered around him.

“But this is not the end. For over a thousand years the Czechs have been here, and long after the so-called thousand-year Reich is nothing but dust and ashes, we’ll be here!” he shouted. “We were here before they came, and we will be here when they’re gone!” A cheer went up around him.

He started to sing the Czech national anthem, “Where Is My Home,” as loudly as he could, and his friends joined in. Soon, voices of other people, standing in small groups around the square, joined in, too, until their voices echoed from the stones and spires of the buildings.

Where is my home? Where is my home?

Water bubbles across the meadows,
Pinewoods rustle among crags,
The garden is glorious with spring blossom,
Paradise on earth it is to see.
And this is that beautiful land,
The Czech land, my home,
The Czech land, my home."

After that, there didn't seem to be anything more to say, and he stepped down, joined his friends, and lit a cigarette. Stamping his feet and waiting, as the morning wore on the crowds in the square became thicker, and the police came and ordered everyone to move on, so they wandered up the street a bit, then back again. After a time, they heard the rumble of vehicles over cobblestone streets, and the first of the invaders appeared. The police worked to clear a path in front of them. First came the dark green vehicles, the cannons, and machine guns, followed by seemingly endless streams of gray clad soldiers, their boots crashing down on the cobblestone streets, arms swinging, and guns over their shoulders, eyes staring straight ahead, their faces bright red from the cold.

Occasionally someone would sob, or shout insults. Now and then strains of the national anthem would start, and then die out. Albert stood with his friends watching the troops as they marched past, then turned and watched as the troops formed a solid line across the bridge and up the hill. Suddenly he felt a knotted ball of anger gather in his stomach and flare up to his head.

"Why don't you bastards march straight into the river!" he shouted in German.

A soldier turned to see who had shouted, lost his footing on the uneven cobblestones, and fell. The troops swept past him as if he were a rock in a stream. One other soldier stopped to help him up. As he struggled to get back up, Albert and his friend laughed uproariously. They had needed something like this to break the tension. The soldier's face was flushed with anger and he pointed his gun at the crowd.

"Who said that?" he demanded. "Say it again, and I'll blow your head off!"

Albert stopped laughing, and suddenly felt a tingle of fear down his spine. The soldier's friend said something to him and then they hurried off to find their places in the ranks.

Albert realized that this was really happening. Suddenly he felt very tired.

"Let's go, guys," he said. "There's nothing we can do here."

CHAPTER 15

The day started like any other workday, except for the snowstorm. Jana woke up to the smell of roasting coffee. Aunt Marie was the first one up, as always, to start the fire in the cookstove, roast coffee beans, and make breakfast.

Jana put a toe out from between the feather quilts, and then quickly pulled it back. It was freezing out there! She grabbed her clothes on the floor beside her, where she'd dropped them the night before, and dressed under the covers, trying not to disturb her sisters, Lili and Anna. She'd be in trouble with her stepmother if she woke them.

She glanced out the window and saw snow swirling around in the gray dawn light. She poured water into the basin. It was icy cold, and she washed up as quickly as possible and then ran downstairs to the warmth of the kitchen.

Max was already sitting at the table. Jana joined him, and Aunt Marie handed her a big mug of hot black coffee. Plates of thick slices of bread, sliced meats, butter, and a jar of homemade strawberry jam were on the table. Jana sat down and spooned several scoops of sugar into her coffee, and half-listened to Aunt Marie's chatter, while sleepily eating her breakfast. Before she finished, Max went out to harness the horses to the wagon.

"Now, bundle up. It's cold outside," Aunt Marie fussed as she wrapped a long, knitted scarf around Jana's nose and mouth, and then handed her Max's lunch box.

When Jana opened the door, a strong gust of wind sent snow swirling into the house. Jana tucked her head down, against the wind, and ran to the wagon.

"Be careful!" Aunt Marie called out after her.

Jana jumped up beside Max and put the lunch box down on the floorboards between them. Then she knelt on the seat and fished around behind the seat and retrieved one of the old blankets they used for padding furniture, and wrapped it around herself. She pulled it up over her head until only her eyes poked out.

"Warm enough?" Max chuckled.

"Not really," she grumbled.

Max flicked the reins, and the horse started on their way.

"Boy, this stuff is thick," he said. "I'm glad the horses know where they're going because I sure can't see much."

The horses trudged through the snowstorm, up the hill to the castle, and they passed people walking to work and standing on corners waiting for a streetcar. Jana noticed that several of the women were crying.

"Did you see that?" she said.

"What?"

"Those women were crying. Did you notice? I wonder why."

"Probably nothing." He shrugged. "Maybe a fight with their boyfriends."

"All of them? I doubt it! Something's going on," she said.

As they approached the castle, the sentries who were usually standing at attention in their guard boxes on either side of the gate instead were standing together, talking. They looked up as Max's cart approached, and motioned them through. Their faces were grim.

When Jana walked into the steaming kitchen in the basement of the castle, she heard a radio blaring out waltz music. That was odd.

Mrs. Sladekova was sitting in a straight-back chair, crying into her handkerchief, her whole body vibrating with sobs. Jana ran to her. "What's wrong, Mrs. Sladekova? What's happened?"

"Don't you know? Haven't you heard? They're coming."

"Who's coming?"

"Those bastards! Those Nazi bastards!" Mrs. Sladekova wailed, then covered her face with her handkerchief and cried some more.

Jana was shocked. She had never heard Mrs. Sladekova use that type of language before.

As the morning wore on, announcements interrupted the music on the radio, warning everyone to remain calm, go about their work normally, and do nothing to antagonize the occupying army.

The next day, Jana stood on the small balcony of the castle, contemplating the scene below. The sky was gray and foreboding, threatening more snow. The trees, red-tiled roofs, and golden spires of the city, which were spread out below, were still covered by clumps of the wet snow that had fallen yesterday. It lay, like rumpled blankets, on the tiled roofs, lined the insides of branches of leafless trees, and mounded, like whipped cream, on the branches of the evergreens.

Far below, the steel gray ribbon of the river mirrored the gray sky, and the German soldiers and army vehicles crossing the Charles Bridge seemed to reflect the gray of the sky and water. From where she stood, they appeared to be toy soldiers. The drone of squadrons of airplanes filled the air. It was an impressive show of force. But few were stopping to appreciate it. The few pedestrians on the bridge hurried along, heads down and shoulders hunched against the damp wind. The cold air made her shiver, and she wrapped her arms tightly around herself. The scene below made her a little uneasy. So much had changed in just one day.

I should be getting back, she thought. Back to the dim, dank basement where piles of potatoes waited to be peeled. Mrs. Sladekova had sent her upstairs with a tray of silverware, napkins, and glasses, which she'd deposited on the sideboard in the dining room. Then she'd stepped out to the balcony, closing the French doors behind her, for a few minutes of fresh air, and to see what was going on.

She heard the door of the dining room open and glanced in. She saw the clockmaker, Mr. Novotny, entering, carrying his small toolbox. She frequently saw him making his rounds through the building, winding the clocks, and making minor adjustments on them, and she'd become friendly with him, greeting him when their paths crossed. She was about to step inside and say hello but hesitated when she saw him glance around, as if not wanting to be observed.

He walked past the French doors of the balcony, and she quietly darted to the other side of the door after he passed so she could continue to watch him through a crack in the drapes. He walked over to the large mahogany grandfather clock at the far end of the room. His back was to her as he put his toolbox on the floor, opened the front of the clock, made a few adjustments, and then closed the toolbox. He glanced around and left, quickly.

After he'd gone, she reentered the room, darted over to the clock, opened it, and peeked inside. She didn't see anything unusual. Disappointed, she closed the clock and left the room. As she walked through the door, the clockmaker grabbed her, digging his fingers into her right arm and stifling her yelp of surprise with his other hand. His hand smelled of clock oil.

"Shhh!" he warned. She nodded, and he removed his hand from her mouth but continued to hold onto her arm.

"What are you doing, sneaking around?" he hissed.

"Let me go!" She struggled, but his grip was like iron.

"Just be still, and I'll let you go." She stopped struggling, and he released her.

"Well, what are you doing sneaking around?" he said.

"What do you mean? I didn't see anything," she said.

"That's an odd thing to say if you really didn't," he said.

"I want to help," she said.

"You have no idea what kind of trouble you're asking for!"

"I know that some people are trying to defeat the Nazis, and I want to help, and not just wait, helplessly, for bad things to happen."

He looked at her appraisingly. "If we can use your help, I'll let you know. For now, just keep your mouth shut, and don't say anything to anyone!"

"Okay. I need to get back to work. Mrs. Sladekova will be looking for me," she said.

After she'd returned to the kitchen, Jana watched in horrified fascination as the two long hairs growing out of Mrs. Sladekova's double chin quivered in indignation and her whole body seemed to expand as she waved her arms for emphasis, like an ungainly bird trying to take flight.

"How many times must I tell you that you need to ask permission to leave the kitchen? You can't gallivant all over the place. You are to remain here unless I specifically send you on an errand, and when I do send you on an errand, I expect you to do it as quickly as possible and then return immediately. Is that understood?" she said.

"Yes, ma'am." Jana stared at her shoes and tried to appear penitent.

"Don't you 'yes ma'am' me. This is your last warning!"

"Now come with me, and help me carry these trays. Our so-called guests require a snack."

Mrs. Sladekova handed Jana a heavy tray, and then picked up the other one. She quickly led the way down the hall, her long skirts billowing around her, like ship sails in the wind. Jana hurried along behind her, amazed that such a big woman could move so quickly.

When they arrived at the large double doors to the dining room, Mrs. Sladekova balanced the tray against one of her ample hips, while knocking on the door. A bored-looking young man wearing a black uniform and a hat with an emblem of a skull and crossbones opened the door.

There were several officers sitting at the oak table. They paused, mid-sentence, and watched as the women entered the room. They put the trays down on the table, and Mrs. Sladekova started to unload the trays.

"Leave it, leave it!" a tall blond man brusquely said, in German. His voice was unusually high-pitched for his size, and Jana looked at him in surprise. Her eyes met his, and his icy blue eyes sent a shiver down her back.

"What are you staring at, you impudent creature?" he snarled in German.

Jana waited for the remark to be translated into Czech, and then said, "I'm sorry, sir," trying to look confused. "I don't speak German."

"Tell her to stay," a dark-haired man with an odd Charlie Chaplin mustache said, pointing to Jana. He addressed the translator, a thin, pale man who wore a smile of strained politeness. "The other one can go." He waved away Mrs. Sladekova. When this was translated, Mrs. Sladekova glanced at Jana, hesitated momentarily, then turned and left quickly.

"Tell her to come over here."

The man with the odd mustache looks familiar, Jana thought. Then she realized he was the one in all the newspapers, the German leader, Hitler! Her legs trembled as she approached him. As she drew near him, she noticed the sprinkling of dandruff on his shoulders. She was a little disappointed. He seemed pretty ordinary. He stared at her for a moment. She noticed that the pupils of his eyes seemed to be unusually dilated.

"Are you a Gypsy girl?" he asked in German.

Although Jana understood him, she pretended that she didn't. She waited for the question to be translated. "No, sir. I'm Czech," she said.

He glared at her. "Do you know who I am?" he shouted.

Jana jumped in surprise but caught herself before replying. The translator repeated the question in Czech.

"Yes, sir, you're the one I've seen in the newsreels, Mr. Hitler," she said.

He stared at her a moment longer, then waved her away, turning back to the other Germans.

"We'll soon be rid of her race," he muttered, and they laughed. "Tell her she can go," he said to the translator.

Jana left the room. As the door closed behind her, she noticed her legs were still shaking. She walked the first few feet down the hall and then broke into a run.

CHAPTER 16

On the way home, Jana chattered to Max as the horses made their way down the steep, twisting streets of the Lesser Quarter. He mostly stared straight ahead, his eyes fixed on the horses until she told him about meeting Hitler in the dining room. That got his attention.

"What!" he exclaimed

"Yeah, I think it was him. He had the mustache, just like in the newsreels, but he didn't seem so important, just sort of ordinary. He said a weird thing, though, something about getting rid of us."

"Getting rid of who?"

"Us, the Gypsies. I think that he was talking about me when he said they would get rid of 'her race.'"

He stared at her, wordlessly, for a few moments, and then resumed staring straight ahead.

"Are you listening to me?" she said.

"You think this is all a big joke, don't you!" he said.

"What? No, I don't. Why?"

"You have no idea how serious this is. Do you? You don't have a clue."

Jana turned away from him in a huff. *What a jerk! I'm not going to talk to him if he's going to react like that*, she thought.

They rode in silence for a few moments then, as they turned on to Újezd Street, Albert stepped out from the shelter of a doorway.

"I was waiting for you. Can I hitch a ride?" he asked.

"Of course," Max said.

He motioned for Jana to move over. She hesitated a second, then slid over next to Max, and Albert jumped up beside her.

"Albert, you know my little cousin Jana, don't you?" Max said.

"I'm not little, or your cousin!" she exclaimed.

Albert laughed. "It's nice to meet you, all the same," he said.

"Where are you heading to?" Max asked Albert.

"I'm going to a friend's house for the night, in Smíchov. I was hoping you could drop me off if it's not too far out of your way," Albert said.

"Sure, no problem," Max said.

"I would walk, but I want to stay off the streets as much as possible. I can't go home, or to my parents' home. I'm a fugitive, I guess," Albert said with a rueful smile.

"What! Why?" Max asked.

Albert looked at Jana and hesitated.

"Oh, don't worry about her. She's all right," Max said.

Jana felt simultaneously pleased to be declared "all right" and annoyed at his dismissiveness.

"Well, as you may know, I used to be a member of the Communist Party, but I was starting to have doubts about it, so when it was outlawed last December, I resigned but, apparently, my name is still on the list."

"What list?" Max asked.

"The list of people the Germans are going to arrest. They came prepared with lists. They're calling it Operation Fence. Anyway, that's what I heard from a friend of a friend who works for the police. So, I've been warned to lie low for a few days, until the whole thing blows over," Albert said.

"Do you think it will?" Max asked.

"I expect so. After all, I resigned months ago. My friend said he would try to get my name taken off the list. Take a right here," Albert directed. "By the way, have you heard about the demonstration on Sunday, at the Tomb of the Unknown Soldier?" Albert asked. "Come if you can. I hope to be there, too."

"Okay," Jana said.

"We'll try," Max said.

Albert directed them to a nondescript apartment building. When they'd stopped, he jumped down. With a flick of the reins, Max sent the horses on their way. Jana slid back across the seat, and they rode together in silence for a few minutes.

"Now do you see how serious this is?" he asked.

Otto was home for the weekend. He sometimes came home late on Saturday night, after work, and then left again on Sunday afternoon. Jana and Otto rarely had a chance to talk to each other privately. They just said hello and engaged in general conversation, along with the rest of the family, like now, while relaxing after an early Sunday dinner. Jana sat with the other women, some ways away from Otto, but she listened with rapt attention whenever Otto spoke. She noticed how his brown eyes twinkled with good humor when he told a funny story, and how his white teeth shone when he smiled, which was often.

A couple of times she felt herself being observed as she listened to Otto, and looked up to catch her father observing her with a slightly amused expression, but then he would quickly look away, pretending to be completely absorbed by the conversation.

Jana hung around after dinner until Otto said he had to go. Then she slipped out, found Max, and asked him if she could go along for the ride when he dropped Otto off at the train station.

"Sure, come along, I don't care," Max said.

The ride to the station, sitting with her shoulder touching Otto's, was an agony of emotion. She was acutely aware every time the cart jostled and caused his arm to brush against hers. When he turned and gazed into her eyes as he said goodbye, she suddenly felt overwhelmed by shyness, looked down, and felt her face grow hot. He laughed softly and kissed her on the cheek. The turmoil of emotion this caused was so strong she barely managed a mumbled "goodbye" as he left. She watched his slim figure and broad shoulders as he walked away.

As they left the station, Max said, "Let's make a detour and stop by that demonstration Albert told us about, at the Tomb of the Unknown Soldier."

Jana's feelings were still in an uproar, but at the same time, she also felt somewhat relieved that Otto was gone so she could relax again. "Okay, why not?" she agreed happily.

The sun was low in the cloudy sky as Max and Jana rode up the hill toward the Tomb of the Unknown Soldier. The imposing granite monument lay, brooding, against darkening clouds. On their way up the hill, they passed people solemnly walking, alone or in small groups, with their heads down.

As they drew closer, they saw several lines of people, each holding a small bunch of flowers. They moved slowly to the front of the line, and then laid their offering on the tomb. A couple of women holding trays of flowers for sale stood at a respectful distance away from the mourners, on the side of the square. Several German soldiers marched back and forth, a short distance away from the crowd.

"Okay, we're here," Max said. He gave Jana some money to buy a bunch of flowers. "Go ahead. I'll wait here with the horses," he said.

Jana jumped down and went to buy a small bouquet of violets and snowdrops, and then joined one of the slow-moving lines. Most of the people moved along silently. A few women were crying into their handkerchiefs. The men removed their hats as they neared the monument. Some people knelt to pray when they reached the front of the line.

Jana waited her turn and laid down her small bouquet down on the heap of thousands of similar bouquets that had been left by others. She didn't quite know what to think or do, so she just stood there uncertainly for a few moments, and then turned and walked away. She looked at the German soldiers, but they weren't watching. They strode back and forth mechanically, like tin soldiers. She walked back to where Max was waiting and climbed back up into the wagon.

"That seemed kind of pointless," she said.

"I know, but at least we did something to show our feelings," Max said. "I wonder where Albert is. I expected to see him here."

Then he turned the horses around, and they headed home. In the distance, they heard boots marching on cobblestone streets and military music echoing off the buildings of Wenceslas Square where a huge German parade—a show of military strength—had been going on all afternoon. It sounded like the distant thunder of an approaching storm.

A couple of weeks later, on a Friday, Max, and Jana saw Albert again. He was waiting for them at the same spot on their way home. He greeted them cheerfully as he climbed on board, but after the smile of his initial greeting had faded, Jana noticed that he seemed different. He was slightly thinner and paler, and his eyes seemed a steelier shade of gray. She looked closer and saw faded bruises on the side of his face.

"How have you been?" Max asked. "We didn't see you for the demonstration at the Tomb of the Unknown Soldier. We were there."

Albert laughed bitterly, and said, "I was a guest of the Gestapo."

"What!" Jana and Max exclaimed, simultaneously.

"Yeah, I was picked up and interrogated."

"Are you okay?" Max asked.

"Yeah, don't worry about me. The Nazis have been arresting thousands of people. At least they let me go after a few days. Others had it much worse, and haven't been released. I could hear their cries. The bastards! Sorry," he said, half turning toward Jana.

"That's okay," she said and shrugged.

"I only spent the night at my friend's house, where you dropped me off last week. I decided it would be safer to get out of town, so I headed up to my parents' summer cottage. Unfortunately, the local gendarme up there, Officer Kepka, was apparently keeping a lookout for any activity around there, since he had the run-in with you and Otto."

"Oh, wow! I am so sorry!" Max said.

"That's okay. It's not your fault. Anyway, I think he was thrilled to get some form of revenge. He went out of his way to check up on me, and I guess I showed up on one of his lists. Then he turned me over to the Gestapo."

"I can't believe it! Was it bad?" Max asked.

"Not as bad as it could have been. The waiting and not knowing what was going to happen was the worst part. They roughed me up, but I kept insisting I didn't know anything, and I guess they believed me. I had to sign an agreement promising that I would not act against the German Reich before they would let me go."

"I guess you signed it," Max said.

"Of course! Why not?" he said. "A promise under duress means nothing." He lapsed into a thoughtful silence.

"Where do you want us to drop you off?" Max asked after a few minutes.

Albert started as if he'd been far off in thought. "Oh, anywhere is okay. I just wanted to talk to you. By the way, have you seen Otto lately?"

"Yeah, he was home the weekend before last. He only gets Sundays off, so he only comes home once or twice a month. Why?"

"Next time you see him, can you tell him I'd like to talk to him?"

"Sure, I'll pass along the message," Max said.

They stopped at the next corner. "Thanks, Max. Nice to see you again, Jana," Albert said. He nodded to her and jumped down.

"Take care of yourself," Max said and waved. Then they continued on their way in silence for a while.

"This is nuts!" Max said.

"What is?" Jana asked.

"You know what I mean—his whole thing, and you getting involved. You're just a girl!"

Jana had just been thinking along the same lines, but the part about "just a girl" annoyed her. "I'm not 'just a girl.' Everyone seems to think I'm old enough to get married, so I must be a woman!" she said.

"What's the difference? The point is, we're getting involved in something that may be dangerous, even deadly—Otto and me, and now you—and for what? What are we going to get out of it? If we do manage to kick these Nazi bastards out of the country, will that be the end of our troubles? The Roma have never been accepted here." He looked at her like she was supposed to have an answer.

"Don't ask me. I'm just a girl," she said, and they both laughed.

"But seriously," she said. "Aren't you the one who said, 'it's our country, too?'"

"I was just repeating what Otto says. He's always been interested in assimilating, maybe because he's light-skinned. He has a dream that if he goes to college and gets a profession, he can move up in the world, but now that's not going to happen. Me, I always knew I'd never fit in, except with our own people."

"What about Albert? He seems to accept you," she said.

"He's a friend. You have to look out for your friends," he said.

"Why are you taking so many chances, then? Carrying messages, and so on?" she asked.

"I don't like Germans. Things were better for our people before the Nazis started interfering. Czechoslovakia had introduced reforms. Now that's all being reversed."

Jana could tell something was wrong even before they got through the gate into the courtyard. She could hear the wailing coming from the house.

"What's going on?" she asked.

"I don't know," he said and slapped the reins to make the horses break into a trot.

They looked at each other, eyes wide with fear. As the wagon slowed, when it neared the gate, she leaped down, opened the gate, and then raced to the house. When she flung open the door, she saw the women huddled in chairs wailing and moaning, the children clinging to them, shrieking in fear, unnoticed by their mothers. Baby Eduard was sitting by himself in a corner, wailing, adding to the general din. Clothes and furniture lay strewn all over the floor. Pictures had been pulled from the walls and tossed on the floor.

"What happened? What's going on?" Jana cried out. She went over and picked up Eduard, shushed and bounced him, trying to calm him. Her stepmother looked up, eyes red from crying. She tried to answer, but couldn't stop crying.

Max walked in behind Jana and saw the bedlam. He went over to his mother, took her by the shoulders, and shook her gently. "Mother, Mother, what is it? What happened?"

Her face was a mask of sorrow. "They took the men," she said.

"Who did? Who took them?"

"The police!" She spoke between sobs. "They were here. They said they were searching for a gun. I told them we didn't have any guns. But they didn't believe me. See what they've done to the place?" She gestured at the mess.

"Who did they take? Did they take Father?"

"Yes, they took him, and Josef, and all of Josef's brothers. They even took Jana's cousin Nicu, and Jana's little brother, Ion. They're only boys!" Her face crumpled, and she put her face back into her apron and started crying again.

"Mother, Mother!" He shook her a little harder. "Did they say where they were taking them?"

"No!" she wailed. "I don't know where they took them."

Max strode to the door. "I'm going to find them," he said as he left.

His mother leaped to her feet and ran after him. She threw open the door and called out. "No, don't go! They'll take you, too!" But it was too late. He'd already gone.

Max ran out to the barn and flung open the door. It was obvious that this area had also been searched. He surveyed the room. Everything had been tossed around. Tools had been swept off workbenches. Wood that had been stacked in neat piles, according to size and type, had been tossed together. Furniture that was being repaired was scattered around; some of it had been broken. A quick look confirmed that the chair with the hollow leg was still there. That was a relief.

Max pulled a flashlight out of the rubble and ran across the room and up the ladder to the hayloft. He went directly to Otto's hiding spot. He had never let Otto know that he knew about it. He tilted back the loose board and there, as he had suspected, was Officer Kepka's gun wedged behind a joist. He pulled it out and stuck it in his waistband, behind his back.

Max raced back downstairs and grabbed an old bicycle that was lying in the corner. This would be quieter than a horse, and quicker than walking or taking a streetcar. It hadn't been used for a while, but it seemed to be in working condition, except for the flat tires. He quickly pumped some air into the tires, rolled it out of the barn, jumped on it, and then pedaled off as fast as he could, racing over bumpy cobblestone streets and across tram tracks.

He started out toward the nearest police station, thinking that if he turned in the gun, they would release his family members. However, before he got very far, he realized that was a very bad idea. Most likely they would just arrest him, too. He would be interrogated, and he probably would get rougher treatment than Albert had gotten since he was a Gypsy. Then he'd be sent to a concentration camp, along with the rest of the family, leaving his mother and the rest of the women and children on their own. This thought brought him to a standstill.

He straddled the bike, resting his forearms on the handlebars, breathing hard to catch his breath. As he stood there, wondering what to do next, Max started to wonder why the police had decided to search his family's home for the policeman's missing gun. The thought occurred to him: *Was it because of Albert?* No! Albert wouldn't have informed on them. But perhaps he'd been forced to do more than sign a statement promising not to work against the Nazis in exchange for his freedom. Max shook his head. No, he couldn't believe that. At any rate, he needed to talk to Albert. Hadn't he said that he had a friend of a friend on the police force? Maybe he could help.

Max got back on the bike and raced to Albert's apartment through the crazy-quilt angles of the streets of Prague, never making a wrong turn. He knew his way around perfectly, due to years of driving the delivery cart for his dad's furniture business. When he arrived, he jumped off his bike, leaned it against the crumbling plaster wall of Albert's apartment building, and ran inside, up several flights of stairs, and down the hall to Albert's apartment. He pounded on the door as he gasped for breath.

The door opened a crack, then, seeing who it was, Albert flung open the door. As usual, the air in the apartment was thick with smoke. A collection of friends sat on chairs and on the floor, talking, smoking, and drinking coffee. They all stopped in the mid-sentence and stared in amazement for a few moments at Max, who stood in the doorway panting, hair disheveled, with a wild look on his face.

Albert grabbed him by the arm and said, "Come in. Come in. What is it? What's the matter?"

Max gasped out between breaths, "Can I talk to you alone?"

"Of course! It must be important." Albert glanced at his friends and made a slight sideways motion with his head. They took the hint and left.

Max sank into a vacated wooden chair at the table. "Thanks," he said.

"So, what's this all about?" Albert asked.

Max pulled out the gun and laid it on the table. For one long moment, Albert and Max sat, silently looking at the gun.

"Why did you bring a gun?" Albert asked.

"That's the reason my father, his cousins, and two of their sons have been arrested."

"Arrested? When did that happen?"

"This afternoon, and I don't know what to do. But we have to do something. This wouldn't have happened if it weren't for Otto and me going up to your father's cottage and running into that policeman."

"You mean . . . this is his gun, and you kept it?"

"Right! Otto hid it, and the police came today and searched for it. They trashed the place—threw everything around—but they didn't find it. I wonder, how did they know we had it?" He looked searchingly at Albert.

"I don't know," Albert said.

"You didn't say anything—maybe blurt something out without meaning to—when they interrogated you?"

"No, of course not!" Albert's face darkened with anger. "How could you even think that?"

"I'm sorry. I'm just so worried. They arrested all the men in my family, and the two oldest boys, too, for questioning, I suppose. I don't know what to do. At first, I thought I should turn in the gun, but decided they'd probably just arrest me as well, and maybe not let any of us go."

"Yeah, you're probably right about that." Albert sat back in his chair and lit another cigarette. "Let's think this over. There's got to be a way to get your family released." After sitting and smoking silently for a few moments, he said, "How did you get here?"

"On a bike. Why?"

"I'm going to try to get my father's car. Where's the bike?"

"In front of the building."

"Wait here. I'm going to go see my dad. I'll be back with the car if I can get it."

"Then what?"

"I'll tell you about it later. Wait here, okay?" Albert said, and left.

Max smoked one cigarette after another and paced back and forth anxiously until he heard Albert's steps running up the stairs. He went to the door and opened it, waiting for Albert to get there. Albert was panting and out of breath when he returned.

"Come on. Let's go. I've got the car. Bring the gun." He gasped between breaths.

Max stuck the gun in his jacket pocket. Albert locked the door, and they raced back down the stairs.

A beautiful, shiny, silver Tatra T87, with its characteristic third, middle, headlight, stood in front of the building.

"Wow, this is your father's car?" Max said, impressed.

"Yeah, and he will kill me if we get a scratch on it. So, we'd better be careful."

"How'd you get him to let you take it?"

"I made up some story about a girl whose family was suddenly emigrating, and who I had to see one last time. I hate to lie to my dad, but I didn't want to tell him more than he needed to know, either."

"This is great," Max said as he climbed in and Albert started the car. "Where are we going?"

"We're going to the cottage to plant the gun, where it will be 'discovered' by the caretaker, who will turn it into the police—therefore proving that you and your brother never had it in the first place, and the police will release your family members," Albert said.

"That sounds kind of risky. Didn't you get arrested the last time you went up there? Anyway, how do you know that the caretaker will find the gun?" Max asked.

"Because we'll tell him where it is. He's worked for us for many years, so I hope he'll do it for me. As far as being risky, I suppose it is, but we'll be careful not to get caught."

"And if the caretaker won't help?"

"I don't know. Let's hope he will. Anyway, we have to try," Albert said.

CHAPTER 17

Spring is finally here, Otto thought as he took a long drag on his cigarette and let it out slowly and luxuriously. It was the first of April, and even in this hellhole of industry, if you got away from the noise and heat for a few minutes, you could tell. He leaned against the wall, hidden behind a stack of wooden pallets, and took another drag on his cigarette. You could even hear a few birdcalls, in spite of the background din of screeching railroad car brakes, the roar of truck engines, and the ceaseless rumble and roar of the conveyor belts and furnaces. A few weeds tried valiantly to grow in the gravel- and asphalt-strewn ground.

It had been a long week. Ever since he'd left home, on Sunday night, he couldn't get the image of Jana's cute little brown face out of his mind. He smiled to himself as he remembered how she had smiled shyly and blushed when he said goodbye. Maybe getting married to her wasn't such a bad idea. He shook his head. *No, I'm going back to school next fall, and the country is in trouble right now. Now is not the time to think of love.*

His foreman, Mr. Jelinek, came striding toward him. He had long since figured out Otto's hiding place. His face was a deep shade of red. "Tucek, get your ass back on the job, pronto, or you won't have a job!" he yelled.

Otto colored in anger but said nothing. He took one last long deliberate drag on his cigarette, dropped the butt, and ground it into the asphalt-contaminated ground. "Okay, okay. What's the rush?"

"You're needed on the job, that's what! Now let's go!"

Otto followed the foreman at an unhurried pace.

The foreman stopped, halfway across the yard, and waited impatiently for Otto to catch up. "They're taking workers out for a meeting, so we're shorthanded. Could you put a little speed into it?" he said.

Otto picked up his pace, his curiosity aroused. "Who's taking who where?"

"The Germans—the new overlords." Jelinek turned away and spat. "They called all of the German workers into an impromptu meeting. As if I can just shut down the line at the drop of a hat." He scurried ahead, again muttering to himself, and shaking his head angrily.

A meeting for the German workers. Otto wondered what that was all about. He knew he'd find out soon enough. He figured the German workers would be only too happy to spill the beans. A couple of glasses of beer in the pub after work and he'd know more than he cared to know. It was Saturday night, which meant payday, and a night of drinking for some.

Later that night, Otto sat on a bench at a wooden table in the pub with a bunch of his Czech coworkers. It was their regular Saturday night hangout—a dim, smoky place with worn wood floors, filled with smoke from cigarettes and fried foods and the din of men all talking at once. If it were not for the tall windows that opened inward in the middle of the room, now open to let out some of the smoke, the place would have been nearly suffocating, as it usually was in the winter.

Over a plate of goulash and dumplings, which he washed down with a mug of Pilsner, he learned the reason for the unscheduled meeting. Across the room, another table was occupied by some of the German workers, and they were chattering away at top volume about how the great General Blaskowitz had stopped in to congratulate the workers on becoming German citizens. The general, they said, had referred to it as their "liberation."

At first, the Czechs pretended not to notice, but then some of them started sending dirty looks across the room. Otto thought it best to get out of there before looks turned into words, and words into fistfights. It wouldn't do to get picked up by the police while living under an assumed name. He wolfed down his food and polished off the beer.

"See you fellows on Monday," he said. Waving off their protests, he made a speedy exit.

So that's how it's going to be, he thought. The increasing presence of German troops was another sign. Soon the Skoda Works would be firmly under control of the German army. It didn't seem that there would be any further chances for sabotage.

He had gone as far as the corner when he heard running footsteps and turned around to see who was following him. "Oh, it's you," he said to Mr. Jelinek and stopped to talk to him.

"Hi, Josef. I was hoping I'd get a chance to talk to you tonight. But you left in such a hurry."

"Yeah. It looked like there might be trouble, and I wasn't in the mood for it."

"I wanted to say I was sorry for jumping down your throat this afternoon at work. It was getting kind of crazy. You know how it is."

"Sure, no problem." Otto shrugged. Jelinek didn't leave, but instead stood there, dug out a cigarette, offered one to Otto, and lit both.

Otto said, "That was really something, the general coming and calling all the German workers together for a little pep talk, wasn't it? They sure seem full of themselves about it."

"You can say that again." Jelinek shook his head in disgust. "I don't know how much longer any of us will have our jobs."

"About that, I was wondering if there have been any repercussions yet?"

"You mean regarding the special matter we took care of?"

"Yeah. Have you heard anything?"

"Nope, not yet. I'll let you know as soon as I hear." After a few more moments, he said, "Do you have some time?"

"I guess so."

"I have something I'd like to propose, and maybe show you. Will you come with me?"

"That depends. Where are we going?"

"You stuck your neck out once. Are you willing to do it again?"

"Maybe," Otto said.

Lately, the thought of going back home, seeing Jana every day, and resuming his studies at the university had become even more important to him. He was increasingly uneasy about his involvement with the sabotage. So far, he hadn't done much. But what if his involvement was known, then what would happen? These thoughts kept him awake at night. It was the waiting that bothered him. He wondered if the guns that had been made with the adulterated steel would explode after a few uses, as the chemist had promised. Had they done it correctly? If so, he supposed the Germans would start checking serial numbers, and figure out that the guns had all come from the same batch of steel. Then there would be hell to pay, and he'd rather not be here when that happened.

"You know what's happening throughout the country, don't you?" Jelinek stopped talking as a group of men passed by, then looked around to make sure they were not being overheard, lowered his voice, and continued, "Arrests, torture, people being sent to concentration camps, and terrified people committing suicide. Even though the censors keep it out of the papers, the word gets out. We need to get the word out to more people."

So that was what Jelinek was getting at—newsletters. Otto had seen a few of these. They spread news gleaned from listening to the BBC, a dangerous practice since it was against the law, and rumors, which were the other main source of news. They were left on seats in streetcars, or on park benches—wherever they could be found anonymously. These were usually one-page newsletters, which had been quickly typed, with misspellings simply left as they were, or struck out and followed by the retyped words, then replicated with a mimeograph machine onto thin sheets of inexpensive paper.

"I guess you're talking about distributing newsletters or some other kind of involvement with the underground press," Otto said.

Jelinek laughed, and said, "Yeah, I guess you could say that. Can you type?"

"Yes."

"I'd like to show you something. If you're willing to help, great, if not, I know I can count on you to keep what you will see to yourself. Are you interested?"

"Sure," he said.

Jelinek led the way through the streets, across a bridge over the Radbuza River, and up a hill to an ancient apartment building. The crumbling plaster revealed the bricks below in several spots. He used a key to open the door and led the way to a door at the end of the hall.

"Is this where you live?" Otto asked.

He shook his head—no—and held his finger up to his lips.

Jelinek glanced back down the hall to make sure they weren't being watched, and then opened the door, revealing a staircase leading down to the lower level. He led the way down, then down another hall dimly illuminated by a single bare bulb hanging from the ceiling.

Several rooms led off from the hallway. They turned into the last one. Otto strained to see what was in the room. As his eyes adjusted to the dark, he seemed to make out a large hulking object.

"Hang on a minute," Jelinek whispered. He felt around on a shelf that was attached to the wall and produced two flashlights. "Here you go." He handed one to Otto.

When they turned on their flashlights, Otto saw that they were in the furnace room. The huge old coal-burning furnace took up most of the room, its octopus-like tentacles spreading out around it.

"Follow me," Jelinek whispered. He crept around the outer edge of the room, ducking under some of the lower arms of the furnace. Otto followed. Behind the furnace was another door. Jelinek unlocked it and, with a wave of his flashlight, motioned Otto through, then followed him and relocked the door behind them. They were standing at the top of a staircase that descended into the darkness below.

Jelinek started down the stairs. Otto shone his flashlight around, to try to see where they were going. The weak beam revealed only uneven stone steps and walls, leading down into the darkness. He followed Jelinek and noticed that the damp air became cooler as they descended the steps. As he descended, he shone his flashlight down, to watch his step, and ran the tips of the fingers of his other hand along the uneven, damp stone wall.

When they reached the bottom, Otto waved his flashlight around. In front of them, he saw a massive, locked iron gate, which reached almost from floor to ceiling. The keyhole was about two inches tall. To their left and right were arched stone tunnels. The air was cool and musty smelling. In the distance, Otto heard running water.

Jelinek shone his flashlight to the right, and whispered, "This way."

After about a five-minute walk, they came to a wooden door on their right, and Jelinek unlocked it. As they stepped inside, Jelinek flipped a light switch and Otto put his hand up to shield his eyes from the sudden light. When his eyes had adjusted, he looked around in amazement. It was an office! A desk, against the opposite wall, was covered with stacks of papers that surrounded a typewriter, and file cabinets lined the walls. A mimeograph machine sat on a table in the middle of the room.

"Now you see why I laughed before when you said 'underground press,'" Jelinek said, no longer whispering.

"Where are we?" Otto asked.

"It's a room in the basement of a building. It was bricked off from the rest of the building at some point during renovations, and forgotten. The way we came is the only way to get here. A friend of mine stumbled on it when he was a boy. He used to play in the tunnels. I had the lock installed."

"Why are these tunnels here?" Otto asked.

"Some of them were built hundreds of years ago, to hide in when the city was under attack. Some are still used to store beer. They also connect with the sewer system. There are several levels and miles of tunnels. It's quite a maze down here. But no one uses this tunnel—at least I've never seen anyone down here, except those I brought. Still, we have to be careful to make sure that we're not followed."

"This is where you produce a newsletter?"

"Not me, personally. I just coordinate it. But yes, it seemed like a good place to work, where the chances of anyone hearing the typewriter and mimeograph, and getting curious, were slim. So, anyway, this is what I wanted to show you. We could use another hand. We have several people who come in when they can, but most of them have families who ask questions if they are away from home too often. You can see how the work is stacking up. So, since you're a single man, I thought maybe you could help."

Otto looked around, his curiosity aroused by the piles of papers on the desk—reports from various informants, he assumed. It would be interesting to see what they said. But still, he wasn't sure he wanted to get involved. Otto hoped that the conflict would end soon, and when it did, Germany would lose. Then he could get back to his normal life. A life, which he now was beginning to hope, would include Jana. "I don't know," he said. "I'll think about it."

"Fair enough," Jelinek said. "I won't say any more about it. You'll let me know if you're interested. But please, don't say anything about what you've seen here today. Lives may depend on it."

"Don't worry, I won't," Otto said.

Otto spent a few crowns on the streetcar to get most of the way back to his room, and then walked the rest of the way. He noticed the light from a cigarette but hadn't paid much attention, thinking it was someone enjoying a smoke in the night air before bed and was startled when a shadowy figure stepped out of the doorway and headed toward him.

CHAPTER 18

The racket in the courtyard, which was below her bedroom window, awakened Jana. She rushed to the window and peered out into the gray twilight of dawn and saw soldiers, horses, and dogs swarming around. Horses reared up in fright, and neighed in terror, as German soldiers attempted to lasso them and lead them out of the stable. Their dogs barked wildly and chased the horses and soldiers. Some of the soldiers were leading horses out of the stable, a couple of them were standing guard on either side of the courtyard gate, which was opened wide to the street, and one was shouting orders at the others.

As Jana threw on her clothes, she heard other voices in the house, as the racket gradually woke everybody up. Doors opened and closed. Everyone was asking, "What's happening? What's going on?"

"Max! Max! Max!" Aunt Marie called out.

"He's not here!" another voice called back.

Someone started pounding on the front door. Jana ran down the stairs but stopped when she couldn't go any farther. The front entry and the first few steps of the staircase were filled with bewildered, frightened women and children crying and clinging to their mothers. They all stared anxiously at the door. Whoever was on the other side continued to pound on it, and demanded, in an officious German voice, that it be opened at once.

Aunt Marie, while tying her scarf over disheveled hair with

trembling hands, pushed past Jana and the others and opened the door. Two soldiers stood in the doorway, a short sergeant in front and a taller private behind him. The sergeant held out a piece of paper and shouted in rapid German. Aunt Marie wrinkled her brow, trying to follow what he was saying. The sergeant thrust a paper toward her, and she took it. Aunt Marie looked at the long document. It was typewritten in German, some parts were in larger bold type, some in smaller print, and a signature was at the bottom. "What is this? I can't read German," she said.

"We're requisitioning your horses!" the sergeant barked.

"Requesting?"

"Requisitioning—taking them. It's all explained there." He gestured toward the form.

Jana examined the tall blond soldier who was standing behind the sergeant. She thought he looked a little embarrassed. He also looked familiar. She wondered where she'd seen him before.

"Jana, come here!" Aunt Marie said. "You know how to read. Can you tell me what this says?"

She made her way through the crowd. The tall blond soldier looked at Jana as she took the paper from Aunt Marie. She looked up, and as their eyes met, she realized, with a start, where she'd seen him before. He was Franz, the man who'd seen her swimming in the woods and then later in town. She could tell by the look of surprise on his face that he remembered her, too.

Jana looked at the document she was holding. "I don't know how to read German," she said in German.

"Find someone who can," the sergeant said and turned to go. Aunt Marie grabbed his arm. "Wait! What do you mean you're taking the horses? You can't take them. We need them!"

The sergeant shook off her hand. "That's not my problem! I'm just following my orders, and if you touch me again, I'll have you arrested."

Aunt Marie started to cry and wailed, "No! No! Please, no!"

The other women caught hold of her and restrained her as she attempted to throw herself on the sergeant. As they tried to calm her, Franz and the sergeant turned and started to walk away.

Jana suddenly realized that she desperately needed the horses to get to work and that she desperately needed to get to work. Most of the men had been arrested, and no one knew where Max was. She was the only wage earner left in the family besides Otto, who was in Pilsen. She ran after the soldiers. "Wait! Please wait!" she cried. They turned toward her. She addressed Franz. "How can you take our horses? How can I get to work without the horses?"

"You can appeal if you have the right paperwork," Franz said and turned to go.

"But how?" she said, following.

"It's all on the form." He glanced at his superior officer, who was glaring at them.

"How can we read it? None of us can read German," she said.

He stopped and looked at her. Jana touched her hair, suddenly aware it was uncombed and falling across her face. His expression softened, as though he felt sorry for her.

"I'll come back tonight. I'll tell you what to do," he said, haltingly, in Romani.

Jana stopped in her tracks, her eyes wide with surprise. Then she nodded and turned back toward the house.

"What did you say to her?" the sergeant asked.

"I just told her the same thing that you told her, that she needs an interpreter."

"But how do you know that gibberish they talk?"

"I picked up a few words here and there, I guess," he said.

Everyone surrounded Jana when she got back to the house and bombarded her with questions. "What did he say? Do you know him? Will he give us our horses back?"

When they finally paused long enough for her to answer, she said, "He said we might be able to get our horses back if we have the right paperwork. He said that it's explained on the form, and he will come back later today and help us read it."

Aunt Marie regarded her with astonishment for a moment, and then said, "Well, if he's coming back tonight I guess we'd better find any paperwork we have that shows ownership. I'll see if I can find ours. How about you, Zofie?" she asked Jana's stepmother. "Do you know where the paperwork is for your horses?"

After everyone left, except Jana and her stepmother, Zofie asked, "Did he speak to you in Romani?"

"Yeah, I guess so," Jana said. "I couldn't believe it, either."

"Do you know him? It seemed like you knew him."

"No, I don't know him. I just saw him once before. I told his fortune, that's all. Do you remember when you, Anna, and I went into the village? It was the first time we saw the German soldiers. I guess he must have remembered me." She wasn't about to mention where, and when, she'd seen him on other occasions.

It took Jana over twice as long as usual to get to work. She walked, then rode several streetcars, and then walked again. When she got there, Mrs. Sladekova was waiting for her, arms akimbo. She glared angrily at Jana. "Why are you late?" she demanded.

"I didn't get a ride today," Jana said, not wanting to go into details. "I had to get here by streetcar, and it took a lot longer. I'm sorry."

Somewhat mollified by the apology, Mrs. Sladekova blustered on for a while, and then retreated, muttering to herself. Jana wasn't really listening. She was mulling over the events of the last couple of days. For once she was happy to get to work, quietly peeling potatoes while trying to sort it all out.

Later that morning, as she was carrying out the garbage, she passed a slender middle-aged man who stood smoking outside the service entrance. He nodded to her as she passed. She recognized him as the maintenance carpenter. She'd seen Max talking to him, but she'd never spoken to him.

"Where's your cousin today?" he asked her as she was about to reenter the building. "I didn't see him drop you off this morning as he usually does."

"I don't know," she said cautiously.

"Will he be here to pick you up?" he asked.

Jana thought she recognized a note of concern in his voice.

"I'm not sure," she said. Now he definitely looked concerned as he took a long drag on his cigarette. She walked past him and went back into the building.

At the end of her shift, she stood by the rear entrance waiting for Max. She stood next to a few pieces of furniture waiting to be picked up for repair. She noticed the chair with the hollow leg was among them. She waited anxiously. *How long should I wait?* she wondered. If she got home too late, she would miss Franz. Would he explain the procedure for recovering their horses to the other women if she wasn't there? What if he wouldn't, or what if they misunderstood him? She was about to give up and start out for home on her own when the door opened and the maintenance carpenter appeared.

"Still waiting?" he asked.

"Yes."

"Would you like a ride home?"

Jana hesitated. Going somewhere, alone, with a strange *Gadjo* didn't seem like a good idea. On the other hand, she desperately wanted to get home quickly, and Max knew him. "Okay," she said.

"Good! I suppose I should introduce myself. I am Mr. Sefarik, the maintenance carpenter."

"Hello. I'm Jana. I work in the kitchen."

"Yes, I know. Your cousin told me. It's nice to meet you, Jana. There is one thing. I wonder if you can help me deliver something on the way. There are five crowns in it for you if you don't tell anyone about it."

"I guess so. What is it?"

"I'll explain in a bit. Wait here while I get my truck."

A short time later, he pulled his truck into the alley and helped her into the passenger side. Then he loaded the furniture into the back. Jana watched through the rearview mirror and saw him bend over the chair with the hollow leg, then stuff a piece of paper into his jacket pocket.

Then he jumped into the truck, and with a grinding of gears, they started off.

"I'm having a hard time getting used to driving on the right-hand side of the road," he complained as he swerved to miss an oncoming car. "The German overlords have to have everything their way."

He stopped at the top of a hill. "There's a house in the middle of the block, number 15—can you walk down the hill and give this to the woman who is waiting inside the window?" He took the folded sheet of paper out of his pocket. "I can't deliver it because I can't drive up to the house and get out without a dozen neighbors noticing."

"Okay, I guess so," Jana said.

"Be disceet. Just act like you are stopping to say hello. Put your hand on the windowsill as you stop to talk, put this in your hand, and give it to her, like so." He demonstrated how she should pass the paper. He folded it into a small square and put it in his palm. Then he put his hand down on the seat and showed how she should push the paper out with her thumb. "Okay? I'll drive around the block and wait for you around the corner, at the bottom of the hill."

Jana took the folded paper from him and concealed it inside her palm. She walked down the hill. When she came to number 15, she saw a woman was seated at a small table inside the opened window.

"Good day," Jana said. "Are you enjoying the nice spring weather?" She put her right hand, the folded paper inside her palm, on the windowsill.

"Very much!" the woman replied, putting her hand next to Jana's.

Jana pushed the paper out from under her palm, and the other woman slid in under her hand. You would have to be watching, very closely, to notice that anything had happened.

"Well, have a good evening," the woman said to Jana.

"Thank you. You, too," Jana said and continued on her way. Mr. Sefarik was waiting for her around the corner, just as he'd said he would.

"How did it go?" he asked.

"Fine, no problem."

"Good!" He pulled out his wallet and gave her the five crowns. "Now remember, don't tell anyone."

"What was on the paper?" she asked.

"You're better off not knowing," he said.

"Does it have to do with the messages my cousin would take out of the chair leg?"

He looked at her with alarm. "So, you know about that."

"Yes, I know about that, and I want to help. I have plenty of reasons not to like the Nazis, and I could use a little extra cash."

"Well, okay, if you're sure. You can take over while your cousin is away."

They drove the rest of the way in silence, except when he swerved to miss an oncoming car, swore, and then apologized for swearing. Jana asked him to let her out a couple of blocks early. She didn't want anyone in her family to see her riding with this stranger.

CHAPTER 19

Albert and Max spent Friday night, March 31, in the summer cottage. They'd taken precautions to avoid calling attention to their visit by taking back roads and using only the car's low beams, as much as possible, on their way there. They'd parked the car behind the cottage, out of sight to a casual passerby, and refrained from lighting the stove at night so smoke from the chimney wouldn't give them away. Consequently, they'd spent the night shivering under as many blankets as they could find in the unheated cottage.

When they awoke, cold and stiff, on Saturday morning, they decided to risk it and made a small fire in the stove to boil water for coffee. They then extinguished the fire as soon as the water came to a boil.

Now they sat, hunched over the table, blankets draped over their shoulders, with their hands cupped around their coffee cups, trying to warm up. They'd found only a few coffee grounds at the bottom of a can, so the coffee was weak, but it still provided welcome warmth. The coffee and some stale soda crackers they'd also found in a cupboard provided their breakfast.

"Where do you think we should hide the gun?" Max asked.

"I don't know. We have to find a place where it could be found by the groundskeeper, but might have been overlooked by the police so his story is believable," Albert replied.

After breakfast, they walked around inside and outside the cabin, discussing various possibilities for a good hiding spot. They rejected inside of drawers or under furniture as too obvious. The same seemed to apply to hiding the gun under the porch. They then explored inside the barn. There were lots of good hiding spots, but Albert thought it might seem odd that the groundskeeper would be digging through stuff in the barn.

"He could say he came in to get tools or something," Max suggested.

"But if we leave it somewhere obvious, like on the tool bench, there's a good chance that the police already looked there," Albert said.

They finally decided to hide the gun in a pile of brush, back by the woods. They thought that if the groundskeeper said that he had been clearing brush when he discovered the gun, his explanation would be believable, and since there were several piles of brush, the police could have missed it during their search.

After the gun was hidden, Max stayed at the cottage while Albert went to see the groundskeeper. Albert was gone for about an hour.

"How did it go?" Max asked when he returned.

"Not well," Albert said.

"What? Why not? What did he say?" Max asked.

"He said he didn't want to get mixed up with the police, that he had to think of his family first. But I got him to agree to at least think about it, and meet me again at ten tonight in the woods at the edge of town. We'll have to persuade him or come up with another plan," Albert said.

"Did you offer him money?" Max asked.

"What? No, I don't have any money, except a few crowns for gas and food. Do you?" Albert said.

"No, I don't have much either," Max said.

They sat dejected for a few moments.

"Wait, Otto gets paid today," Max said. "Let's drive to Plzeň and tell him what happened. I know he'll help."

Albert agreed it was worth a try, so they decided to go to Plzeň right away and wait in a tavern rather than sit here in the cold. They checked around the cottage and tried to put everything back the way it was when they'd arrived to erase any evidence of their overnight visit. Then they locked up the cabin, got in the car, and drove to Plzeň.

After a long afternoon spent slowly sipping a few beers to justify taking up a place in a tavern, Max and Albert drove to the street where Otto lived and sat in the car, waiting. After a time, Max got tired of sitting and got out to stroll up and down the street. He stopped in the doorway of a courtyard and cupped one hand around a match to light a cigarette. When he looked up, he saw Otto approaching.

He stepped out to meet him. "Hi, Otto," he said.

"What? Oh, hi, Max, it's you!" Otto said. "How did you get here?"

"We drove. I came with Albert. Come on, he's parked just up the street."

Max led him back to the car.

Later that night, in the pale light of the moon, Albert stood in a clearing near the edge of the woods. He took another ten-crown note out of the pay envelope that Otto had given him and added it to a growing stack of bills in his hand, and then held them out to the groundskeeper, but the money seemed to have the opposite effect that Albert had hoped for. Every time another ten-crown was added to the pile, the groundskeeper, Mr. Muller, seemed more determined to refuse the offer. He started to inch away while he continued to apologize.

"Everybody in town knows that something is going on! There's no way to keep a secret around here." He twisted his hat, which he held in his hands, and shook his head no again. "I can't afford to get involved in this! I'm sorry. I heard some talk in the pub this afternoon and saw the sidelong glances. I know they were talking about me, and wondering what was going on. I'm sure your morning visit was noticed. I can't get involved. I have to think about my family. I'm sorry!"

He stood there, silent for a few minutes, dejectedly staring at the ground. "I have to go now. My wife will wonder where I am," he said, and then he turned and strode off into the darkness.

Albert stood looking after him for a few moments before heading back to where Otto and Max were waiting for him.

"Is he going to do it?" Otto asked.

"No." Albert sighed and shrugged disconsolately. "He says he's afraid for his family."

"What now?" Otto asked.

Albert thought for a few moments and then said, "I guess I'll have to talk to my father and see if he can help. I don't know what else to do."

"Should we go back for the gun first?" Otto asked.

"I think so. I don't know who knows what, or if we can trust Mr. Muller not to talk, especially after a few beers," Albert said.

They walked back through the woods to the car and drove back to the cottage.

Otto and Max searched under the brush pile, while Albert held a flashlight. The cold, damp night air penetrated his jacket, and his hand holding the flashlight was getting numb. He shifted it from hand to hand and put the free hand into his pocket to warm it up.

"Are you sure this is where you left it?" Albert asked.

"Yes, I'm sure," Max said.

"Well, where is it?" Albert asked.

"I don't know," Max snapped. "Hold the light still."

Otto kept feeling around under the brush and said nothing.

"Here, you hold the light, and I'll look," Albert said to Max.

Albert started grabbing armfuls of brush and throwing it aside.

"Hey, look out where you throw that stuff!" Otto said.

"Sorry, but I think it'll go faster this way. I'm freezing out here," Albert said.

"Okay, if that's the way you want to do it, but it'll look pretty obvious that this brush has been moved."

"I don't care. What difference will it make?"

"All right." Otto shrugged, got up, brushed off his knees, and started moving armfuls of the brush onto the new pile.

Within a few minutes, they'd moved the pile. Max moved the flashlight back and forth where the brush pile had been. "Where's the gun?" he asked. "I don't see it."

"Do you think it might have gotten caught up in the brush?" Albert asked.

"I don't know—could be. I suppose it could have," Otto said.

They looked at each other, then reluctantly started moving it, piece by piece, back to where it had been. Finally, they were thoroughly cold and damp and had to stop searching and admit that the gun wasn't there.

"Where is it?" Albert asked. "Do you think Mr. Muller took it?"

"Who else?" Otto said, after a pause.

"Come on, let's get out of here," Albert said. "At least we can warm up in the car. Do you want us to drive you back to Plzeň, Otto?"

"No, I'll go home for the night and take the train back tomorrow," Otto said.

CHAPTER 20

The Saturday night crowd was getting louder and more boisterous when Franz finished his second beer and told Rolf and Paul that he was tired and was going back to the barracks.

"Are you serious? We finally get a night off, and you call it a night after only two beers? I'm worried about you," Paul said.

Franz laughed. "Yeah, yeah. I know. I'm a lightweight. You guys have fun. I'll see you later." He dug in his pocket and tossed a few marks on the table to cover his beer, then headed out. However, instead of going back to the barracks, he caught a streetcar to Jana's house.

He didn't want his buddies to know where he was going. For one thing, they would think it was pretty strange and would ask a lot of questions that he didn't want to answer, partly because he really wasn't sure he understood his own actions. For another thing, it was against regulations, and Rolf could be gung ho about regulations.

Franz hopped on a streetcar that was heading southeast and rode it to the end of the line. He ignored the stares from the other passengers. Some looked angry, but most just looked curious. After getting off the streetcar, he proceeded further on foot. All day long he'd asked himself if he was crazy to get involved in something that really wasn't any of his business. He finally decided that since he'd told them that he would come back, in spite of his doubts, he was going to follow through.

He noticed that the farther he walked the shabbier and farther apart the houses became. When at last he arrived, he opened the gate cautiously, remembering the dogs they'd encountered that morning. Sure enough, they came running toward him, barking. He stood still and held out one hand for them to sniff, hoping they wouldn't bite it off. The door of the house opened and a large, friendly woman called out something to the dogs, and they all turned and trotted away.

"Come in. Come into the house," she called out in a welcoming voice, waving him forward.

He took off his hat as he stepped into the small entryway. Curious little faces peeked at him from the stairs. An older woman, who seemed to be in charge, scolded and gestured toward them with the dishtowel she held in her hand, and they ran, giggling, up the stairs and out of sight.

"Come into the parlor," she said. They stepped inside the dimly lit room, which overflowed with upholstered chairs and couches. A brightly patterned rug covered the floor, and a couple of oil lamps provided the light. One of the lights was on a table, placed against the far wall. The table was surrounded on three sides by wooden chairs. Beside the light lay a pile of papers, a bottle containing some sort of beverage, and a plate of pastries. A single glass and plate were set to one side, and several glasses and plates were piled separately.

Franz was surprised to see that there were only women in the room. Aunt Marie introduced herself, Grandma Berta, Zofie, and Jana.

"I made a special trip to the get some pastries, this morning, just for you," she said. "We want to take good care of you. I saved some for kids, for later. Provided they stay upstairs and stay quiet."

"Come, sit down," Aunt Marie said, and gestured toward an

overstuffed chair. "Would you care for some blackberry brandy and a pastry?"

"Yes, thank you," he replied eagerly as he sat down and placed his hat on the end table next to his chair. He realized that he was hungry and thirsty after his long walk.

Aunt Marie poured a large portion of the liquid into a glass. He noticed his glass and plate were a different color than the others and recalled that he heard that some Gypsy families kept a separate set of dishes for those who were not Gypsies. She brought him the refreshments and then brought some to Grandma Berta. Jana and Zofie helped themselves.

Earlier, Aunt Marie had told Jana she could have a half glass of brandy. Normally, it was only for adults, except for a spoonful now and then when you were sick. Jana took a sip and felt the warmth spread through her body, calming her. She'd worried all day about this stranger whose help they so desperately needed. Could they trust him? She watched him as she sipped her drink and ate her pastry, trying to discern his motives.

Franz took a sip of the brandy, and nibbled on the pastry. "This brandy is both sweet and potent. It's delicious!" he said.

"Thank you. My husband makes it," Aunt Marie said.

"Will your husband be joining us?"

"No, he's not here. They've all been arrested."

"Arrested? Who's been arrested?"

"All of the men—our husbands and sons."

"When did this happen?"

"Yesterday. Didn't you know?"

"No, I wasn't involved in that. I imagine it was the police?"

"Oh, that's right. I'm just so confused. It's all been so confusing!"

Aunt Marie covered her face with the towel. They all sat silently for a few awkward moments.

Franz cleared his throat and said, "I'm sorry. Well, I suppose I should have a look at those papers."

Jana, who hadn't said a word until now, jumped up and said, "Oh yes, we should. I can help you with that since I can read a little Czech, unless . . . Do you know Czech?"

He looked at her, clearly surprised, as if he'd forgotten she was in the room, and then said, "No, I'm afraid I don't. I've picked up a few words, but I could use your help."

They settled down across the table from each other, the oil lamp and the stack of papers between them, and started to sort through the papers. Zofie, Berta, and Aunt Marie refilled their glasses and retreated to a corner where they sat together in the shadows and talked in low tones.

"Basically, what we're looking for is proof of ownership, and proof that the horses are needed for your work," Franz said.

They handed papers back and forth. He asked for her help with Czech words and phrases. She tried, as best she could, to read and translate them into German. He read and explained the German phrases in documents.

Jana studied his face when he wasn't looking, and decided that he was rather nice looking, in a pallid sort of way, with his blond hair and blue eyes. When he smiled his slightly goofy smile, his eyes crinkled almost shut and his mouth opened wide, showing rows of white teeth. He looked like a farm boy. *If he had any hidden motives, he hides them well*, Jana thought. She started feeling more relaxed as she continued to sip her brandy, and she started to think that maybe he was as sincere and nice as he seemed and that he just wanted to help them. She asked the question she'd been wondering about all day.

"How did you learn to speak Romani?"

The sudden silence from the other women showed that they were also interested in his answer.

"My parents own a vineyard, and Gypsy people would help with the harvest. As a child, I played with the Gypsy kids, and I picked up a few words and phrases from them."

"There are not many others who can speak our language. You must have a good ear."

"I suppose so," he said.

They were engaged in their work, with his blond head bent toward her dark head, laughing together over their attempts to pronounce foreign words, when the door opened and closed, and Max and Otto walked into the room.

"What's going on? Who are you?" Otto demanded.

Franz stood up and bowed stiffly. "Good evening," he said. "I am Private Franz Schmidt."

All the women rushed toward Otto and Max and started talking at once while Franz stood uncertainly by the table. Otto held up one hand, and they fell silent.

"Mr. Schmidt is trying to help us get our horses back," Jana said.

Otto stared at her for a moment. His face was a mask of neutrality, but Jana sensed his anger, and then he turned toward his mother without responding to Jana.

"Mom, what's going on here?" he asked.

"It's like Jana said—this gentleman is trying to help us, Otto. The army took our horses, and he offered to help us to try to get them back."

"The army took our horses?" Otto asked.

Otto turned to Franz with an expression of confusion and suspicion. "What is this all about?" he asked.

Franz walked over to where he had first been seated and picked up his hat. "The young lady can explain," he said, nodding toward Jana. "Perhaps I should be going."

"Please, don't go just yet. I'd like a chance to discuss this with you if you have a moment," Otto said, his voice stiffly polite.

Turning to the women, he said, "Max and I will handle this."

"But I—" Jana began, but she was silenced by an angry look from Otto. She turned and ran up the stairs. The older women went into the kitchen.

Jana stopped at the top of the stairs and tried to hear what they were saying, but they were speaking in low tones, and she couldn't make it out. A few moments later, the front door opened. She peeked down the stairs and saw the three of them walking out the door. A short time later, Max and Otto came back into the house without Franz. Jana flounced off angrily to bed. *How dare they treat me like a child!* she thought.

Albert brought the car back home and sat through a Sunday dinner, making small talk with his parents. He waited anxiously for an opportunity to talk to his father, alone. Finally, when his mother went into the kitchen to make coffee, and he and his father went into the living room, he seized his chance.

"Dad, I need to talk to you."

His father looked up, startled by the urgency in Albert's voice, and paused in his search for his reading glasses. "Of course. What is it?"

"Not now. Can I meet you tomorrow for lunch?"

"I guess so. But what's this about? Do you want to come to my office, or meet somewhere?"

"How about the pub on Nerudova, at noon?"

"All right, I'll see you there tomorrow."

Albert's mother came bustling back into the room; they both stopped talking suddenly.

"What are you two up to?" she asked.

"Nothing, just talking politics," Albert said.

"Politics! I hate politics," she said as she started to pour the coffee.

Albert had arrived early, anxious to talk to his father, and had been sitting with a cup of coffee and a newspaper he tried unsuccessfully to read for over ten minutes before his father arrived and walked down the few stairs from street level into the small coffee shop.

"Good day, Father," he said.

"Well, what's this all about?" his father asked after getting settled.

Albert hesitated as the waiter approached and they both ordered the daily special, listed in chalk on a small blackboard on the wall, and another coffee.

After the waiter left with their order, he leaned toward his father, and said in a low tone, "It's regarding the summer cottage."

His father looked surprised. "Again? Now what?"

"Well, there have been some developments, some repercussions caused by the activities of our recent visitors."

"I'm not sure I'm following."

There was another pause as the waiter brought Albert's father his coffee.

"I'm talking about when my cousin and his family stayed in the cottage. Well, I sent some friends up to bring them supplies, but when my friends got there, my cousin and his family weren't there."

His father glanced quickly from side to side, without moving his head, and then gave Albert a warning look.

"Oh yes. Well, let's discuss the repair plans after we eat. Can you walk me back to my office?"

"Sure, I guess so," Albert said, slightly confused by his father's manner.

Albert's father steered the conversation toward sports and the weather while they finished their food. After they'd left the café, they headed west into the brisk spring breeze.

"You never know who might be listening," his father said.

"Oh, right."

"Now tell me the whole story."

"Remember when Alois and Heda and their baby stayed at the cottage?"

"Yes."

"I asked my friends Otto and Max, who rescued them in the first place, to bring supplies to the cottage, but when they got there, no one was around. It was late, so they stayed until morning. The local policeman must have noticed smoke from the chimney or something, and he confronted them."

"Were these friends of yours Gypsies?"

"Well, yes, but that's not the point."

"That explains the phone call I got from an Officer Kepka—about Gypsies and a stolen gun."

"What phone call?"

"I got a phone call from Kepka. It must have been the next day."

"Right! Apparently, they were confronted by Kepka, but somehow, they got his gun away from him and locked him into the outhouse while they got away."

"In the outhouse!" his father said. He looked incredulous and then chuckled.

"I guess he's had it out for them ever since. He somehow managed to track them down. Now there have been further complications."

"What kind of complications?"

"Well, the police searched their place for the gun, but they didn't find it. Otto and Max weren't home at the time, but they arrested all the other men of the family—their father, their uncles, and two boys.

"Max came to me for help and brought the gun with him. We thought that if we could make it look like the gun really wasn't stolen, but had just been lost, that the Nazis would let everyone go. That's why I borrowed your car."

"So, it wasn't to visit a girl?"

"No, I'm sorry. I lied about that. I didn't want to get you more involved in this, but now I don't know what else to do. I'm hoping that you can help, somehow."

"So, you drove to the cottage? Why?"

"Well, first Max and I went to the cottage and hid the gun, and tried to get our groundskeeper to 'find' it and turn it in. I talked to him twice, but he wouldn't do it, even when I tried to bribe him. He said he was afraid for his family."

"Bribe him? Where did you get money for a bribe?"

"I got it from Otto. Max and I drove to Plzeň to get Otto. He's working for Skoda."

"I see," his father said. "So now our groundskeeper knows that you have something to do with the disappearance of Kepka's gun."

"I'm afraid so. I know it sounds like a dumb plan, but it was the best we could come up with."

"Where's the gun now?"

Albert didn't answer. His father stopped walking, grabbed his arm, and said, "Well?"

Albert took a deep breath and said, "That's the problem—we don't know. We went back to search for it. We'd hidden it under a pile of brush, but it was gone. I don't know where it is."

"Of all the stupid . . . How could you get mixed up in this?"

"I know! I'm sorry, but I had to try to help them. After all, it was because they helped my family that this all happened."

"Right. Well, I'll have to give this some thought," he said as they started to walk again. Soon they arrived at Albert's father's office building. "Well, here we are. I guess I'll see you later," he said.

"Do you think you can help?" Albert asked.

"I don't know. I'll see what I can do," he said and went into the building.

CHAPTER 21

Every breath that Jana took of the April morning air was cool and fragrant as she rode beside Max on her way to work. The morning sunlight slanted across drifts of white pear blossoms blanketing the hills, accented by an occasional spray of pink apple blossoms. Mist still shrouded the sparkling waters of the Vltava River below. The wooden wheels of the cart clattered over the cobblestone streets, and the clip-clop sound of the horse hooves on stone echoed through the quiet streets. Jana and Max barely noticed any of it, as they rode, lost in their thoughts.

A couple of their horses had been returned for work purposes after Otto and Max made numerous trips to various agencies and filled out reams of paperwork. The others were gone, replaced by vouchers redeemable after the "glorious victory of the German Reich." A victory that none of them believed in, and fervently hoped would never happen.

Jana's concern and worry over what had happened to her father, brother, and her other male relatives, as well as the loss of the horses and what that might portend for the loss of her family's mobility, could not completely eradicate the joy of having Otto nearby. He had never returned to Plzeň and his job at Skoda Works. Now he was needed at home to keep the family business running, until his father and the other men were released. He and Max were trying to find out where they had been taken, and how they could get them out.

Soon they arrived at the castle gate. Jana jumped down and presented her ID to the soldier at the gate. Though he saw her every day, he scrutinized it carefully, and then arrogantly looked her up and down, before waving her through. She carefully avoided reacting as she took back the ID and passed through the gate. *If only he knew,* she thought and smiled to herself. *I might be helping get important information to the resistance this very day.*

That afternoon Jana examined the trays of dirty dishes left behind from meals she had delivered earlier in the day before she loaded them onto the trolley. On one of the trays, the fork and knife were crossed at right angles. This was a signal from Joseph Novotny, the clockmaker, that there was a message to pick up. She finished loading the trolley, glanced around her, and then stood still for a moment, listening for any approaching footsteps. Hearing none, she crept over to the large grandfather clock in the corner of the room, opened the front panel, and reached up inside between the wooden case and the face of the clock. She felt around and found the thin, rolled-up piece of paper tucked onto the ledge, removed it, and then quickly hid it in the pocket of her apron. As she quietly closed the front panel, she heard footsteps approaching, dashed back to her cart, and calmly finished wiping off the table, while her heart pounded wildly. The footsteps continued past the door.

Jana finished her rounds, rolling the cart down the wide, marble-floored halls and into ornate dining rooms and offices, picking up other trays. At the end of the hall, she went through the door to the back stairs and into the service elevator and rode it as it slowly descended to the basement. As usual, she stopped at the incinerator room to dispose of the trash before returning the dishes to the kitchen. Once inside the dimly lit, damp-smelling room, she darted back to the darkest corner and pulled out a loose brick, revealing a small cavity behind it. Before she stuck the paper in the hole, she unrolled it and squinted in the dim light to try to make out what was written on it. It seemed to be a simple letter that started, "Dear Aunt, as I wrote in my last letter, we have been busy preparing for the wedding. As you will surely understand, it is difficult in times like this to obtain enough ingredients to prepare a reception meal for our guests . . ." Jana realized that this seemingly innocent letter must contain some sort of coded message. She quickly rolled it up, tucked it into its hiding spot, and replaced the brick.

When Max picked her up in the evening, she noticed that the chair with the wooden leg was once again in the cart. She wondered if the message that she'd picked up earlier that day was now hidden in it, but knew that she couldn't ask. Neither Max nor anyone else in her family was aware of her covert activities.

"You'll never guess who I saw today," she said.

"Who?"

"A big fat fellow with a big mustache. I know he was important because of all the decorations on his uniform, and the number of people following him around. Later I was told that he was Baron von Neurath, the so-called Protector."

"No kidding? What was he doing?"

"He was just walking down the hall when I saw him. Apparently, they had some meetings. All I know is that the kitchen was in an uproar with twice as many meals to prepare as usual, and Mrs. Sladekova was in a foul mood. I was running all over the place delivering meals and picking up dishes, and she kept complaining that I was taking too long."

"I heard on the news that he'd arrived and was taking over from the army," Max said. "I guess the Germans plan to stay awhile. Hopefully, it won't be for as long as they think. The war will start soon, the Germans will lose, and then they'll have to pack up and leave."

When they arrived at home, her brother, Ion, and cousin Nicu ran out to meet them. Jana jumped down and grabbed Ion, and hugged him.

"How are you? Are you okay? Where's Dad?"

He shoved her aside with mock irritation. "I'm fine, I'm fine. Don't make such a fuss!" Without answering her second question, he ran to help with the horse and wagon.

She watched him as he ran with a slight limp; it looked like there were several bruises on his face and neck. She started to get a queasy feeling. She ran into the kitchen to find Aunt Marie.

"Aunt Marie, the boys are back! Where are my dad and the rest of the men?" A single look at her aunt's face gave her the answer. She shook her head silently, lips pressed firmly together, took a deep breath, and said, "I don't know. The boys don't know, either. They weren't kept together." She turned back to the dough she was kneading, and after standing there a few moments, not knowing what to say, Jana silently turned and left the room.

Her stepmother, Zofie, was sitting in the living room, bouncing baby Eduard on her knee. He was teething and was fussing and chewing on his little fist. She looked even more wan and worn out than usual. Jana took the baby from her and sat with him on the floor, jangling some keys in front of him to distract him.

"It's nice to see that Nicu and Ion are safely home," Jana said.

"Yes, but they don't know what happened to your father or the others," Zofie said.

Jana cooed at the baby as he lay on his back on the floor, and jangled the keys. He calmed down a bit and reached up, trying to grab them.

"Does Otto know?" Jana asked. She tried to sound nonchalant. Just saying his name caused her heart to beat faster. She hoped it didn't show.

"Yes, he knows," Zofie replied. "He was home when the boys arrived. They've been together, out in the barn, for most of the afternoon."

"Well, maybe he'll figure out what to do," Jana said. As she said it, she realized that she really believed that he would figure out what to do, and that everything would turn out okay.

"Yes, maybe he will," Zofie agreed. Jana's optimism seemed to lighten her mood a little, and she held out her arms for little Eduard, who had started to cry again.

"Here, give him to me. I'll see if he's hungry." She picked him up and carried him into the kitchen to get some milk.

Jana trailed after her and then continued out the back door to find out what was going on in the barn. The door creaked as she opened it, and Otto, Max, Ion, and Nicu all stopped talking and looked at her.

"What were you talking about?" she demanded.

"None of your business," Ion said. "Go back to the kitchen."

"Forget it, I'm staying," she said as she dragged an old wooden box over next to them and sat down on it. Out of the corner of her eye, she thought she noticed Otto smiling at her.

"Anyway, you should be nice to me. I was worried about you," she said to Ion.

Ion picked up a handful of wood shaving and threw it in her direction. It landed on her skirt and she brushed it off.

"Tell me about Dad and the uncles. Do you know where they are? What are we going to do?"

"*We* are not going to do anything," Max said. "At least you aren't. This is not something that a girl should be messing around with."

Jana thought about how she had hidden the secret message today and smiled to herself. *If only Max knew, then he wouldn't think of me as just a girl*, she thought.

Jana glanced up and noticed Otto looking at her appraisingly, with a mixture of amusement and irritation on his face. Their eyes met, momentarily, and then they both quickly looked away.

The conversation turned to horses and weather. Jana could tell that they wanted her to leave so they could talk freely among themselves and that they weren't going to say anything more about her father and the others while she was there.

Jana pushed her seat back a few inches into the shadows so she could watch without it being too obvious. She noticed how small and tired Ion looked. The bruises on his face were barely visible in the dim light. A surge of anger swept through her body. *My father and uncles are missing, and my brother has been tortured. There must be something I can do*, she thought.

"Jana! Jana!" Aunt Marie called from the back door.

"Okay, I'm leaving," she said as she reluctantly got up and left. She glanced back before she closed the door, and they sat watching her leave. As soon as she closed the door behind her, she heard the scraping of chair legs as they drew them closer together to continue their conversation.

Later that evening, as Jana was taking out the trash, she saw Otto crossing the yard from the barn to the house. His head was down and he appeared to be deep in thought. When he was within a few yards of her, he suddenly noticed her, glanced around to see if anyone was watching, and then approached her.

He stopped in front of her and looked down into her eyes. Jana, startled by his approach and the serious look on his face, didn't move. He reached out and grasped her shoulders. His fingers pressed into her flesh.

"You know I'll do everything I can, don't you?" he said.

"Yes, of course." She shrugged her shoulders to loosen his tight grip.

He looked at his hands as if suddenly noticing where they were, and released her. "Just don't do anything you shouldn't. I mean, don't do anything that might be dangerous."

"No, I won't," she said.

He looked at her a moment longer, as though he had something more to say, and then abruptly turned away and went into the house. Jana stood there for a few moments taking in deep breaths of the cool evening air to compose herself, before finishing her chore and returning to the house.

CHAPTER 22

Jana pushed aside the drapes of the third-floor conference room and peeked out at the jumble of red tile roofs and golden spires that covered the hills below and reflected the morning sunlight. This conference room was seldom used, and the heavy brocade fabric of the drapes smelled of dust. Nevertheless, the ornate grandfather clock, standing against the far wall, was wound regularly, as were all the clocks in the castle. Jana heard the clockmaker opening and closing doors as he headed in this direction.

Jana's heart was thumping in her chest and her mouth felt dry. She tried to remember what she'd planned to say—she'd gone over it again and again in her mind—but now she was drawing a blank. Mr. Novotny rattled his keys outside the door and, in a moment of panic, she stepped behind the drapes.

From the crack between the drapes, she watched as he entered the room, crossed over to the clock, and wound it with the large key he wore on a chain hanging from his vest.

She stepped out from behind the drapes as he finished and turned to go. "Hello, Mr. Novotny," she said.

He stopped and turned. "Oh, it's you, Jana! You must stop scaring me like that! I'm an old man; I might have a heart attack. What are you doing here?"

"I'm sorry. I came to talk to you." She hesitated for a moment, then crossed the room and stood close to him so they could talk quietly, in case someone passed in the hall.

"It's about my father and other relatives. They've been arrested, and I—"

Mr. Novotny looked alarmed, put his finger to his lips, and glanced around. "I'm sorry to hear that. You must be very worried about them, but I'm sure everything will turn out okay."

Jana was startled by his response, but then realized he was afraid someone might be listening. "Yes, I . . . I hope so," she stammered.

"Well, we need to get back to work. Shall we?" He walked her to the door and held it open for her. When they were in the hall, he leaned down and whispered, "Can you meet me by the fountain in front of the summer palace about noon?"

She nodded, and they went their separate ways.

She hurried to collect the dishes from the second floor and rushed downstairs with them. Mrs. Sladekova greeted her with a scowl.

"Can't you ever do anything quickly?" she asked.

"Sorry," Jana mumbled and went back to work. She tried to work as quickly and quietly as possible and kept her eye on the clock. When it was nearly noon, she took off her apron and mumbled something to Mrs. Sladekova's back about going out for a bit of fresh air.

"Well, don't dillydally, like you always do! I'm making some soup for our lunch," she said and continued to grumble to herself.

Jana dashed out, down the long hallway, up an old stone staircase, and out a small wooden back door. The bright noontime sun momentarily blinded her, and she paused for a moment in the doorway, waiting for her eyes to adjust. It was a crisp, beautiful spring day, and she had a fleeting desire to forget everything and just run in any direction that her feet cared to take her. Instead, she took a deep breath and walked across the courtyard and through the arched entrance to the long garden that ran alongside the castle. A few minutes later, she arrived at the fountain. It was empty and dry because it had not yet been filled and turned on for the summer season. Mr. Novotny sat perched on the edge, smoking a pipe. He looked up casually as she approached.

"Hello, Jana. Isn't it a beautiful day?"

"Yes, I suppose so," she said, looking around without really seeing anything.

"Try to look casual," he said. "Let's keep this short. Tell me what happened."

"My father, his cousin, and my uncles were all arrested, and we haven't seen them or heard from them. My brother and cousin were arrested, too, but they let them go," she said.

"When were they arrested?" he asked.

"On Friday, March 31."

"What are their surnames?"

"Their what?"

"Their last names, the family names."

"Oh, they're all Benaks; my father is Josef Benak, my uncles are Emil, Tony, and Martin Benak; except my father's cousin is a Kovac, Vaclav Kovac," she said.

"Okay, Benak and Kovac; and you haven't heard from them since their arrest?" he asked.

"No."

"What would you like to know?"

Jana hadn't really thought about it. She hesitated a bit, then said, "I guess I'd like to know where they are, and if they're well? And what can be done to bring them home."

"Okay, I think I know someone who may be able to help. If I can set up a meeting, it will be in front of the Astronomical Clock, in the Old Town Square. I'll let you know when; I'll leave a note for you in the usual way. Now, continue walking around the garden so it looks like you just stopped for a brief chat."

"All right, thank you," Jana said. She started to turn away, but then she turned back. "But how will I know who I'm meeting?"

"Don't worry. He'll find you. You just need to be there at the specified time, and don't do anything to draw attention to yourself."

"Okay, I understand."

Jana walked along, trying to slow down to an appropriate stroll, and stopped to sit on a bench, pretending to admire the view. She hoped that Mr. Novotny would be able to help, and wished she could do something to make everything work out. She tried to remember a prayer that the nuns had taught her, years ago, when they had stopped near a village for the winter and the nuns would give them lunch if they came to Sunday school, but all she could remember was "Our Father, who art in heaven." She kept repeating that, followed by "Please help us."

For the next several days, every time Jana collected dirty dishes she expected to find a sign that there was a note waiting for her. She was beginning to think that maybe Mr. Novotny had been unable to arrange a meeting, when one day, as she was stacking dirty dishes onto a trolley as usual, she saw the crossed silverware, a sign that there was a message waiting for her. She opened the clock, stood on her tiptoes, and felt around inside the grandfather clock. She found a small piece of paper, torn out of a small notebook and folded into a square, tucked into the usual spot near the face of the clock. She opened it and read, "Tomorrow at 5:00 p.m."

The next day at breakfast, she mentioned to her family that she would have to work late, to help Mrs. Sladekova get ready for a dinner party. This was not out of the ordinary and, as she hoped, aroused no suspicion.

"What time should I pick you up?" Max asked.

"Around six thirty," she said.

"Okay, I guess I'll have time for a beer—or two. Too bad." He laughed.

His mother eyed him while drying her hands on her apron. She put her hands on her hips and said, "It's a good thing the horses know the way home."

Jana watched the large clock on the wall throughout the afternoon. As it got close to four thirty, she said, "I have to leave a little early today, Mrs. Sladekova. I have to shop for my mother before I go home. She isn't feeling well."

"Okay, have a nice day off," she said and waved dismissively. The radio was blaring announcements about tomorrow's "holiday" in honor of the *Führer's* birthday. Mrs. Sladekova had the volume turned up too high and barely glanced up as Jana hung up her apron and hurried out.

Jana had to leave by the back exit as usual, to avoid unnecessary attention, though it would have been much quicker to go out of the front gate. She hurried down the steps from the castle, through the twisting streets, and across the St. Charles Bridge. The soot-covered statues of the saints, blackened by many years of burning coal to warm houses and buildings through the cold winters, watched impassively and, as she neared the end of the bridge, the figure of the crucified Christ seemed to stare down sorrowfully as she hurried past.

When she arrived at the Old Town Square, she noticed that there were groups of German soldiers everywhere. She had gotten used to seeing them around the city during the past month, but there seemed to be many more of them than usual here today.

Standing apart from the soldiers, a small crowd had gathered in front of the Astronomical Clock, located on the side of the Old Town Hall, waiting for the chiming of the hour. There were fewer people than would have normally have been here on a warm spring afternoon because of the German soldiers, who clustered together, talking loudly amongst themselves.

When the clock struck the hour, two doors slid open and statues of the twelve apostles glided by, while four statues depicting the evils of life danced and shook below. While the crowd watched this hourly show, a serious, slender man of medium height, wearing a Masaryk cap, approached Jana. He leaned slightly toward her and quietly said, "Meet me on the other side of the Hus monument in a few minutes."

Jana nodded once, in agreement, waited a few minutes, and then followed him. As she walked across the square, she noticed the swastika flags and banners that hung from flagpoles and the fronts of the buildings facing the square. As she walked around the Hus monument, she saw a huge picture of Adolf Hitler mounted on a stand, erected behind a podium and surrounded by more swastika flags.

The man she came to meet sat on the bottom steps of the Hus monument, and she walked over to join him. "Hello, my name is Jan. Care to join me?" he asked. He motioned for her to take a seat to his right.

"Pleased to meet you; my name is Jana."

"I know. Our mutual friend described you well, a pretty young girl of about fifteen or sixteen, with long dark hair."

Jana felt herself blush. To change the subject she said, "This must be where they will be holding some of the ceremonies for Hitler's birthday."

"Yes, it is." He smiled slightly.

She was surprised by his reaction. "Is that amusing?" she asked.

"No, it's not that. It's just that they are going to get more in the way of decorations than they are planning for."

"What do you mean?"

"Just that some of us are planning a peaceful demonstration, to remind the invaders that this is not their country. We're going to cover this monument with flowers." He gestured expansively. "The centerpiece will be a huge wreath with the national motto, "Truth shall prevail." His smile broadened.

"Anyway," he said and resumed his usual serious expression, "your family members are okay. They're in a work camp, in Germany, doing road construction. Here's where they are." Turning toward her, he took a folded piece of paper out of his pocket and slid it along the step to her.

"Don't look at it here," he warned. "I have a contact who spoke to them, and they want you to know that they will find a way to get a message to the family as soon as they can."

Jana slipped the paper into her pocket. Then Jan got up, tipped his cap, said goodbye, and walked off.

Jana sat there for a few minutes, suddenly feeling happier and lighter than she had for weeks. She gazed around her, enjoying her surroundings. The warm summer evening had lured people out. It seemed as though people were trying to resume their normal lives, in spite of the occupation. They seemed to ignore the Nazi decorations.

She saw that tables that had been set up under awnings outside restaurants were starting to fill. She noticed a group of three German soldiers sitting at one table, and the surrounding tables were empty. It looked as though people were not anxious to get too close. One of the soldiers seemed familiar, and then she realized, with a start, that it was Franz! She jumped up, her heart beating fast in her chest, and hurried off, hoping that he had not noticed her.

Her legs trembled, and she wanted to run, but she forced herself to walk. She remembered Mr. Novotny warning her not to do anything to call attention to herself. She walked across the square, through some narrow, winding streets, and into a small park, which was between several tall buildings, that had once been a courtyard. A walking path wound around the perimeter of the park, surrounded by numerous benches and flower beds. Tulips and other spring flowers were blooming, but it was still chilly in the shaded garden, and there were only a few people strolling or sitting here. Jana sat down on a bench, away from the others, took the paper out of her pocket and unfolded it. It contained two words "Buchenwald, Weimer."

She refolded the paper and returned it to her pocket. The words didn't mean anything to her. She wondered what she should do next. She thought she should tell someone. But who? If she told anyone in the family, they would want to know how she got the information, and that would mean trouble. How could she explain meeting with a strange man, or even how she'd contacted him? She certainly couldn't say anything about the clockmaker and her extra activities at the castle. Anyway, Jan had said that her father and uncles would send word soon, so why not just wait?

As she sat there, trying to figure it all out, the church bells chimed at six o'clock, and she realized that she'd better get back to the castle in a hurry, to catch her ride home. She sprang to her feet and hurried back the way she'd come.

She got back to the castle before Max and had time to catch her breath and try to look tired and bored, as she normally would after a long day's work. Fortunately, Max didn't pay much attention to her. He'd stopped for a couple of beers, and he launched into a long story about some old pal he'd run into in the pub. She barely listened, and he didn't seem to notice that she wasn't listening.

When they got home, her stepmother, Zofie, was more perceptive. "What are you smiling about?" she asked.

"No reason. Am I smiling?" Jana said and tried to look impassive.

Zofie looked at her suspiciously, then shrugged, and said, "Come into the kitchen with me and I'll get you something to eat. Here, hold Eduard. He's been cranky all day. See if you can entertain him."

CHAPTER 23

Franz, Rolf, and Paul sat at a table in the Old Town Square enjoying their beers and the warm spring evening. They'd spent the day helping set up for tomorrow's big celebration of Hitler's fiftieth birthday. They didn't mind. It was a change from the usual routine of standing guard duty on street corners or in front of buildings.

They discussed the latest rumor, which was that the brass believed that there wouldn't be a mass rebellion, so they'd be pulling out soon. Sure, there were nuisance disturbances, like swastika flags torn off cars, so swastikas were painted onto the sides of the vehicles, instead; and signs had been defaced or torn down, but for the most part, it was thought that the Czech police could keep order.

Tomorrow they were required to show up for the ceremony, and that would entail more hours of standing around.

"At least there would be bands and speeches, for a change of pace," Franz said. "Although I could do without the speeches."

"I hope wherever they send us, we get in on some excitement," Rolf said. "So far all I've done is march around, stand around, and sit around." He fidgeted in his chair.

Franz had known him since they were both little kids, and he had always been full of nervous energy. "Enjoy it while you can," Franz said.

"What do you mean?" Paul asked, with a worried expression.

"Who knows where they'll send us next—maybe Poland, and that may not be the cakewalk that this has been. I like it here. The beer is good, and most of the people speak German," Franz said.

"When they want to!" Rolf snorted.

"I hope they send us back to Germany," Paul said. "Wouldn't it be great to be home?"

"Not yet. I want to go home with a chest full of medals," Rolf said.

Franz tuned them out while they argued about where they'd like to be stationed next. *I'll bet no one will ask us*, he thought. He looked around the square at the people out for an evening stroll, enjoying the nice weather. They stopped to chat with their friends and neighbors who they met along the way.

He noticed a couple sitting on the steps of the Hus monument, which was in the middle of the square. The girl looked familiar. She was small and had long dark hair. The young man sitting next to her was wearing a gray jacket and a Masaryk cap. *It's Jana!* he realized with a start. *I wonder what she's doing here.* He continued to watch her while appearing not to.

"Hey, Franz, what do you think?" Paul asked.

"Think about what?" he asked.

"See, I told you he wasn't listening," Paul said to Rolf. "One beer and he's off in the ozone."

"Yeah, I guess so," Franz agreed, good-naturedly.

"Hey, do you want to do some shopping?" Rolf asked. He was never happy sitting still for long. "We might not get another chance, and I'd like to stock up on cigarettes and buy some gifts to send back home. There's so much stuff here in the shops, and the prices are good."

"Sure, I guess so, as soon as I finish my beer," Franz said. He looked back at the step where Jana had been sitting, but she and the young man she was talking to were both gone.

* * *

The next day's ceremonies went off without a hitch. The German command made every attempt to make the celebration a memorable one. Every Czech of German nationality was required to attend, and all members of the German army were there in their dress uniforms, along with the black-uniformed SS. The Czech population mostly stayed away, except the politicians who were required to be there, or those who wanted to curry favor with their new overlords. The rest of the people went about their lives, as they would on any day off from work.

The weather had turned gray, cloudy, and windy so that the words of the speakers were sometimes lost in the wind. No one seemed to mind—it was the usual self-congratulatory tripe that they had been hearing day and night, blaring from every radio set and street corner loudspeaker.

Sometime during the night, people had deposited piles of flowers on the base of the Hus monument, as a sign of protest. At first, it was ignored by the Germans, who mistook it for a tribute, until someone pointed out that the wreath was emblazoned with the Czechoslovakian national motto, "Truth shall prevail," and then a Czech police officer was sent to remove the wreath.

Albert sat across the table from his father, Karel, in a coffee shop. They exchanged pleasantries as the waitress took their order and returned with coffee and pastries. Albert took a package of cigarettes out of his shirt pocket and offered one to his father.

"No thanks. I'm trying to stick to only smoking one pipe of tobacco after dinner. Your mother is always after me. She claims it's bad for my health."

A moment later he continued, "I considered the matter we discussed." Karel glanced around to see if they could be overheard, but there were only a few other people in the coffeehouse, and they weren't seated nearby. "I learned that your friend's family was transferred to a work camp in Germany called Buchenwald."

"For how long?"

"I don't know. It could be months or longer."

"Is there any way to get them out?"

Karel fell silent and pensively stirred his coffee. When he replied, he spoke so quietly that Albert had to lean forward to hear him. "Possibly, but it would take money, lots of money; the right palms would have to be greased, and I don't have that kind of cash. The bank has put a hold on our account. It's only possible to withdraw small amounts."

"But if we could raise the cash, you could arrange it?"

"I don't know if I could, but I could try." He hesitated, staring into his coffee cup as if searching it for answers. "Albert, I'd like you to consider leaving the country," he said, at last.

"What? Why?"

"It's not safe here. You know that. Young Czechs may be drafted to fight for the Germans, as we were made to fight for the Austrians in the Great War. It's still possible to get you out through Poland, but how much longer that route will be an option, no one can say."

Albert thought of his recent arrest by the Gestapo, and what they would do if they found out that he was working against them. "Where would I go?" he asked.

"To England. You could stay with your cousin Alois's family, or possibly to France. I understand that they are forming a Czech division of the French Foreign Legion."

"What about you and Mom?"

"Oh, don't worry about us. We'll be all right. I have contacts, and I always keep an ear to the ground."

"I don't want to," Albert said. "I have friends here. It seems cowardly to flee the country and leave everyone behind, and I would have to drop out of school."

"Well, think it over. Anyway, see if your friends can raise some cash. If they can, let me know and I'll put the wheels in motion. Oh, and one other thing," he said and paused.

"What?" Albert asked.

"It may not be important, but it seems that a young girl—a family member, I assume—has been making inquiries. There's been no harm done, so far, but it's probably best if we don't get too many cooks stirring the broth, if you know what I mean."

"A girl?" Albert thought for a moment. "What girl? Did they say who she was?"

"No, just a description: small, dark, good looking, about fifteen or sixteen years old."

"Oh, I think I know who she is," Albert said. "I'll take care of it."

The next few days, Jana desperately wanted to tell someone in the family her secret. The words "Don't worry; they're safe" almost flew out of her mouth when she walked into a room and saw someone crying or gazing sorrowfully off into the distance. But each time she told herself that they would soon learn the truth, and it would just cause more trouble for everyone if she told them what she knew.

One evening, after a week of keeping the secret, Jana and Max were on their way home when they noticed Albert waiting for them on a corner. Max pulled the horses over and stopped.

"Hi, can I get a lift?" he asked.

"Of course." Max nodded. Jana moved over to give him room, and Albert jumped up.

"I've got some great news! I know where your relatives are," he said.

Jana and Max both turned toward him in astonishment. "What! Where? How are they?" Max and Jana peppered him with questions.

"Okay, okay, give me a chance to tell you. They're in a work camp in Germany, a place called Buchenwald. They're building roads," Albert said.

"How did you find out?" Max asked.

"I asked my dad to see what he could do, and he pulled some strings. I need to talk to you and Otto about that. Can you come up later tonight to my place?"

"Of course! Absolutely!"

"Well, I'd better get going then. Say, you don't happen to have a cigarette, do you? I'm out," he said.

"Yeah, sure, just a second." Max patted his jacket pocket.

While he was distracted, Albert slipped a note from his left hand into Jana's right hand. She looked at him questioningly, and he gave a slight shake of his head and a warning look. She understood that Max should not know, and slipped the note into her pocket.

"Here you go." Max handed him a cigarette.

"Thanks. See you later," he said and jumped down.

"Okay, hand it over," Max said after Albert was gone.

"What do you mean?" Jana asked.

"Come on! Do you take me for an idiot?" I saw Albert pass you a note. So, hand it over! Why is he passing you notes, anyway?"

"I don't know. I haven't read it yet. Anyway, it's none of your business," she said, and she pulled the note out, unfolded it, and read, "Don't get involved. It may complicate things."

Max tried to grab the note from her as she held it out at arm's length to try to keep it away from him. The horses kept clopping contentedly along while they wrestled.

"Give me that!" he said as he grabbed her arm and yanked the note from her hand, leaving her holding a ragged edge.

"What does he mean 'don't get involved'?" Max asked.

"How should I know? Maybe you should ask Albert," Jana said.

"Maybe I will. Let's get him, and ask him right now." Max pulled up on the horses, but Albert was nowhere in sight.

CHAPTER 24

Otto and Max sat on mismatched wooden chairs around Albert's kitchen table. It was against the wall under the window that overlooked the courtyard below, which was now shrouded in darkness. A single light bulb hung from the middle of the tall ceiling of the room and cast shadows around the kitchen as Albert opened and closed cupboards, retrieved a half-full bottle of brandy and three glasses, and put them in the middle of the table; and then he emptied the ashtray and placed it next to the bottle. Before sitting down, he opened the bifold window, to let out the smoke and let in the cool night air. Then he sat down and poured drinks for the group and they each lit their cigarettes. The kitchen chairs scraped against the wooden floor as they settled back and got comfortable.

After some initial small talk, a brief silence fell over the group. Albert cleared his throat, tapped the ash off the end of his cigarette, and said, "As you know, my father has been in contact with some men who may be able to secure the release of your father and your other relatives. But it will be expensive, possibly as much as 6,000 CKD."

"Wow!" Max said.

Otto whistled and raised his eyebrows in surprise.

"I know—it's a lot," Albert said. "I guess there's a lot involved. The right paperwork must be prepared. Several people will be involved, and they will all need to be paid. If it doesn't seem legal, things could turn out worse than they are now. They could be arrested and charged with escaping, or something. They could end up somewhere worse, or even dead."

"I suppose you're right," Otto said. Max nodded in agreement.

"The first problem is raising the money," Albert said. "My father says there is a strict limit on how much can be taken out of the bank."

"Of course," Otto said, "and we don't expect your father to finance this, anyway."

"Oh, I know," Albert said, looking relieved. "Of course, he'll do what he can. After all, what happened started because I asked you to help my family and that eventually led to the arrest of your family members. But it looks like we'll need to raise some money. Do you have any ideas?"

Otto and Max looked at each other. Otto took a long drag on his cigarette and very deliberately knocked the ash off the tip into the ashtray while he thought it over. As the older brother, he knew he was expected to speak for the family. "We probably have some things we can sell. I don't know exactly what or how much we can get for them. I'll have to talk to my family," he said.

In fact, he'd already talked to his mother, and the other women, before he came, and had a pretty good idea of how many gold coins were sewn into the seams of their skirts and how many pieces of gold jewelry they owned, but he wasn't ready to reveal everything he knew. Albert was a friend, but he was still a *Gadjo*, and reluctance to completely trust those outside of the people was as natural to him as breathing. He knew that the women would gladly sell everything they owned to free their husbands or sons, but he also knew that, as night follows day, another emergency would follow this one. So, it would be wise to hang onto something for tomorrow.

"Do you have any other sources of income, or ways to raise money?" Albert asked.

"Just our work," Otto replied, "and that has been slow. What with the occupation and the threat of war, people are putting off buying furniture or having it repaired. It's been kind of slow," he repeated. "In fact, I've been thinking of trying to get my job back at Skoda and leave Max to keep things going at home, with the help of some of the older boys; and, of course, there's also Jana's job," he added.

"Do you have contacts? I mean, do you know where you will sell your items to get the best price?" Albert asked. There was a note of eagerness in the way he asked. "I'm wondering if you have discreet sources, where things could be sold without drawing any unnecessary attention."

"I think so," Otto said.

"The reason I ask is I know people, people who don't have your connections, who would be willing to pay a middleman to help them sell things. As you know, some people had to go underground after the invasion—ex-military, German refugees, and so on."

"Yes, I know."

"Which means they are undocumented and can't work or travel freely, and that they don't have ration cards, so the problem becomes how to survive. They're being helped, of course, but those helping them don't have unlimited resources.

"I've been working with people who are facilitating the exchange of goods for food from farmers, for example, but we'd like to also be able to exchange some items for cash and find ways to get the correct paperwork for these people—under assumed names, of course, so their situation wouldn't be quite so precarious. Do you think you might be interested in acting as middlemen?"

Max and Otto looked at each other and shrugged slightly.

"Possibly," Max said.

"We might be able to make some connections," Otto said.

"Okay, let me know. As I said, if you can, there would be some money in it for you," Albert said.

"Up-front money?" Otto asked. "Because, obviously, the sooner we can get something going, the better."

"I'll see what I can do. Let's get together soon and see what can be arranged."

With business taken care of, they poured another round of drinks, lit their cigarettes, and Albert got out the radio to listen to the BBC, an activity that was both very common and highly illegal.

The next evening, Otto and Max sat in their living room talking to their mother, and Jana's stepmother and aunts. Jana had been sent upstairs with the other children, in spite of her protests that she was "old enough." This had been ignored, and she'd stomped off, angrily, and then crept back to the top of the stairs to try to listen in. But their voices were too low, and the kids, who had been sent upstairs before they were ready to go to sleep, were making a racket behind her.

She finally gave up and slipped between the comforters with her sisters. She'd see what she could find out from Max and her stepmother tomorrow, she decided. As the kids gradually calmed down and fell asleep, she heard the murmur of voices below, until she, too, fell asleep.

In what seemed like only a moment later, Aunt Marie was leaning over her and gently shaking her shoulder to awaken her. She held a finger up to her lips, indicating that Jana should not wake up the other girls. "Hurry!" she whispered.

Jana rushed to get ready and was sitting at the kitchen table, hurriedly eating bread and jam, washed down with sweet black coffee.

"Why the rush?" she asked.

"Max is dropping Otto off at the railroad station before he takes you to work," Aunt Marie said.

"He's leaving? Why?" She tried not to sound too interested, but she could tell that Aunt Marie had noticed the slight quaver in her voice.

"They say that the woodworking business is kind of slow right now, and Otto thought he'd try to get his job back," she said.

Max opened the back door to the house, leaned in, and said, "Come on, it's time to go." And left again.

Jana took one more gulp of coffee, folded the bread over into a sandwich, with jam leaking out of the edges, and took it with her to finish on the way. Otto was sitting next to Max in the cart waiting for her. He reached down to help her up.

"Your hand is sticky," he said, and laughed as he licked the jam off his fingers.

"Sorry," she said, blushing.

"That's okay." He shrugged and turned toward Max. They continued their conversation about the latest news from the BBC and rumors of troop movements. Jana didn't pay much attention as she hurriedly finished her breakfast and surreptitiously licked the jam off her fingers and dried them on her skirt. She was just happy to be sitting next to Otto, listening to the sound of his voice, and feeling his shoulder bump against her as the cart rattled over the cobblestone streets.

She'd heard a lot of this kind of speculation; it seemed to be the favorite topic of conversation these days. Everyone was talking about when the war would begin and fervently hoping it would be soon. It was widely believed that once the war started, the Germans would quickly be defeated, President Beneš would return, and everything would go back to normal.

"Okay, we're here," Max said as he pulled up to the curb.

Otto reached behind him and pulled out his bag. "I'll see you soon. Try to get along without me," Otto said to Max, with a laugh.

"Yeah, yeah, I'll try," Max said

As Otto turned and started to get up, he paused, and said to Jana, "Don't look so serious. I'll be back before you have time to miss me."

She blushed, embarrassed that her face had given her away, and blurted out, "Don't worry about me. I'll be fine!"

Otto laughed, kissed her on the cheek, and then clambered past her and jumped down. He strode toward the station door, his bag slung over one shoulder, and, as Max started to pull away from the curb, he turned and waved goodbye.

He seems awfully happy to be leaving, Jana thought, and she fought back tears. Jana and Max didn't speak for most of the rest of her way to work as she stared, unseeingly, at the usual morning scene of people hurrying to work and onto crowded streetcars. Max glanced at her from time to time with an expression that was a mixture of amusement and pity.

As they rode up the hill to the castle, Max cleared his throat. Although Jana didn't want to talk, he seemed to have something he wanted to say. "I've been thinking," he said.

"About what?" she asked.

"I know you're more involved in stuff than Otto knows. I know that you've been asking questions and trying to see how you could help get your father and the other men released."

"So what?" she said.

"Don't get excited. I haven't told Otto, or anyone else. Of course, Albert already knows, as well as everyone else you've talked to about it."

She gave him a puzzled look. "I guess so," she said. "What's your point?"

"Well, since you're already involved, you might as well know, we met with Albert, and he said his father knows people who may be able to help us but it will take a lot of money, more than we have. That's why Otto is going to try to get his job back. I'm going to try to sell whatever I can, and we'll be using your salary, too—just about anything we can do to get some money together. I just thought you should know." He seemed to want to say more, but he hesitated.

"Okay, thanks for telling me," she said. "Is there anything I can do to help?"

He glanced at her out of the corner of his eye. "Maybe," he said. "But don't go off half-cocked, talking to everybody about it. If there's an opportunity, a safe opportunity where you can be useful, I'll let you know. Okay?" He turned to look at her, waiting for her reply.

"Okay," she said.

"I mean it!" he said. "If I find out that you're sneaking around behind my back . . . I don't know what I'll do, but you'll be sorry. Don't mess this up, okay?"

"Okay! I said okay! Just remember, I'm not a kid anymore," she said.

"Yeah, yeah, okay, kid." He laughed as he pulled up to let her out. "See you later."

CHAPTER 25

A huge throng of people had turned out on this lovely Saturday in early May for a holiday celebrating the reburial of the Czech poet Karel Hynek Mácha. Jana, Otto, Max, and Albert sat on the grass on the edge of the crowd.

This was Otto's first weekend home in a couple of weeks since he'd gone to Plzeň and gotten his old job back at Skoda. He normally worked Saturdays, but he'd taken this Saturday off so he could take part in the day's events.

The night before, Otto had explained the importance of the day to Jana and Max. He'd said that Mácha was an important national figure who had lived a short life, died, and had been buried over one hundred years ago in the northern Bohemian town of Leitmeritz. The Munich Agreement, which was signed last October, put that town into German territory. At that time, his remains had been removed and brought to Prague, and now were going to be reburied in Vyshehrad Cemetery with much pomp and ceremony.

Throughout the city, the population celebrated the day as a national holiday, with Czech flags flying and no swastikas in sight. Otto and Max had been out the night before and had told her they saw the city's historic monuments lit up, just like they were for national holidays before the invasion. It was easy to imagine that things were getting back to normal.

Jana shifted her weight on the rocky ground, trying to get

comfortable. They sat near the top of a gradual incline, which surrounded a platform. An altar had been erected on that platform, and a priest was saying a dedication Mass. He droned on in Latin, and they stood, knelt, and sat, following along with the rest of the crowd. Jana heard only snatches of what he said, when the wind blew in their direction, carrying the sound along with whiffs of incense, and she didn't understand what he was saying, anyway.

Her mind drifted as she watched the clouds float by and birds fly across the clouds and sky, and she snuck sidelong glances at Otto, studying his profile when he wasn't looking. She noticed the chiseled features, the light tan skin, and the black hair falling rakishly over one eye. She'd thought he was probably the most handsome man she'd ever seen! Her heart beat faster every time she looked at him.

After the priest had given the final blessing, he invited the crowd to sit, and he and the altar boys took seats in a row of folding chairs at the back of the platform. A pompous man strode up the steps and over to the lectern. In answer to her questioning look, Albert leaned over and whispered.

"He's an actor from the National Theatre. He's going to recite 'May.'"

"'May'? What's that?" she whispered back.

"Mácha's famous poem." They were getting looks and shushing from those seated around them. "I'll tell you more about it later," he whispered.

The actor began.

Late evening on the first of May
The twilit May—the time of love,
Meltingly called the turtle dove,
Where rich and sweet pinewoods lay."

Jana liked the rhythm and the rising and falling inflections of the sentences, but much of the meaning of the poem was lost to the wind in the trees, and she soon tired of trying to follow it. She gathered it had something to do with love, violence, and death. It seemed to be a very long poem, with no end in sight. She fidgeted, trying to get comfortable on the hard ground.

Albert and Otto seemed to be hanging on every word, while Max had assumed a neutral expression and seemed to be waiting, like Jana, for it to be over. At last, it was finished and the crowd burst into prolonged applause, before slowly forming into a long line.

Jana was just glad to be moving, although slowly, as they shuffled along, waiting for their turn to file past the draped coffin, which was covered with the Czech flag, with a floral lyre hanging over it, and guarded by students with golden rapiers. It was all very grand and somber, but at the same time, the mood of the people seemed both cheerful and defiant.

Jana thought it was a rather odd way to spend a sunny Saturday in May, but she was happy to be spending the day with Otto, although he seemed almost unaware of her presence. She fell behind the others as they started to leave, and Otto stopped to wait for her.

"Are you coming?" he asked.

"Otto," she said, feeling like she would burst if she didn't ask the question that was on her mind. "Do you like me?"

He looked down at her, then suddenly put his hands on both sides of her face, leaned down, and kissed her, gently.

She stepped back, her face flushed when he released her.

"Does that answer your question?" he asked.

A single, bare light bulb, hung on a long dusty cord from the middle of the ceiling, dimly illuminated the subterranean room. Otto sat, his hands resting on the keys of the typewriter, trying to compose an opening line for the lead story for *The Truth*, the newsletter he'd been spending most of his free time writing since he'd returned to Plzeň. He gave it up for the moment, and instead sorted through the bits and pieces of notes; some he'd been given by others, and some he'd jotted down himself, most of them related insults and outrages recently perpetrated by the Germans.

One recent incident was the arrest of fifty Jews and fifty "Czech Marxists" following an alleged throwing of acid at a German soldier. Since the individuals involved had gotten away, the German policy of "community responsibility" caused one hundred people to suffer for what amounted to a few holes in a German uniform. That was a good story, he thought; one that demonstrated Nazi methods to the outside world, and showed that the Czechs did not welcome the German occupation, as the Germans wanted to pretend.

It was a good story, all right, but he decided to lead with a recounting of the events of last weekend in Prague—the reburial of Mácha. Though most people were already aware of the events of that day, it was something encouraging. Perhaps a slight indication that things would be back to normal soon.

In the opposite corner, a serious-looking young woman stood at a counter, improvised from an old door laid across two sawhorses, turning the crank on a mimeograph machine, making copies of the previous newsletter. As the copies came off the machine, a young man laid them out to dry, and then gathered them up into piles a few minutes later. They rarely spoke to each other, but something about the way they worked together and glanced at each other made Otto think they were a couple.

Otto leaned back and closed his eyes for a few moments, trying to compose his thoughts. He was dimly aware of the odors of ink and stale coffee, mixed with dampness and dust. The young couple interrupted his thoughts as they gathered up the finished newsletters and got ready to leave. They nodded and said goodbye as they left, then headed out into the darkened tunnels, which they'd all learned to navigate with the help of the flickering beams of flashlights.

Otto didn't know their names, and they didn't know his. Nor did he know what they did with the copies of the newsletter once they left, or how they were distributed.

To Otto, the secrecy seemed extreme, but that's the way Mr. Jelinek, the Skoda foreman who oversaw this newsletter, wanted it. "It's safer that way," he'd said.

As the two sets of footsteps receded, the quiet closed around Otto. He pushed the old wooden chair back from the desk, across the uneven stone floor, and tilted back. Lacing his fingers together behind his head, he reflected on all that had happened in the past few weeks.

He'd gotten his job back, of course. Since he knew about Mr. Jelinek's clandestine activities, it hadn't been difficult to convince him to rehire him. Not that he'd said anything; he didn't have to. Mr. Jelinek had been visibly relieved to see Otto again. After Otto had disappeared, he'd worried that he might have gone to the authorities with what he knew. Not that Otto could use that information without implicating himself in the process, so their secrets were safe with each other. They had to be.

As part of the deal, Otto had agreed to help with the newsletter. Mr. Jelinek had agreed to pay him for his efforts after hearing the reason Otto needed extra money, and the reason he'd quit and then came to ask for his job back. So here he was, trying to compose the lead story.

He imagined he was at home, sitting with his family around the stove in the barn, talking and laughing. Sitting on the edge of the group was Jana. Her little face, so quick to smile and to frown, changed from moment to moment. Then he remembered how she'd looked at him after he kissed her. With an effort, he pushed the thoughts aside. *Those things will just have to wait. Soon, perhaps, but first we must get our fathers, and the other family members, out of prison*, he thought.

He pulled his mind back to the present and the task at hand. He decided to write the story about the Mácha burial and call it a night. He had a few more days until this edition was due. He pulled his chair up to the desk, and the silence was broken by the sound of the typewriter keys striking the page.

"On a beautiful spring Saturday, all of Prague stopped to remember that we are Czechs," he began.

Jana had been badgering Max to find her something she could do to make extra money. Every day as he drove her to and from work she questioned him. "Do you have something I can do?" she asked. "You promised!" she reminded him. After two weeks of this, he was clearly getting fed up.

"If you ask me that again, I'll make you walk the rest of the way to work!" he threatened.

"Don't you dare! If you do, I'll tell your mom what you have hidden in the leg of that chair you keep hauling back and forth," she said.

He tried to grab her, but she ducked out of the way. "Come here, you little brat!" He tried to grab her again; she twisted away from him and jumped down. She started running up the hill toward the castle, then stopped, turned around, and called, "See you after work."

Cursing and smiling, he urged the horses into a trot and caught up with her, "Okay, okay, get back up here." After she climbed back on, he said, "I'll see what I can do."

"Today?" she asked.

"Yes, today. Well, I'll try, but no promises," he said.

When Max returned that evening to pick her up, his carefully controlled expression told her that he had some news to tell her.

"So, what did you find out?" she asked, after enduring a few minutes of suspense.

"Find out about what?" he asked.

"Come on, you know what I mean," she said.

He laughed, and then said, "Well, I was racking my brain, trying to come up with something to make you happy so you'd stop bugging me, when one of my customers happened to mention that they would be shutting down the Sokols soon."

"Shutting them down. Why?" she asked.

"The usual reason—the Germans probably don't want the Czechs to have a place to congregate and talk politics. Anyway, I recalled what a kick you got out of playing with those puppets, and I swung by there to have a talk with the manager, Mr. Kopecky. He asked about you immediately."

"Really? He did?"

"Sure, he thought you did a great job. So that was a good start. We started talking, and he said they are doing a puppet show this coming weekend, maybe their last for a while, and invited you to help out. I told him that you would like to be paid for helping and the reason why, and he agreed! I'm supposed to bring you by on our way home today to seal the deal. What do you think about that?"

"Oh, that is so great!" she exclaimed, and then jumped up onto her knees on the seat next to him, and gave him a big hug.

"So, I guess it's okay, then," he said and laughed.

They were presenting two fairy tales for a children's matinee that Sunday afternoon: *The Enchanted Forest* and *The Tin Soldier.* Jana's job was to be sure that the puppets, some of whom played more than one role, were in the right costumes for their parts, and ready to go when they were needed.

The Enchanted Forest was a story about an evil wizard who captures the princess and holds her hostage and tries to force her to agree to marry him. The prince and the clever clown, Kasparek, who advises the prince, set out to rescue her. They have to fight a dragon, but in the end, they are successful, and the princess falls in love with the prince and invites him to "Come with me to my country where eternal spring prevails, and where treason is unknown." He agrees, and they set off together to live happily ever after.

Mr. Kopecky explained that there was a nationalist message hidden in the play. He said that the prince, princess, and Kasparek represented the Czech people and the evil wizard represented their oppressors. Jana thought that adults, who had come to the show with their children, might be aware of the message, but the kids probably just liked the story. She peeked through the curtain and laughed to see them gasp and fall back when the dragon breathed fire at the prince and Kasparek. This was just the reaction she'd hoped for when they'd practiced this effect.

The Tin Soldier was a sad story. Jana felt a few tears well up for the poor tin soldier, even though she was busy behind the scenes. In this story, a tin soldier falls in love with a paper dancer, but before he can tell her how he feels, he falls out the window of the playroom, into the street below. After further adventures, he returns home, but the toy's owner doesn't want him anymore because he is battered and worn by his adventures, and throws him into the stove. Before he is melted, someone opens the stove door, and the paper dancer is picked up by a gust of wind and blown into the stove. They are together at last, but only for a moment.

At the end of the show, the puppet characters came out for one last bow, and "sang" the Czech national anthem. The audience stood and sang with them. Then Mr. Kopecky came out from behind the curtain and thanked everyone for coming.

"I am sorry to say that this is our last performance for a while," he said. "However, I will not say it is our last. Some of you may recall, as I do, that we suspended our productions during the last war. Let us hope that the time will soon come when once again I can welcome you back." His voice shook a little, and his large bushy mustache quivered. "Thank you for coming." He bowed and exited the stage.

The audience leaped to their feet and the applause seemed like it would never end. Finally, Mr. Kopecky came back out and went into the audience to shake hands and greet the people. Then the applause ceased and many members of the audience crowded around him, saying goodbye and wishing him well.

When everyone had finally left, and Jana helped pack away the puppets, Mr. Kopecky came over to talk to her. "Thank you, Jana, you did a great job. We couldn't have done it without you. I think you have a real knack for this."

"Thank you, I enjoy it. It's fun."

"Indeed? Well, maybe there will be more opportunities to help us out," he said.

"Really? But . . . I thought this was the last show," she said.

He looked at her appraisingly for a moment. "Can you keep a secret?"

She nodded.

"We may be holding some impromptu shows next spring and summer as we did during the Great War. Would you be interested in helping out with that? It's not without risk, of course." He then quickly added, evidently noticing that she hesitated, "Perhaps you should talk it over with your family first."

Jana was thinking of how Otto always insisted that she stay out of danger. But surely he didn't mean something as harmless as entertainment for children. Anyway, what gave him the right to boss her around?

"I'm sure they won't mind," she said.

"Do you want to take a few of the smaller ones home with you? You can put on shows for the kids in your family over the winter, and then we'll be in touch."

"I'd love to," she said.

"Then it's settled," he said.

CHAPTER 26

Albert rode his bike over the rough cobblestones and through the winding streets and worried about how much time he was spending on underground activities. *My grades are going to suffer,* he thought. *I need to study, too, or my parents will start asking questions. I'll stay up late tonight and try to get caught up,* he promised himself.

He stopped in front of the café where he was meeting his contact. He leaned his bike against the wall, sat down at an outdoor table where he could keep an eye on his bike and watch for his contact, and ordered a pint of beer. Although they'd met several times, he didn't know his contact's name. They'd decided at their first meeting that, as a precaution, they wouldn't exchange names, so he just thought of him as "my contact."

He took a deep draft of beer when it was served. It was a hot afternoon, and he was thirsty from the bike ride. They'd agreed to meet at this out-of-the-way spot because here Albert was unlikely to bump into people he knew, but it was a long ride over rough, dusty streets. As he fumbled with lighting a cigarette, a young woman, hatless, and wearing a summer dress, slid onto the bench across from him.

"Hi," she said.

He looked at her with surprise and mild alarm. He glanced around; the few other people sitting on the terrace all seemed to have noticed them. A woman in this place was a curiosity. "Hi," he said. "Actually, I . . . I . . ." he stuttered.

She laughed. "Yes, I know, you're meeting someone, and it's not me."

When she laughed, he noticed the dimples in her cheeks and the mischievous gleam in her blue eyes. Her light brown hair was pulled back, but a few stray curls had escaped and framed her pretty face.

"He sent me. I'm not allowed to say who." She laughed again, as though this was all just a silly game. "But here's a picture of us together that he gave me for proof." She pushed the photograph across the table. Albert picked it up. It was a picture of his contact and this girl, standing outdoors with their arms linked, squinting into the sun and smiling for the camera.

"He's not well; nothing serious—probably just something he ate—so I was sent in his place to give you the information. The address is on the back of the photo. Anyway, I guess it's an address, even though it's in some sort of cipher. How dramatic!" She laughed again.

A giddy teenager! Albert thought, with irritation. He put the picture in the inside pocket of his jacket. *It doesn't seem wise to get her involved.*

The waiter approached, and she ordered a lemonade. After he'd left to fill her order, she said, "We should act like a couple so we don't arouse suspicion. Act like you know me, and talk to me. You can call me Lída," she said. "You know, like the movie star Lída Baarová. After all, you have to call me something."

Albert was rattled by the sudden turn of events and racked his brain for a few moments for something safe they could talk about, but before he'd thought of a subject, she continued.

"Do you know who Lída Baarová is?"

"Yes." He nodded.

"She's my favorite—well, one of my favorites, anyway. She's so pretty. I've seen every movie she's been in. Do you know that there is a rumor that she is having an affair with some German muckety-muck, someone named Goebbels, but I don't believe it. She is so beautiful and he is so ugly."

Albert was startled to hear her casual mention of the German Minister of Propaganda. He started listening more closely, but that that was all she said on that subject. She rattled on about some new American film, *Gone with the Wind*, that she was hoping to see. She seemed to know all about films and film stars. Albert had little interest in the subject but enjoyed her smile and laugh. An occasional monosyllabic "yes" or "no" seemed to be all she required from him. Watching her, he realized how serious everyone around him had been lately. When they finished their drinks, she got up and he followed.

She leaned toward him and said softly, "Take my arm, and make it look natural." He offered her his arm, and she slipped her arm through his and they walked out together.

"Okay, bye," she said, and abruptly dropped his arm as soon as they reached the corner. He felt a slight twinge of regret as she turned, smiled one last time, waved goodbye, and then walked away.

The sun was high in the noonday sky when they were told to put down their tools and line up for lunch. Josef wearily dropped the shovel he'd been using to shovel wheelbarrows full of gravel all morning long. Every day was the same, only a few miles farther down the road. Occasionally, if they were lucky, it was cool and breezy, but as spring had turned into summer the days were longer and hotter. He went to stand in a long line of men who shuffled along wordlessly, too tired to talk or complain about the horrible food. Anyway, they were used to that, too. The lunch was always the same, a thin, tasteless soup made of mostly water with a few cabbage leaves and pieces of turnip in it. Josef held out the battered metal bowl and received a ladle of soup. *It looks like there are a few shreds of pork in it! I'm lucky today,* he thought.

He looked around to see if he could find his brothers Emil, Tony, Martin, or his cousin Vaclav, but he didn't see them. So, he found a grassy hillock to sit on and pulled a piece of bread out of his pocket. Their bread was given out in the morning for the whole day. Some men ate theirs right away, but he liked to save a piece so he'd have some energy for the afternoon. He was used to going hungry sometimes, especially in the winter, so he didn't suffer from hunger as much as some of the others who seemed to talk of nothing else but food.

He noticed that he was getting thinner and thinner, though, and his ribs were starting to stick out. *I used to be, not fat,* he thought, *but substantial looking; the way a head of a family should look, but not anymore.* As Josef ate his meager lunch, he daydreamed about the wonderful stews and roasted meats that his wife, Zofie, used to make over the campfires for him. He could almost smell them now. He let his mind drift back to those evenings around his own campfire, his wife waiting on him, and his children nearby, playing and laughing. He remembered how, after eating his fill, he'd relax and smoke a cigarette, completely contented. He was startled out of his reverie and stiffened as he saw the foreman marching purposefully toward him. *What does he want?* he wondered, searching his mind for something he may have done to get in trouble. The only time the man ever spoke to him was to yell orders or threats, often followed by blows from the cudgel he always carried with him.

"They want you to report to the office at the end of the day," the foreman said.

"What?" Josef asked.

"Are you deaf, or just stupid?" he yelled. His face turned its customary color of crimson and the veins stuck out on his neck. "Go to the main office when we get back to camp. Is that clear?"

Josef wanted to ask more questions, but he knew better, so he just nodded and said, "Yes, sir."

All afternoon, as he shoveled gravel, questions, hopes, and fears of what this could mean made the long, hot day seem endless. They turned in their tools at the end of the workday and were marched back to camp. After they'd arrived, he walked over to the main office and, with trepidation, entered the waiting room. A young, bored-looking German soldier was sitting at a desk sorting through stacks of papers and rubber-stamping them. An oscillating fan sat next to him on the floor. It moved from side to side ruffling the piles of papers on his desk, held down with paperweights, at each pass, but his heavily pomaded hair didn't move. He glanced up, holding the rubber stamp suspended in mid motion. "Yes?" he asked, with a mixture of boredom and irritation,

"I was told to report here," Josef said.

"Your name?"

"Josef Benak."

"Oh, yes," he said, consulting a list. He riffled through the papers on his desk and pulled out an envelope and handed it to Josef. "You're being released. Your ID and paperwork are in the envelope. You are to gather your things and report to the front gate tomorrow morning at 6:00 a.m. sharp. Don't forget to bring this envelope with you. Sign here," he said and pushed a clipboard, a form on it, toward him. Josef stood, stunned, staring at him for a few moments.

"Do you know how to sign your name?" the soldier asked with growing irritation.

"Oh, yes, yes," Josef said, and then carefully wrote his name on the dotted line and returned the clipboard to the soldier. As he stumbled out of the office and back into the sun, he felt dazed and happy, like a man reborn. He was momentarily unaware of the aches from the long day's work or the gnawing hunger that had oppressed him for these past several months. He felt nothing at this moment but happiness. Then he thought of his brothers and his cousin. *Are they also being released?* he wondered and set out to look for them. He started to run across the grounds, then thought it better not to attract any attention, and forced himself to slow down to a fast walk.

The next morning, after roll call, Josef waited at the front gate in the cool morning air with his three brothers and his cousin Vaclav. They each clutched small bundles of belongings and shifted anxiously from foot to foot. They'd talked about all the possibilities last night. Was it a trick? Were they being taken to someplace even worse, if that was possible? They'd asked Vaclav, the only one who could read and write more than his name, to look at the forms they'd been given. He said that it looked like they were being sent home, but they were all afraid to believe it.

A short time later, a truck pulled up, the gate was opened, and they were ordered to get into the back. No one got in with them to guard them; that was a good sign. As the truck turned around and drove back through the gate, they looked at each other and their looks of disbelief changed to broad smiles. Soon they were laughing, hugging, and clapping each other on the shoulders.

They bumped along for hours and crossed several checkpoints. At every checkpoint, a soldier would jump up into the back of the truck and demand their papers. They held out their envelopes and he would riffle through the contents, while they held their breath, fearing that some reason would be found to send them back, but each time the envelopes were handed back to them without comment. However, at the final checkpoint, they were ordered to get out of the truck and take their stuff with them. They climbed down fearfully, wondering what would happen next.

"You're on your own now," the truck driver said. "You're back in the Protectorate."

"What?" Vaclav said, looking around at the fields surrounding the road. "But, how do we get pack to Praha?"

"That's your problem," he snarled, jumped in the truck, and turned around with a spray of gravel.

The sun was high in the sky as they stood alone on the gravel road. They hadn't had anything to eat since the night before, or anything to drink since early that morning. Josef looked around and noticed a line of trees ahead and to the right. He guessed that might mean that there was a river or a stream hidden behind the trees. "Let's get moving," he suggested. He motioned to the tree line. "Maybe we can get some water and shelter in that direction, and then figure out what to do next." The others nodded or shrugged, and they turned and started to walk along the dusty gravel road.

Josef noticed a cloud of dust in the distance, indicating that a vehicle was approaching. Something about it seemed odd. It seemed to be moving fast, too fast to be a farmer's truck or tractor. *Perhaps it is a German official in one of those black Mercedes they usually drive*, Josef thought. As it approached it slowed and Josef was amazed to see that it was a silver Tatra, covered with a thin coating of dust. It slowed further, and then stopped alongside them. The front doors opened on both sides and out jumped Albert and Otto!

Otto ran to hug and kiss his father. He was shocked by how thin, ragged, and tired his father looked, but tried not to show how he felt. Then he turned and greeted his uncles and Vaclav. Albert shook hands with everyone and soon everyone was talking, laughing, and crying at once.

"We should get going," Albert said when the din died down a bit. "We need to get you home. Everyone is waiting."

"But how did you know we'd be here?" Josef asked.

"We'll tell you all about it," Otto said. "But hop in. We'll stop at a tavern in the next town so you can wash up and get something to eat, and we'll tell you the whole story."

A small argument broke out as Otto insisted that his father take his place in the front seat and Josef, in turn, insisted that Vaclav, as the eldest, should take that seat. When Vaclav finally accepted, the rest of the men crowded into the back seat and they set off.

When they stopped in the next village and walked into the tavern, the proprietor and the few patrons who were there all turned to look at them. The looks were not welcoming. Otto approached the proprietor and pulled out a roll of bills. At the sight of the cash, his expression changed to one of obsequious friendliness. Josef, Emil, Tony, Martin, and Vaclav were shown into the back and given water, soap, and towels to clean up while Albert and Otto ordered sandwiches and beer.

Otto smiled at how elated Josef was to see the pitchers of beer and plates of sandwiches brought out for them but he, and most of the others, knew better than to eat or drink too much after their prolonged fast.

"You'd better take it easy. Eat only a little. Our stomachs need to get used to food again," Josef said.

Vaclav had seldom gone hungry before, and Martin was young and impetuous. Both of them were eating as fast as they could. Upon hearing Josef's advice, they slowed down and ate and drank only a little, while Otto filled them in on how they'd gotten them released and the part that Albert and his father had played.

Albert waved off their effusive thanks. “It was nothing,” he said. “Your families came up with the money. For example, Otto worked extra shifts.”

“Everyone helped get the money together,” Otto said. “The women sold everything they could sell, and Max and Jana looked for ways to earn extra money. Jana was hired to help out with another puppet show at the Sokol.”

Albert said, “I’m just sorry that Max couldn’t be here, instead of me, but my father insisted that only I could drive the car. It’s his pride and joy, and I’ll be in deep trouble if I put a scratch on it. I figured we needed as much space for the five of you as possible, but that we still should have at least one family member here to greet you, and we thought it should be Otto since he’s the oldest.”

After they’d eaten a little, they had the rest of the food wrapped up to take with them and left, with regretful glances at the unfinished beer left on the table. It was a long journey home for the former prisoners, as they waited to see their families for the first time in months.

The women and Max were waiting to greet them when they arrived. Albert dropped them off, refusing their importunities to join them. “No, no, I have to get the car back. I promised my father I’d return it as soon as possible. If I don’t, I won’t have much luck the next time I need it,” he said. So, with many thanks, much handshaking, and promises of future help if he needed it, at last he could leave, and the family closed in around their missing family members and drew them back into the courtyard.

Albert drove off, relieved at missing what would surely be an emotional family scene. *Anyway, I should study*, he thought.

CHAPTER 27

One day in August, Franz and his comrades were told to pack up and be ready to move out in the morning. The spring and summer had passed pleasantly enough. When they were on duty, they'd stood guard on sidewalks in front of banks, hotels, post offices, and other public buildings of Prague. Leave time had been spent in sidewalk *cafés*, bars, stores, and parks, but that was about to change.

Although the sun wasn't up yet, they stood at attention in the schoolyard. The morning air was cool and moist, but it promised to turn into another hot and muggy day. There had been the usual running, rushing, and barking of orders as his company was lined up outside of the school, which had served as their barracks for the past several months.

Soon they were marching through the quiet, early-morning streets of Prague. Their hobnail boots rang on the old cobblestone streets, and the sound echoed against buildings that were still shrouded in mist. The occasional passerby paused for a few moments, and watched impassively as they marched past.

Franz recalled how different it had been when they'd marched into the city in the early spring amidst falling snow and surrounded by angry and bewildered crowds. Despite the continued, thinly veiled hostility of the populace, he had mostly enjoyed his stay and wondered where they were going to be sent and what would happen next. Whatever it was, he was afraid it wouldn't be good.

Rumor had it that they would be marching into Poland soon. The British and French had warned Germany that if they did, it would mean war, but almost everyone Franz talked to didn't believe it. After all, the British and French hadn't done a thing to prevent the German occupation of the Rhineland, Austria, or Czechoslovakia. Why should Poland be any different?

The city was waking up, and the streets were becoming busier by the time they marched onto the train platform, which was full of noisy activity. Weapons, machinery, supplies, and horses were being loaded onto freight cars. Some of the horses bucked and shied away as their handlers tried to load them into cattle cars. Some of the most skittish ones had to be blindfolded and then several men, working together, pushed them up the ramps and onto the train.

The morning sun moved higher into the sky as Franz and his buddies stood, smoking cigarettes and watching the organized confusion. They were getting hotter and hungrier as the morning wore on. They hadn't been given breakfast before their sudden departure. Instead, they'd been given some provisions for traveling, and Franz considered whether he should have something to eat now or wait until he was on the train. He drank some water from his canteen and decided to wait.

Finally, everything was loaded, and they boarded the train. Franz settled into a window seat and, ignoring the chatter of Rolf and Paul, watched the scenery change as the train headed east. As it picked up speed, the spires of Prague receded into the distance. He felt a twinge of regret and wondered if one day he would be able to return.

Jana's image appeared in his mind's eye. He remembered the sound of her laugh as they sat across the table from each other at her uncle's home, when he went there to try to help them get their horses back, and how she looked, later, sitting on the steps of the Jan Hus monument in Old Town Square. He realized that he hoped they would meet again.

I wonder if they ever got their horses back, he thought. He'd never found out. Her cousins had made it clear to him they didn't want him to talk to Jana, or have anything more to do with her, that night when they'd come home and found him sitting across the table from her. He shook his head, dismissing the memories.

"Hey, what's on your mind?" Paul asked, breaking his reverie.

"Not much," he replied.

"That sounds about right," Rolf said with a laugh, winking at Paul.

Franz joined in the laughter. *I'll have to wait and see what fate will bring*, he thought, and then he pulled some bread and cheese out of his rucksack and settled in for the journey.

Otto sat in the subterranean stillness. In the distance, he heard the rumble of traffic. Nearer he heard the scurrying and scratching of rodents in the walls. He welcomed the quiet and dim light. Outside, the August heat and searing light was oppressive. He was alone today. The young couple who duplicated and distributed the newsletter came in only once a week, so they rarely crossed paths. He took a sip of lukewarm, bitter coffee, and stared at the blank sheet of paper rolled into the typewriter in front of him. The weekly edition of *The Truth* was due, and he would have to stay until it was done. This weekend he would not be going home.

He thought he should include something about troop movements, of course. Everything he'd seen and read, sent to them from eyewitnesses, especially in Slovakia, indicated that the Germans were massing troops in the east. Despite the German takeover of Slovakia, the news still got out. It was difficult to control the rugged countryside between the two countries. It was clear the Germans were getting ready to invade Poland, in spite of official denials.

The whole country seemed to be holding its breath as the summer dragged on. Countless petty acts of aggression occurred daily, such as Czech signs being replaced with German signs, even in places where there were few, or no, German-speaking residents. Then there were the outrages, the disappearances of those suspected of opposition, and wholesale violence, such as what took place in Kladno, after the suspicious death of a German soldier. There the mayor and numerous other innocent citizens were killed in retaliation.

Everywhere Czechs met and talked, they expressed the hope that war would come soon. They were confident that once it started, the Germans would quickly be defeated and they would get their country back. At least they had been confident, until recently.

The most recent bombshell was the signing of the Soviet-German Nonaggression Pact on August 23. He wondered what Albert thought of that! He wished he could talk to him about it. It was a truly bizarre event—an analysis would make for some good copy. As he saw it, it was just another indication that an invasion of Poland was at hand. The Soviets would, no doubt, like to get in on the dismantling of Poland. Albert, who was a former member of the Communist Party, and still a party sympathizer, was bound to see it differently.

This turn of events had seemed to stun most people he talked to and threw cold water on their eagerness for war. Many had hoped that England and France would form an alliance with the Soviet Union against Germany, but now that seemed a forlorn hope, and the outcome of the war, if and when it came, seemed far less certain. Some people had even started talking about how they'd have to make the best of the current situation and learn to live with the German overlords. He needed to somehow convince people to hold onto hope.

His mind ablaze with ideas, his fingers began to fly across the keys, and the copy started to pile up. By the time he was done, he had a stack of ten pages. He stretched his muscles, tense from hunching over the typewriter, and ready for a break. He looked at his watch and, to his surprise, discovered it was now past five in the afternoon. He pushed back his chair. *I'll have to do the rewrite later*, he thought. *First I need a beer and something to eat.*

The blazing August sun temporarily blinded him as he left the building, and the muggy afternoon heat enveloped him. Once his eyes adjusted to the light, he turned and headed in the direction of a nearby tavern. He took a seat at a table on a shaded patio, outside the tavern, and a waiter took his order. It was a little cooler in the shade, but without a breeze, it was still oppressively warm. He knew, though, that it would be even worse inside. Soon he was gratefully swallowing cool drafts of beer. He looked up in surprise as Mr. Jelinek sat down opposite him. He had always insisted that they keep their meetings to a minimum, outside of work, to avoid suspicion.

"Hello, Josef," he said, addressing Otto by his pseudonym.

"Good evening, Mr. Jelinek. Will you join me?"

"Don't mind if I do," he said. He took off his cap, dropped it on the table, and then wiped his brow with his shirtsleeve. "Hot, isn't it? I wouldn't mind a cold beer." He looked tired. "Have you heard? I've been replaced."

"No! When did that happen?"

The waiter delivered Otto's plate of potatoes, cabbage, and meat, all smothered in thick gravy, and took Mr. Jelinek's order.

"I'll have the same," he said, indicating Otto's order. After the waiter left, he continued. "Just today. Of course, I've been expecting it for some time. I'm surprised it took this long. I guess it's not so easy, right now, to find spare Germans with knowledge of metalwork," he said, wryly. "It might be for the best, although I don't know what I'll do to earn a living."

"For the best?" Otto asked.

Mr. Jelinek glanced around; everyone seemed engaged in their own conversations and not paying any attention to them. "Because of the altered, shall we say, shipment we sent out a while ago," he said, in low tones. "Who knows where it went, or when, or what the repercussions will be. We'll talk more about it later."

Otto nodded in reply and changed the topic to the Nazi-Soviet Pact. This had been in the news and was the topic on everyone's mind, so they felt free to discuss it, like everyone else. The Nazis touted it as a great victory for Hitler's diplomacy, of course. Their spin was that it would produce peace since the Poles would certainly now know they needed to knuckle under to demands for some of their territory, and the French and English would know better than to interfere. Otto and Mr. Jelinek discussed all the possible scenarios, without touching on their own particular knowledge of the troop movements, which seemed to argue strongly for war.

The air began to cool, and a breeze sprang up, as Otto and Mr. Jelinek finished their dinners, followed by another round of beer. They left together and, as they walked toward the main square, Mr. Jelinek fell into a thoughtful silence and then said, "Take my advice—go home."

"What? Why?"

"If that adulterated metal is traced back to our plant, and I'm sure it will be—the Germans are nothing if not good record keepers—there will be hell to pay. God willing, some of it was made into guns, and those guns will be in the hands of Nazi soldiers. As you know, the adulteration makes the metal brittle, so after they shoot a gun a few times, the barrel will fracture and injure, or kill, the soldier who is using it."

Otto thought about this for a moment. The thought made him kind of queasy. He tried not to visualize the person behind the gun when it exploded. *This is war*, he thought, mentally scolding himself for softness. *There will be casualties; after all, they are the enemy.*

"What about the newsletter?" he asked. "Who will take over writing it?"

"I think we have to suspend publication for a while, just to be on the safe side. I don't want to put you, or the others, in any unnecessary danger. Who knows, perhaps after the war starts, the Nazis will be quickly beaten, and we can get back to life as it was before this all began," he said wistfully. "At least let's hope so."

They paused in front of St. Bartholomew, where their ways parted. "Goodbye, my friend," Mr. Jelinek said. "I hope we will meet again in better times."

"Yes, I hope so, too. Goodbye," Otto replied as they shook hands and then parted. Otto walked away, slowly, thinking regretfully of the pages of copy he'd left sitting on the desk, only hours before. He wished he had at least taken the time to proofread the copy, in case one last issue of *The Truth* was delivered. He hoped it would get out. His steps slowed as he decided to go back and get the newsletter copy. He stopped abruptly and turned around, his stride quickening.

If Mr. Jelinek is getting cold feet, perhaps Albert can help me find a way to continue this work in Praha, he thought.

Early the next day he packed his things, said goodbye, and paid for his stay. He took the precaution of stuffing the pages of the newsletter, which he'd retrieved the night before, behind the lining of his suitcase, by loosening one of the lower edges a bit. It was not very well hidden but would pass a casual search. He'd taken the train back and forth many times and had not been searched, although he'd seen it happen to others.

Later that morning, as he waited to board the train for home, he watched German soldiers doing spot checks of luggage before it was loaded onto the baggage cars. They also had all the passengers line up in front of the tables set up in front of the trains, where they checked all carry-on luggage. There must have been some sort of threat, or perhaps it was just a new procedure.

Otto was directed to stand in the line forming in front of one of the tables. Behind the table, two harassed-looking German soldiers were directing people to put their carry-on luggage on the table. He watched as they dug through the contents of each suitcase and bag. Would they notice the loose lining inside the suitcase, or hear the crinkling of the paper as he opened it on the table?

"Next!" the soldier said, motioning him forward.

CHAPTER 28

The war was supposed to start today, August 26, 1939. Franz was with the troops that had been moved to their starting positions yesterday, where they'd set up temporary camps. They were roused before dawn this morning and rushed through reveille and breakfast. They tore down and stowed the tents. Trucks were loaded, and Franz and the rest of the troops strapped on their gear and lined up, ready to go. Then they were left standing there for several hours. Eventually, when Franz had thought he might fall asleep on his feet, officers made the rounds shouting that they should fall out.

"I guess Hitler got cold feet," Paul quipped.

Franz laughed, and Rolf shot both a dirty look. Later they learned that Paul was right. Great Britain and France had announced, on the twenty-fourth, that they would declare war on Germany if Germany attacked Poland, and Hitler blinked. He didn't want to fight a two-front war. He had been confident that Great Britain and France would back down again, as they had when he seized Austria and Czechoslovakia. Now, however, the British and French guarantees to Poland made him hesitate.

So here they were, living in tents in the middle of a field, on the German side of the border. Between exercises, they sat, played cards, smoked cigarettes, and complained about boredom and the stupidity of everyone involved in the planning. They'd been told to leave their gear packed, ready for their marching orders. Those orders finally came on the morning of September 1. The day began before dawn as it had a week before—officers yelling, trucks revving their engines, and horses neighing. The postponed invasion was on!

After a hurried breakfast, the men were organized into lines and began marching east. Franz felt both relief and anxiety. At least the waiting was over, but what would happen next? They'd been briefed to expect hostile resistance from the population, and they'd heard, and read, many reports of atrocities against the ethnic Germans who lived in Poland. They'd been ordered to report any suspicious activity to their officers.

They'd been marching for days now, and this morning's march was as uneventful as the previous days had been, just like a training march. They walked along a dirt road that disappeared into the distance, between two rows of scrawny trees and the surrounding flat fields. Ahead, in the distance, Franz heard the booming of artillery and, occasionally, a squadron of German planes flew overhead.

He shifted his pack again. The handle of his folding trenching shovel hung down below his pack and bumped against his leg with every step, and it was becoming painful. He thought that he would try to reposition it when they stopped for lunch. They were approaching a village, and the landscape had become hillier and wooded. He saw the smoke from the chimneys, probably from the preparation of the noon meal, he thought and realized he was getting hungry. He hoped they would stop for their lunch soon. He dug in his inner pocket for a cigarette.

Suddenly, shots rang out, and a man fell, about twenty feet in front of him, clutching his stomach and screaming. Blood oozed out from around his hands. There were shouts of "Medic!" and "Take cover, take cover!" He ran and crouched behind the closest small tree, keenly aware that it only covered a portion of his body. His hands were sweaty and shaking as he grabbed his rifle and scanned the landscape. Three horsemen were disappearing across the top of a hill. Before he could raise his gun, shots rang out, and one of them fell from his horse; the other two disappeared over the ridge.

A few minutes passed without any more shots being fired, and they were reassembled. Some men were sent up the ridge to see if they could spot where the horsemen had gone and find out if the man they'd shot was dead or alive.

They returned to say they didn't see which way the escaped gunmen had gone, and the other man was dead. Shortly thereafter, they were ordered to go into the village to round up all men and boys over the age of fifteen for questioning.

Some men were sent to guard the church, where the Poles would be held for questioning, and some were sent to guard the perimeter of the town so no one escaped. The others were told to form groups of three and go house to house, sending the men and boys to the church.

Rolf and Franz had lost track of Paul, so they asked Hans, a young freckle-faced kid who they'd played cards with, to join them. The three of them were sent to the south end of the village to start from the last house and work their way toward the center of town.

The streets were deserted as they set out. Everyone had gone inside and pulled their curtains closed. He saw window curtains twitching as they walked past the houses. When they got to the last house at the end of the main road that ran through the town, they started knocking on doors and, by shouting and gesturing, got the men and older boys out into the street and walking toward the church in the center of the village.

They successfully cleared two houses without incident. As they approached the third house, they saw an old couple running across their courtyard from the barn to their house. Franz, Hans, and Rolf started running, too, but the old couple beat them to their house, ran in, and bolted the door. Franz and Hans knocked on the door and shouted for the man to come out. Franz stood a few feet to the left side of the door. For some reason, he noticed that the geraniums in their window boxes needed to be watered, and had a momentary impulse to tell the old couple. There was no response to their knocking from inside the house. Then Hans and Rolf started kicking at the door, but it didn't give way.

"Wait, let's go through a window," Franz said.

"Are you crazy?" Rolf said. "They'd blow your head off before you got in!"

Hans aimed his gun and, before the others had a chance to react, fired a series of blasts at the door. Inside they heard the woman start to scream. Rolf and Hans resumed kicking the door and, with a groan of splintering wood, it gave way. Inside, the small kitchen was splattered with blood. The old man lay on his back on the floor, his eyes wide open, and a gaping hole in the side of his head, surrounded by a pool of blood. The old woman was crouched under the kitchen table. She was splattered with blood and screaming wildly. Hans pointed his gun at her.

"No!" Franz said, and knocked the gun aside. "Let's get out of here."

They left her there, still screaming, and continued toward the fourth house. Franz felt his stomach heave, and his legs were shaky. He noticed that the freckles stood out against the paleness of Hans's face. Rolf was looking down. "We'll have to report this, I suppose," Rolf said.

That night they set up camp at the edge of a field, near a grove of trees and a small stream, guards were posted, a meal was cooked and eaten, and then water from the stream was heated in the field kitchen and used for washing up.

Franz cleaned up as best he could, using his allotment of hot water, and crawled into his tent. He was so exhausted that as soon as he had lain down, he immediately fell into a deep and dreamless sleep.

He was startled awake by a hurricane of sound: stampeding horses, shouting in Polish and German, gunfire exploding from every direction, and screams of pain! German officers shouted, "*Schnell! Schnell!*" He struggled to unroll himself from his blanket. In the early morning semidarkness, he knocked elbows with the other three occupants of the small tent as he shoved his feet in his boots and groped for his rifle.

Outside of the tent was chaos. Thick gunsmoke hung in the air. The acrid smoke filled his nose and burned his eyes. Polish soldiers on horseback rode through the camp. The horses snorted and whined, wild-eyed, nostrils flaring. Some Polish troops were shooting rifles. Others slashed down with sabers at the German soldiers running between the horses or, galloping at full speed, ran them through with lances. The German soldiers shot at the men on horseback or tried to stab upwards with their bayonets.

Amidst the screams, Franz heard a familiar voice. It was Rolf. He turned and saw his friend raise his gun and fire. A flash of light and Rolf fell to the ground.

Franz raised his rifle and shot at the mounted Polish soldier who galloped toward him. A glint of metal, a vicious downward slash of a saber, then a blinding flash of pain was the last thing he remembered before everything went black.

That evening, as Franz regained consciousness, he gradually became aware of the moans of other wounded men, and the murmuring voices of medics. He realized that he was in a field hospital. In the flickering light of hanging lanterns, he saw medics moving from bed to bed treating their patients.

He tried to sit up, but the movement caused electric jolts of pain, and the tight bandages around his back, and right thigh, restricted his movement. His heart raced as he lay back against his pillow again, and he called out for a medic. One came to his bedside, and he asked, "Can I have a cigarette?"

The medic gave him one and lit it for him. Franz held the cigarette in a trembling hand, inhaled deeply, and let the smoke out slowly, waiting for his heart to start beating normally.

He slept for a time. When he next awakened, Paul was standing near his bed.

"Hi, how are you feeling?" Paul asked.

Franz turned toward Paul, and grimaced at the pain caused by this slight movement. "I've been better," he said and tried to smile. "Have you seen Rolf? He was the first one out of the tent, as usual. I saw him fall, I think. Is he okay?"

Paul looked away. "He's . . . he's dead. I'm sorry to be the one to tell you."

"Dead? How?"

"They said his gun exploded when he fired it—a freak accident, I guess."

Franz felt like his heart would break. He fought back tears. "Oh, man, what rotten luck! I'm going to miss him. I know you will, too. How about you? Are you okay?"

"Yeah, I'm okay. I don't know what I'll do without you guys, though. They're going to send you home, you know, so at least you'll be okay."

"I'll be back," Franz said. "Meanwhile, take care of yourself."

After Paul left, Franz lay back and stared, unseeingly, at the canvas ceiling, and thought of Rolf. He had been so full of life and energy. He would never see him again. *My friend is gone*, he thought, as tears fell on his pillow.

CHAPTER 29

It was before dawn on the morning of September 1. Albert had tossed and turned all night. He finally gave up and got up to make a pot of strong coffee. Then he lit a cigarette, poured some of the coffee into a cup, and took it back into his bedroom. He dug the radio out from where he kept it hidden under a pile of dirty clothes in a basket in his closet, set it on the small writing table in the corner of the bedroom, plugged it in, and pulled up a chair.

This is how he usually started his day, by listening to foreign radio programming with the volume turned up only loud enough so he could hear it with his head bent toward the speaker. He knew that if he was discovered, it could mean prison, or worse. Suddenly, he heard an announcement on the BBC that Germany had invaded Poland and was bombing Polish airports!

The pact between Stalin and Hitler in August had been a serious blow to the resistance, and their activities had virtually stopped. Albert and his friends had hoped Germany would invade Poland. They were certain that if the French and British lived up to their promises and aided Poland, Germany would quickly lose the war, then they would be pushed out of Czechoslovakia and life would return to the way it had been, before the invasion.

Albert couldn't wait to meet his friends later that morning at their usual coffee shop, to discuss the latest developments and start planning a memorable way to mark the anniversary of the Munich Agreement.

September 30 would be one year since that agreement was signed; the agreement that had been the beginning of the end of Czechoslovakia.

He was startled by the sound of footsteps coming up the stairs and down the hall. He turned off the radio and paused, cigarette suspended in midair. There was a knock at the door. He unplugged the radio and stashed it in its hiding place.

Another knock sounded, more insistently. "Just a minute," he called out. He scanned the room, looking for anything that would look out of place. He closed the closet door, carried the coffee cup and ashtray into the kitchen, and opened the door.

"Oh, it's you, Dad! What are you doing here so early in the morning?" Albert ran his fingers through his hair, aware that he was in his pajamas and bare feet. He stepped aside and said, "Come in."

His father was his usual well-groomed self, wearing a hat, tweed suit, and vest, with a folded newspaper under his arm. But instead of his usual jovial appearance, his neatly trimmed mustache was turned down and there were worry wrinkles on his brow.

"Thank you. I'm sorry to bother you so early, but I wanted to catch you before you went out."

"That's okay. Have a chair. Would you like some coffee?"

"Yes, thanks." He took off his hat and dropped it on the table, sat down, accepted a cup of coffee, and then took out his pipe and started filling it.

Albert excused himself and then came back a few minutes later, wearing a robe and slippers. His dad was drumming his fingers nervously on the table and emitting puffs of smoke.

"Have you seen the headlines in today's paper?" his father asked.

"No, does it have to do with the invasion of Poland?"

"In a way. How do you know about that?" his father asked, looking at him suspiciously.

"Everyone knew it was coming." Albert shrugged.

His father unfolded the paper and handed it to Albert. The headlines declared that one thousand prominent Czech citizens would be arrested and held hostage to ensure the good behavior of the population.

"It says they will be executed if there are any actions the Germans deem to be treasonous," his dad said, gesturing at the newspaper. "This is barbarism."

"You're right, it is. But it's not too surprising, I guess," Albert said. He stopped, turned to his dad, and said, "You don't mean . . . You're not going to be arrested, are you?"

"There are some advantages to obscurity," his father said. "Some of my contacts will certainly be on the list, though. I came because I want you to leave the country."

"Dad, we talked about this. I don't want to leave. You know that. I have my studies. Besides, I'm needed here, and now that war has started, it'll be over in a matter of weeks."

"Weeks? That's what they said about the Great War, and you know how that turned out," his father said. He stopped and puffed quietly for a few moments. "I'm thinking mostly about your mother. We only have you, and it would kill her if something happened to you. It's getting more and more difficult, but it is still possible to get you out of the country. Obviously, going through Poland is no longer an option. Soon it may not be possible at all.

"I'm sure that they will be forming a Czech regiment in England soon. You can do more for your country by staying alive to fight rather than endangering your life by doing something symbolic."

His father stayed for another half hour trying, without success, to convince Albert to leave the country. Finally, he got up to leave. "Well, promise me that you will at least think about it," his father said.

Albert hated to see his father look so worried. "I'll think about it again at the end of the term if the war isn't over by then," he said.

His father looked a little more cheerful. He pointed to the newspaper that he left on the table. "One last piece of advice—read that, and think about it carefully. Don't do anything rash."

Later that morning when Albert met some of his friends at the coffee shop, he had a hard time feeling as jubilant about the Polish invasion as he had earlier. His father's cautions had tempered his enthusiasm. His friends were talking, laughing, and openly gloating about how badly the Germans were going to lose as soon as the French and the British joined the fight. He glanced around to see if anyone was listening in, but there seemed to be only a few students and old pensioners in the coffeehouse at this hour.

"We need to meet for a study group tonight," he announced. This was their code for a meeting at his apartment.

"Why? I thought the test had been canceled," Jan Opletal said, and laughed. He was a popular, cheerful, easygoing young man who always leaned toward looking on the bright side.

Albert smiled a little. "I hope that's true, but I think we should be prepared for a pop quiz," he said. The others chuckled, nodded, and indicated that they would be there. Then the topic changed to an upcoming hockey game.

Otto had stood, waiting anxiously, his suitcase open on the table in front of him. A young German soldier, who looked extremely bored, poked around in the bag. *Had he heard that rustling or noticed the loose lining?* Otto wondered, forcing himself to look only slightly annoyed at the delay.

"Are there any metal objects in your bag?" the German soldier asked.

"Yes, I suppose there are, in my shaving kit," Otto replied.

The German soldier took the kit out of Otto's bag, opened it, and glanced inside of it, then waved a metal detector over the suitcase—no beep this time. Otto suppressed a sigh of relief. The German soldier tossed the shaving kit back into the suitcase, shoved it aside, and motioned for the next person in line to step forward, calling out, "Next!"

Otto quickly closed his bag and walked to the train. He forced himself to walk at a measured pace, though he felt like running, and to keep a neutral look on his face.

The train was very late leaving the station by the time all the bags were checked, so Otto was quite late getting home. Max was waiting for him, sleeping on the bench of the delivery cart, his head resting on his chest. When Otto woke him, Max was grumpy and didn't want to talk. When he asked how everyone was at home, he just got a grunted, "Fine," and they rode the rest of the way together in silence.

At home, everyone had already gone to bed. His mother got up to fix him something to eat, mumbled a few pleasantries, and then went back to bed, leaving him to eat on his own. As soon as he'd eaten, he went to bed and slept until late the next day. He didn't see Jana until she came home from work the following day.

When she walked into the house in the evening, he stared at her with open-mouthed surprise. Her hair had been cut to shoulder length and was curly. She was wearing a skirt just long enough to cover her knees, with bobby socks and saddle shoes.

"Hello," he greeted her, looking her up and down in amazement. "You've changed your appearance."

She blushed. "Dad and Mom said it was okay. I wanted to blend in."

He looked at Josef, who shrugged and smiled. “She pestered us relentlessly until we gave in.”

“Why do you want to blend in?” he asked Jana.

“I don’t know. I just got tired of people always noticing me. It doesn’t really matter, does it?” she asked.

“No, I guess not. You can always let your hair grow back, I guess,” he said.

“I have no intention of letting it grow! I like it like this,” she retorted and stormed out of the room.

CHAPTER 30

"One Hundred Six Executed for Skoda Sabotage" read the headlines on the front page of the September 18 paper that was lying on the table in the café where Otto and Max had stopped for lunch while making their delivery rounds. Otto's hands shook as he picked it up. He scanned the paragraphs looking for a list of names. When he found it, he slowly read through the alphabetical list. With a slight gasp, he came to the name that he had hoped would not be there—Jelinek, Josef, age forty-two, foreman.

"What is it? What's wrong?" Max asked.

Otto passed him the paper. "It's Mr. Jelinek. He's on the list. He was my foreman at Skoda. He's the one that warned me to leave. If he hadn't, my name would have been on the list, too." He stopped and took a few deep breaths. "Come on, let's get out of here. I need some air."

"What about lunch?" Max asked.

"Forget it. I lost my appetite," Otto said.

They walked silently while Otto struggled to compose himself. He couldn't escape thinking about what the last few minutes of Mr. Jelinek's life must have been like, bloodied and bruised from days of torture, his eyes blindfolded and hands tied behind his back, falling in a hail storm of bullets in a bleak prison courtyard.

They passed two black-clad SS men, striding along, arrogantly hogging the sidewalk. Otto felt an iron core of anger and hatred growing inside of him as he stepped aside to let them pass.

"He was a friend; that's all. You know." They walked in silence for a while, and then he said to Max, "Come on, let's get a drink."

They stepped out of the bright September sunshine into a dark pub, sat down at a table, and ordered a couple of beers.

"Are you going to get something to eat?" Max asked.

"No, I'm not hungry," Otto said.

"Do you mind if I order something?" Max said.

"No, not at all, you didn't know him," Otto said.

Otto drank his beer and ordered another one, while Max ate his sandwich and drank his beer. Suddenly Otto remembered the typewriter, mimeograph machine, and other supplies that were probably still sitting in the subterranean room in Plzeň. He described the room and its contents to Max.

"We should go get it," Otto said.

"Get the typewriter and stuff, you mean? How?" Max asked.

"We'll ask Albert to borrow his dad's car again. I know where the key to the room is, so it should be easy," Otto said.

Now that he had a plan, Otto felt a little better. Suddenly he was hungry, and reached over and grabbed the other half of his brother's sandwich.

"Hey!" Max objected.

"Never mind. Hurry up and finish. I'll buy you another sandwich later after we finish our deliveries. Then you can drop me at Albert's place before you pick up Jana," Otto said.

Mrs. Sladekova was in the kitchen surveying a stack of boxes when Jana arrived for work. "So, there you are—it's about time! Come and help me put these groceries away," she said.

Jana glanced at the clock. It was only two minutes after eight, which hardly qualified as late, in her estimation, but she didn't respond. She'd learned that Mrs. Sladekova often fussed at her out of habit. At any rate, she had more important things on her mind. Otto was back and had been with Max and her while she went to and from her job every day. Then the two brothers continued on their way, picking up and dropping off furniture. Otto mostly just ignored her, but she was keenly aware of his presence and looked forward to sitting next to him but, at the same time, she wished she had an excuse to avoid him. She felt like her secrets might slip out and, if he learned about the messages she'd been delivering for the past months, he would hate her for breaking her promise to him to avoid dangerous activities.

Jana was still startled when she caught a glimpse of herself in a store window. She looked just like any other young Czech girl, just a little darker than most. Of course, she hadn't been able to tell anyone why she had made the change, least of all Otto or her family. Max suspected, she thought, but he hadn't said anything. She told anyone who asked her that she just wanted to look like the girls she saw in the magazines.

"I don't know what to do with all of this stuff," Mrs. Sladekova said. "At home, we can't get enough of anything. We must stand in line, ration cards in hand, for our puny portions. Here there's such abundance I'm running out of places to put things."

Jana looked skeptically at Mrs. Sladekova's ample posterior and thought she could afford to make do with less.

"Mrs. Sladekova, I have to go out for a bit on my lunch break. I'll try to be back on time," Jana said.

"What! Again? Do you know that there are a hundred girls who would love to have this job?"

"I know. I'm sorry, but I need to visit a sick aunt and see if she needs anything."

"Oh, spare me the excuses! No one has as many sick relatives as you do," Mrs. Sladekova said. "You're not fooling me."

Jana felt a chill of fear run through her body. "What do you mean?" she asked.

"I bet you're seeing a boy. Don't think I haven't noticed how you've dolled yourself up lately."

Jana looked at her, wide-eyed. She couldn't believe her good luck! Not only would she not have to come up with any more lame excuses for her lunchtime outings, but she could be a few minutes late getting back to work, without arousing suspicion.

"Don't worry!" Mrs. Sladekova chuckled. "Your secret is safe with me. I was young once, too, you know." She went on talking about when she was a young girl and the boys that she'd dated, but Jana had stopped listening. She was thinking about her lunch hour errand.

For the past several weeks, there had been fewer messages left for her to deliver to the house down the hill. Fewer meetings were being held in the castle, and when they were, the participants were being more careful about leaving information behind. However, she'd started a new activity a few weeks ago, riding the streetcars to deliver messages. Mr. Novotny, the clockmaker, had approached her several weeks ago, to see if she was interested, and she had agreed.

Mr. Novotny had arranged another meeting for her, with Jan, and again they met at an appointed time in Old Town Square, at the Hus monument. There were always a lot of people crisscrossing the square, and many stopped to sit on the steps of the monument, so two people meeting there didn't draw any attention.

"Hi, Jana, thanks for meeting me. Before we go any further, I must warn you, this could be dangerous, and it is imperative that you act with discretion and blend into the crowd as much as possible. Are you sure you want to do this?" he said.

"Yes, I'm sure. After what the Nazis did to my family, I want to help get them out of the country."

"Good, but to blend in, I suggest you alter your appearance, with a haircut and a more mainstream wardrobe. Are you willing to do that?"

Jana hesitated. "But what will I tell my family? They'll want to know why. I can't just show up one day looking different. That would make them suspicious." She thought for a moment. "I suppose I could say that I want to look like other girls, and like the girls in magazines. I bet I could convince them."

"Okay, you work on convincing your family and, if you can, let me know in the usual way, and then I'll tell you more," he said.

Since then, she'd gotten a new look and had her picture taken. She picked up messages that gave her instructions about which streetcars to get on, and what to do to be recognized by her contact. Several times a week she received and delivered messages to and from passengers as they got on and off the streetcars. This week she was told to wear a pink scarf.

When it was Jana's lunchtime, Mrs. Sladekova waved her on her way with a knowing smile. Jana ran up the stairs, out of the building, and down the hill to wait for the designated streetcar. *Yuck!* she thought as she pulled the scarf out of her purse and put it on. She didn't care for pink.

She also dug the streetcar punch pass out of her bag, ready to show it to the conductor. Jan had it made for her, with her picture on it but another name. According to the pass, she was Milada Novakova. Jana stared at the picture. She hadn't seen many pictures of herself, and this one almost looked like it was of another person—someone with dark, curly hair, brown eyes, and a wide, unsmiling mouth who stared back at her with a slightly challenging look.

Soon the streetcar stopped, she got on, took a seat, and started to watch those getting on, while trying to look casual. A few stops later, a tall young man with thinning brown hair got on and sat next to her. "Is this car stopping at Mala Strana?" This was the question her contact was supposed to ask.

"Yes, it will stop very close to it," she said. This was how she'd been told to reply.

She moved her bag over so it was between them, and under it, he handed her an envelope. She left it lying in her lap while she opened her bag, pulled out a compact and checked her appearance, and then she put it back into her bag along with the envelope.

When they got to the next stop, she got off and crossed the street to wait for the returning streetcar. As she stood there, Max and Otto happened to pass by in their delivery wagon.

They turned the cart around, and they pulled up next to her.

"Hi, Jana. What are you doing here?" Max asked. "Hey, that's a pretty scarf."

Jana felt her stomach fall and her heart start to race. She touched her scarf and tried to think of a response. "I . . . I . . . ah," she stuttered.

"Are you on your way back to work?" Max asked, helpfully. She nodded mutely.

"Hop in. We'll give you a lift," he said.

"Oh no, I don't want to take you out of your way. I'll just wait for the streetcar," she said.

"Don't be silly; it's not far. Come on, get in," Max insisted.

Not wanting to make Otto suspicious by being overly obstinate, Jana reluctantly climbed on board, keenly aware of the envelope in her purse. She wondered what was in it, and what she should do with it. At the same time, she frantically tried to think of an explanation for being on the corner waiting for a streetcar.

"I was walking during my lunch break, and I lost track of the time, so I was going to take the streetcar back. Mrs. Sladekova gets so upset if I'm late, but do you know what?" Jana said. "Today she said she thinks I must have a boyfriend who I see during my lunch breaks, and that's why I'm sometimes late, so she won't mind as much. Isn't that funny?"

Max and Otto both laughed, but she thought they were scrutinizing her when they thought she wasn't looking, as though they sensed she was lying.

"I might be a little late picking you up tonight," Max said when she got off. "I have to drop Otto someplace first."

"Oh, okay," she said, trying not to show her disappointment that she wouldn't be riding home beside Otto tonight.

She found Mr. Novotny, the clockmaker, making his rounds that afternoon, and she gave him the undelivered envelope and told him what had happened.

"I don't think it's safe for you to continue this job," he said. "I'll talk to Jan."

"No, no! It's okay. I like doing it."

"No, your cousins will be watching for you now. It will be a problem. We'll find something else for you," he said.

When Max picked her up that night, she could tell there was something was on his mind.

"Tell me what you were really doing this afternoon," he said as soon as she climbed aboard.

"I already told you," she said.

He looked at her skeptically. "Well, you'd better be telling the truth. I'll be keeping an eye on you."

In return for the car keys, Albert's father had extracted a promise from him that he would leave for England before the end of the year unless the war had ended. Albert hadn't tried to come up with a lie for why he needed the car this time. He just said that he needed it to pick up some publication materials, and his father, happy that Albert had agreed to leave the country, didn't ask any more questions.

After Otto, Max, and Albert returned from retrieving the printing equipment and supplies from Plzeň, they installed them in the student newspaper office. The extra typewriter and mimeograph machine were used to crank out handbills and mimeographed leaflets announcing a transit boycott on September 30, to commemorate the one-year anniversary of the Munich Agreement. These publications were left on park benches, posted on walls, and handed out in taverns, coffee shops, and *cafés* owned by patriotic Czechs, and distributed in every way possible. By the end of the month, there wasn't anyone in Praha who didn't know about it, including the Germans and the SS, who threatened all sorts of violent retaliation if there was any disorder.

The message of the handouts was that the populace should walk, bike, or find other ways to get to and from work that day or take a vacation day. They were told to wear their National Solidarity pins and dark-colored clothing to indicate that this was a solemn remembrance, but to remain calm, and not do anything to invite violent retaliation.

Excitement grew as the day drew closer and, to improve participation in the boycott, rumors circulated that the Saturday fares would be donated to the Nazi Winter Help Fund. Picket signs were created for volunteers to carry by each tram stop.

Throughout the month of September, the early enthusiasm that the war in Poland would end with a swift German defeat began to look less and less likely with one German victory after another. Great Britain and France had declared war on Germany on the third of the month, but after that, they had done virtually nothing to help Poland. Despite the depressing war news, enthusiasm for the upcoming transit boycott helped keep spirits high.

The day before, on Friday, a group of parishioners processed out of church singing the national anthem, "Where Is My Home," although this was strictly forbidden, and the tune was taken up by those who heard it, and then by others until throughout the city you could hear snatches of it.

The Saturday of the boycott dawned bright and sunny. Albert, Otto, and Max set out to their assigned spots with picket signs reminding people that there was a transit boycott today in remembrance of the Munich Agreement. SS troops and German soldiers who guarded the doors of hotels, banks, and other public buildings watched impassively as they walked by.

Throughout the day, masses of people walked as buses and trams stood still and empty. At the end of the day, citizens gathered in pubs to celebrate one small victory against their oppressors.

"I can't believe how smoothly that went," Max said.

"I know. I think they're losing their grip on us," Otto said. "We'll have to plan something even bigger for October 28, Czechoslovak National Day."

The next day there was no mention of the boycott on the front pages of the controlled press. On inside pages, there was a brief article about it, twisted for Nazi propaganda purposes. The article claimed there had been a partial transit boycott because the subjects of the Protectorate were angry that Jews were still allowed access to mass transit, so measures would have to be taken to ban them.

CHAPTER 31

Otto sat in the smoke-filled headquarters of the student newspaper and proofread the first sentence of the leaflet he was writing. "Since Nazi propaganda claims that we acquiesce to being held as a Protectorate, we must show the world that the Huns have lied again." He smiled as he crushed his cigarette out in the overflowing ashtray, pleased with his first sentence. He wrote on, fingers flying over the typewriter keys, throwing the typewriter carriage at the end of each line, urging a peaceful protest on National Independence Day, Saturday, October 28.

"All Czechs should wear dark-colored clothes and black ties that day," he wrote, "as a sign of mourning for their lost independence, and wear their national colors in their buttonholes or their National Solidarity pins. The day would end with two moments of silence at 6:00 p.m. at the top of Wenceslas Square."

Albert, Otto, and their friends, encouraged by the success of the transport boycott, hoped to make the Independence Day protest an even bigger event. They worked feverishly to produce leaflets, flyers, and posters, and to distribute them throughout the city to spread the word. The student newspaper office had become their unofficial headquarters, while the faculty advisors ignored their efforts, staying at a discreet distance.

Their published material also urged other actions on Independence Day, including boycotting the streetcars, because the notice boards were printed first in German; not buying beer and cigarettes that day, because some of the tax went to the Germans' war effort; and contributing to collections for Czech charities that would be taken up throughout the day.

These plans were well known by both Czech and German authorities. They issued strongly worded warnings over the radio and on posters that they plastered all over town, often covering the posters that urged protest. They threatened severe penalties for violation of the laws against sabotage, and infringement on the honor of Germany.

October 28 began quietly with most people going to work as usual but wearing their Sunday clothes and black ties or black armbands and National Solidarity pins on their lapels, or Masaryk caps, a style popularized by the father of Czechoslovak independence.

Otto and Max went to Wenceslas Square early in the morning to hand out flyers. At first, the crowd was thin but grew throughout the morning. By late morning there were throngs of people processing, silently and somberly, around the square. From time to time chants of "long live Beneš" or "we want freedom" would reverberate throughout the crowd. Smaller groups cried, "Long live Stalin, " but this chant wasn't taken up by the majority.

Albert, breathless from running through the crowd, found Otto and Max. His usually serious face was flushed with excitement, his eyes gleaming. "Isn't this great? Can you believe the size of the crowd? The streets are filled all over the city. You should see what's happening in front of the Palace Hotel."

"You mean the living quarters of the Gestapo? Why, what's happening there?" Otto asked.

"Crowds are blocking the entrance and chanting, 'The bloodhounds live here.' I didn't see it, but I've been told that there's also a large crowd protesting outside of Petschek Palace, headquarters of the Prague Gestapo."

"Oh my God!" Max said. "Aren't they being arrested?"

"No. Apparently, they're letting the Czech police handle crowd control, and they're on our side." Albert laughed. "It's probably part of their propaganda effort to portray Czechoslovakia as a peaceful backwater in need of German protection."

Just then groups of ethnic German young men, wearing swastika armbands, jostled their way through the crowd. One of them reached out and ripped the National Solidarity pin from Otto's lapel. He was wearing it upside down, as had become the custom, as a sign of protest. When worn that way, the *NS* became *SN* and was understood to mean "*Smrt Nemcum*"—"Death to Germans." Another one of the Germans knocked off Albert's Masaryk cap.

"Hey, what do you think you're doing?" Otto said, just before a punch landed on his chin.

Their leaflets flew up into the air and scattered under trampling feet. A melee broke out around them as more Czechs and Germans joined into the brawl. The Czech police, who had been standing on the sidelines, observing impassively, waded in, blowing whistles, waving cudgels, and pushing the combatants apart. "Do you want to cool off in jail?" they yelled.

As soon as they could break away, Albert, Max, and Otto took off and ran down the cobblestone streets to Old Town Square. The crowd was just as thick there. They laughed about their narrow escape, despite their bumps and bruises.

"I guess we're done passing out leaflets. I'd say, let's get a beer, but I guess we can't break the boycott. After all, it was our idea," Otto said.

"Let's go to my place," Albert said. "I have another box of leaflets, and beer, too."

When they got to Albert's apartment, bottles of beer were distributed, and they sat back to relax for a few minutes.

Soon, Albert excused himself. "It's getting a little chilly. I'm going to put on a warmer shirt," he said and went into his bedroom. He closed the door and went to the closet. Standing on his tiptoes, he reached up to the back of the top shelf, felt around, and pulled out a gun. It was Officer Kepka's gun.

He had picked it up when he went with Otto and Max to find the gun. As they argued with each other, he'd slipped it into his jacket pocket without being noticed. He hadn't told anyone that he had it. His plan was to turn in the gun if his father hadn't been able to secure the release of Otto's family members, as sort of a last-ditch effort to free them. He was glad that things turned out as they did, so he hadn't had to try it.

Now, he'd decided to take the gun with them, for protection. He stuck it into the back waistband of his pants and put on a large, loose shirt, covering it.

When they returned to Wenceslas Square, they found that the Czech police were clearing it. A cordon of both mounted police and others on foot pushed the crowd back to the sidewalks and into the adjoining streets.

"Please clear the square. A permit has been granted for a group to parade here at one o'clock," the street loudspeakers blared, and the police repeated this as they rounded up groups of demonstrators and escorted them out of the square.

From the bottom of the square, the hated sounds of the "Horst Wessel Song" issued forth as the SS battalion *Leibstandarte* Adolf Hitler came goose-stepping down the square, their swastika banners flying. Under their hats, their beefy faces scowled as they stared straight ahead, ignoring the hisses and catcalls that issued from the crowd.

"Can you believe those jerks?" Max asked as the parade passed them. "They just love to prance by, lording it over everyone."

"Their day of reckoning will come," Otto said.

The battalion paraded to the top of the square, marched around the statue of St. Wenceslas, and started back down the square when a small group of young men surged past the police line, grabbed some of their banners, and trampled them underfoot. Some of the SS men broke ranks and attacked the Czechs.

The Czech police, anxious to prevent bloodshed, sprang into action separating the SS men from the Czechs and arresting the instigators. The parade finally disappeared between police lines at the end of the square, strains of "Deutschland Über Alles" echoing behind them.

After the SS parade was done, the police let the crowds reoccupy the square. The people resumed their peaceful protest and, when the appointed time for the protest to end neared, Otto, Max, and Albert made their way forward through the crowds, toward the steps of the National Museum, where Albert planned to thank the crowd for coming and lead two minutes of silent prayer and reflection.

At that moment, a black Mercedes-Benz sped through the crowd as people jumped frantically to get out of its way; it stopped at the foot of the stairway of the National Museum. Karl Frank, the German State Secretary, stepped out of the car and strode up the steps, surrounded by SS bodyguards. He was tall and thin, with a ferret-like face, contorted now in hatred. He held a whip in one hand and a bullhorn in the other. "Clear this area immediately," he screamed into the bullhorn.

The demonstrators stopped, confused, and turned to look at him.

"Clear this area immediately, or you will be arrested," he shouted.

Most of the demonstrators started slowly moving toward the adjoining streets.

Suddenly, German police detachments, in full riot gear, appeared from all sides, shouting in German, waving their guns into the air, and clubbing people with truncheons. Pandemonium broke out as people screamed, running in all directions while trying to ward off the blows.

Shots rang out.

Max, Otto, and Albert, who had been standing on the upper edge of the crowd, froze for a few moments, stunned by the sudden outbreak of violence.

"Let's get out of here," Albert said, and they turned and ran in the direction of Old Town Square.

As they turned to go, Otto thought he glimpsed a familiar figure in the crowd out of the corner of his eye. *Was that Jana's pink scarf?* he thought.

"Go ahead, I'll meet up with you later," he said and ran toward her. He pushed his way through the crowd that was running in all directions, trying desperately to find her.

Otto sensed, rather than saw, a German policeman running up behind him, turned, and ducked just in time to avoid being hit by his truncheon. He changed direction, trying to guess which way Jana would have run, if that was, in fact, Jana whom he had glimpsed.

He heard bullets whistling by as he ran, and then felt a hard bang on his left shoulder, as though he'd been kicked by a horse. The next thing he knew, he was lying on his back while the crowd separated and swept past him. He felt his shoulder, and it was wet. He looked at his hand and saw it was red with blood.

"Can you stand up?" Jana asked as she leaned over him.

"What? What are you doing here?"

"Never mind that. Can you stand up?"

"I think so." He sat up groggily.

"Here, let me help you."

He smiled a bit at the thought of her, a head shorter and half his weight, helping him get up. He used his good arm to help himself up and stood, dizzy and blacking out from the pain.

"Here, lean on me," she said. "Let's get out of here before we're arrested, too." Suddenly Max appeared beside them.

"Where did you come from? Where's Albert?" Otto said.

"I followed you. Albert took off. I told him it was okay. If he gets arrested again, it'll be bad for him."

Albert ran down the street by himself. Suddenly, he was pushed and buffeted by people leaping out of the way as Karl Frank's black car bore down on the crowd.

Now's my chance to rid the world of one evil man, he thought. He pulled out the gun and aimed at Frank's head as the car tore by. His arm was jostled just as he fired, and the shot went wild, striking the rear door of the car.

He stuck the gun back into his waistband and sprinted away from the scene, darting around other fleeing people. The crowds thinned as he approached the river. He half ran, half slid, down to the water's edge, and then slumped down, gasping for air. The steel-gray water moved sluggishly.

Bitterness welled up in Albert. *Everything has gone wrong*, he thought. He had wanted to make a difference, but what good had he done? Sure, he'd helped his cousin and his family get out of the country, but Otto, Max, and his dad were the ones who'd gotten that done. *I'm all talk*, he thought, *and when I finally get a chance to do something, I foul it up.*

He pulled the gun out of his waistband and flung it into the river.

Max and Jana led Otto to a small park in an enclosed courtyard, next to Old Town Square. He sat down on a bench, his jacket and shirt half-covered with blood.

"We should get you to a hospital," Max said.

"No! No way. That's just asking for trouble. Just get me home."

"How? You can't walk that far, and we don't have our wagon."

"Wait here," Jana said. "I'll go get Mr. Sefarik, the castle carpenter. He has a truck."

"Not so fast! He's probably gone home by now," Max said. "You stay here with Otto, and I'll try to get a taxi. I'll be back as soon as I can." He left at a trot.

"We should put something on your wound to stop the bleeding," Jana said after Max left.

"How about that pink scarf you're wearing?" Otto said. "Of course, you'll probably never get the stains out."

"That's okay. I hate it," she said. They both laughed a little.

"Ouch, it hurts to laugh," he said.

"Here, let me help you get that jacket and shirt off," she said.

She helped him ease out of his jacket, then unbuttoned his shirt and slid it off his left shoulder, handling it gingerly to avoid getting blood on her hands. Her curly black hair cascaded forward as she removed her scarf and leaned in to get a closer look at the wound. She winced at the sight of the deep, jagged gash across the top of his shoulder.

"At least you don't have to worry about removing a bullet. It looks like it went through," she said. "Do you have a handkerchief I can use to stop the bleeding? Then I'll tie it on with this," she said, indicating her scarf.

He pulled one out of his pants pocket and handed it to her. She pressed it against his wound, lightly at first, and then with more pressure when he didn't wince.

"Here, hold it in place while I tie it on." She folded her scarf so it had several layers in the middle and tied it over the folded handkerchief.

He felt her breath on his cheek as she bent over her work. A gentle gust of wind blew strands of her hair against his face, and he brushed it aside with his right hand.

"Sorry," she said.

"That's okay," he said.

"It's not very secure, I'm afraid, but it should be okay until we get home if you sit still," she said as she pulled his shirt back in place and helped him rebutton it.

"Thanks. I won't move a muscle," he said. "Why were you in Wenceslas Square?"

She paused for a moment, and then said, "I knew that you and Max would be here, so I came after work. You said I should walk home because you were both going to be busy, but it's a long walk. So, I took a chance that I might find you. Besides, I wanted to see what was going on. Everyone was talking about it."

"I told you to stay away from danger," he said, turning toward her. He grimaced as the movement aggravated the pain.

"Hold still! You're just making it worse," she said.

"I don't care; listen to me," he said. "I don't want you to get hurt." His dark eyes blazed with passion.

Jana took a sharp breath in as she gazed into his eyes.

Max ran back into the park. "Come on, I have a taxi waiting for us. Here, throw my jacket over your shoulder to cover the blood," he said to Otto. He took Otto's jacket and folded it to hide the blood. "Here's a little something to take the edge off." He unscrewed a bottle of whiskey and handed it to Otto, who took a couple of stiff drinks and then handed it back.

"Thanks, that's just what I was hoping for."

Jana trailed along behind them, seeming to be deep in thought, as Max helped his brother to the taxi.

CHAPTER 32

Jan Opletal was dead! The news spread like wildfire. This friendly, well-liked student had been shot, and seriously wounded, on October 28. He had died in the hospital two weeks later.

You could feel the tension in the air. The city had been tense since the Independence Day protests. Once again, news of the protests had been downplayed by the Nazi-controlled media, but everyone knew what had happened—that protestors had been shot down in the street. Thousands had seen it firsthand. Others had heard about it or read about it in the handbills, which, though illegal, were printed and passed from person to person.

Otto did his part to make sure everyone knew about it, and every other scrap of news that his network could uncover. He sat in a haze of smoke, alternately taking a drag on a cigarette and pecking out words, sentences, and paragraphs with his good arm, oblivious to the bustle of activity as people came and went, and the relentless *thumpa-thumpa-thumpa* of the mimeograph machine as it turned his copy into stacks of newsletters.

These were loaded into the bags of the students who came and went, and distributed all over the city. He was proud of the fact that some of the news that he reported even made it out of the country, via short-wave radios that the Nazis had not yet located and shut down.

"Hi," a voice suddenly said.

Otto looked up in surprise. "Oh, hi, Albert. What are you doing here?" He hadn't seen Albert since the Independence Day protests.

"I want to talk to you. Can you take a break? Maybe we can go get something to eat?"

Otto took a closer look. He saw that behind the wire-rimmed glasses, Albert's gray eyes were a little bloodshot.

"Sure, give me a few minutes to finish this page," Otto said

"Okay, I'll meet you out front," Albert said.

When Otto came out to meet him a few minutes later, Albert was leaning against the side of the building, hands in his pockets, his shoulders hunched against the chill of the day. As they walked to a nearby coffee shop, Albert studied the sidewalk in silence.

"I haven't seen you lately. How have you been?" Otto asked.

"To tell the truth, I was avoiding you. I'm embarrassed by the way I acted during the protest. We should have stuck together," Albert said, blushing and avoiding eye contact.

"Don't worry about it. I was the one who took off," Otto said.

"Yeah, I know, but I could have gone with Max when he followed you. The thing is, I got scared." He looked at Otto with a small apologetic smile. "How's your arm, by the way?"

"It's fine, healing up," Otto said. He paused to think, and then said, "I get it. You were scared. We were all scared. But you've been through it already—being arrested by the Gestapo, I mean—so you have more reasons to be scared than the rest of us," Otto said.

"Yeah, okay." Albert shook his head and then shrugged.

Albert stayed silent until after they were in the coffee shop and started to eat. Then he said, "I've decided to go to England. My parents want me to go, and maybe I can do some good from there. I hear they're putting together Czech army units."

"When are you going?"

"At the end of the semester. My dad's working on getting the paperwork I need. He wants me to leave sooner, but I want to at least finish this semester. I only need one more year after this one. I just want to finish. Maybe after the war," Albert said. He fell silent again for a few minutes.

Suddenly he exclaimed, "It's not fair, this whole damn thing, it's not fair! Nazi bastards!" Then he laughed, drank his beer, and sat back. Looking more relaxed, he said, "Meanwhile, put me to work. I'll do whatever is needed. I want to help out as much as I can."

"No problem. When can you start?" Otto asked.

"Right away," Albert said.

"Great! I'm not the fastest typist in the world with this bum arm. We can use your help."

After lunch, they headed back to the student newspaper office, together.

To their surprise, the Student Senate had gotten permission for a funeral procession on November 15. They had to promise there wouldn't be any anti-German demonstrations and/or any other trouble. Otto had been a little nervous about publicizing the event. He suspected there was an ulterior motive for granting permission for it. If it caused further unrest, he was sure the Nazis would not hesitate to overreact. However, the death was so well known, it was impossible to downplay the funeral. He did all he could to warn his readers to stay calm and avoid further incidents. In addition, the Czech police had agreed to provide security for the funeral, rather than the German police, to avoid any unnecessary provocation.

The day of the funeral dawned gray and cold. Long before the Institute of Pathology building was open, a line of students started to form outside the building in the shrouded predawn light. Among the first to arrive, Otto, Max, and Albert leaned against the wall in front of the building, their shoulders hunched against the cold. They smoked cigarettes and nodded hello to friends and acquaintances as they arrived for the viewing.

When at last the doors were unlocked, Otto, Max, and Albert shuffled up the stairs and into the building. The coffin lay on a bier in the middle of the large rotunda, surrounded by candles and honor guards, who were volunteers from the Student Senate. The cold wind rushed through the open door and swirled around in the large open space; the flames of the tall candles flickered, as they walked past the coffin.

Otto looked down at Jan Opletal, hands folded across his chest, his blond hair neatly combed. He thought that he looked like he was sleeping and imagined that he might open his eyes and sit up at any moment and look around in amazement at the line of mourners. Otto wasn't sure if it was the cold breeze, or the sight of Jan in his coffin, that gave him the chill that ran down his spine as he walked slowly past the coffin on one side, around the top, and then past it again on the other side, before heading toward the door again.

"Come on, let's get something to eat," Otto said to Max and Albert when they were back outside. "It will be a while until we can start for the train station."

After they left, throughout the cold morning, lines of mourners shuffled in and out of the building, as thousands came to pay their respects. As the time of the funeral procession neared, an ever-increasing number of mourners arrived. When Otto, Max, and Albert returned, they were surprised to see a large number of mourners milling around in front of the Institute of Pathology.

Many of the faces were grim and pinched with cold, as the long, slow procession formed, and set off down Albertov St. Most of the mourners followed the coffin to the train station, where his body would be transported to his hometown for burial. But a small group broke away and gathered in Charles Square to sing the national anthem and other patriotic songs.

The Czech police, who were lining the route of the procession, quickly broke up this demonstration, and the crowd dispersed into smaller groups. Some of the mourners caught up with the funeral procession or went home. Others, chased by the police, escaped through Prague Technical University, onto Ressel St., and marched along the river embankment, tearing down German street signs and tram destination boards, throwing them into the river.

Eventually, a group of over one hundred students ran along the embankment to the Mendel Bridge and into the Law Faculty building of Charles University, where they barricaded themselves inside the building and refused to come out.

Otto, Max, and Albert were unaware of these disturbances. They were near the beginning of the procession and continued to the train station without incident. After a brief ceremony, the crowd dispersed, and they headed home. By this time, a light drizzle had started, driven by a cold north wind. They hurried along the cobblestone streets, hands buried deep in their pockets.

Suddenly a group of about a half-dozen ethnic Germans jumped out of an alleyway and began pummeling them with their fists, sticks, and rubber truncheons. A stinging blow connected with Otto's injured arm, and he started to black out; another blow from behind knocked him to the ground, and his assailants started kicking him. He tried to push himself up with his good arm, at the same time trying to keep his injured arm angled away from his attackers, but was knocked back down.

Suddenly, several Czech police ran toward the group, blowing their whistles and waving their truncheons, and their attackers fled. Otto got to his feet, and they listened and nodded as the police asked for their IDs and berated them for fighting in the street. They didn't try to explain that they'd been attacked. They all knew it was pointless. The police couldn't do anything against their attackers. They were just happy that they'd come along in time to save them from a worse beating.

"Let's get a drink," Otto suggested after they'd gone. His arm was throbbing, and he felt like he needed to find a place to sit down for a while. Max and Albert agreed, and they headed to a nearby tavern. Albert was squinting and holding a handkerchief to his nose; blood spatter covered the front of his coat. He'd taken off his glasses before the first blow had been struck. Max's coat had been torn open and was missing several buttons. He combed back his hair with his fingers.

After a couple of beers, their moods improved. "Too bad the police broke it up," Max said. "I was about to kick the crap out of the fat kid." They all laughed.

Albert's nose had stopped bleeding, and he was more cheerful than he'd been in a long time. "Did you see that tall kid? I stomped on his foot and then punched his face when he doubled over," he gloated.

A radio sitting on a shelf behind the bar was blaring out the latest news, and the announcer said something about Charles University. "Shh, shh!" Otto held up his hand. "I want to hear this."

"A group of student radicals has occupied the Law Faculty building!" the announcer said. "This illegal activity will be met with severe countermeasures, according to sources in the Protectorate government." They looked at each other with alarm.

Max and Albert looked at Otto. "What should we do?" Max asked.

"I'm going to go see if I can talk them out of there," Otto said.

"You won't be able to get near the building," Albert said. "They probably have the whole block cordoned off."

"Maybe." Otto nodded. "But I want to check it out. You guys should go home."

Max and Albert looked at each other. "Oh no, if you're going, we're going," Albert said. Max nodded in agreement. They were heading toward the university when the sound of gunfire stopped them short.

"What was that?" Max asked.

"Sounds like gunfire," Otto said, just before another volley of shots echoed through the streets. They stood for a few moments, unsure of what to do.

"I don't think we should go any further," Albert said.

"I agree," Otto said. "We should head home. Stay on the lookout for German police or the SS." Otto and Max nodded goodbye to Albert and headed home.

"Wait here for a minute," Otto said and ran back to talk to Albert, and then back to Max.

"What was that all about?" Max asked. There was another burst of gunfire.

"I told him I thought he shouldn't wait but should try to get out of the country as soon as possible. His dad has been trying to convince him to go, but Albert said he wants to finish the semester. I don't think anyone will be finishing the semester now."

CHAPTER 33

The night after Jan Opletal's funeral, Max and Albert sat in the living room, listening to the radio with other members of the family. Otto's injured arm was starting to throb, and he took a quick swallow of brandy to ease the pain, and then a drag on his cigarette. He looked up and caught Jana watching him with an expression of concern, but when he noticed her, she quickly averted her gaze.

The radio announcer excitedly delivered the news in bad Czech, with a heavy German accent. "Armed student radicals held the university's Law Faculty building for several hours until SS guard battalions arrived in full battle gear and cleared the building. In the resulting gunfight, three students were injured. This radical action will not be ignored by the Protectorate government."

I've heard enough, Otto thought. He slipped out the back door and walked across the courtyard to the barn. He started a fire in the stove, threw in a few larger logs, and then pulled a chair up to the stove. He sat staring into the flames, visible through the grate in the stove's door, smoked a cigarette, and reflected on the events of the past few days.

Not too much time later, Otto cursed and moved his injured arm, trying to find a comfortable position.

"Can I help you with that?" a voice asked. Otto whipped around to see Jana walking toward him.

"What? No! What are you doing here?" he asked. He sounded

angry, but he could see on her face she knew it was because he was in pain, and didn't retreat.

"I just slipped in. Can I help you with your arm? I can get some water and new bandages and rebandage it."

After a moment's hesitation, he said, "Okay, go ahead, and bring me some brandy, too."

A few minutes later she returned, alone, clearly having managed to get everything she needed without being noticed.

"Here's the brandy." She handed him the small bottle. He unscrewed the cap and took a stiff drink. Then he unbuttoned his shirt and pulled it back from his left shoulder.

Jana carefully removed the old bandage, flinching a bit at the sight of the inflamed wound. "I don't know if this will help," she said as she worked. "You might have to go to a doctor. It looks like it might be infected." She gently washed the wound and started to rewrap it with fresh bandages.

"I'll be fine. There's no way I can go to a doctor with a bullet wound, now," he said.

"Okay, well if it doesn't start to get better, my stepmother might be able to help. She knows a lot about herbs, and maybe some of them can be used to clear up infections. I wish that I'd paid more attention when she explained it to me."

Otto took another drink and leaned back in his chair. The strong drink and Jana's gentle touch relaxed him. He smiled to see her face fixed in concentration, unruly wisps of hair escaping from her scarf and framing her face. Suddenly, he was overcome with a wave of emotion. "Oh, Jana, if only things were different," he said.

She looked up, clearly surprised by the sudden change in his voice; their eyes locked for a moment, and her face reddened. He wondered if she was aware that her right hand still held the unfinished bandage against his left shoulder. She tore her eyes away from his and finished wrapping his injured shoulder. She worked as if she could feel his eyes on her, and he could see her hands trembling as she tore the end of the bandage and tied it as securely as she could.

"There, all done," she said, trying to sound casual, but her voice wavered. Otto stared at her with a strange intensity. She started gathering her supplies, refusing to meet his gaze. "Jana, come here," he said, his voice gentle.

"I better not stay," she said, not moving.

"Just for a few minutes," he said.

She walked over to him, still avoiding his eyes. "What is it?"

He reached out and pulled her to him. The basin and the bandaging supplies that she was holding clattered to the floor, spilling soapy water across the floorboards. He felt her heart beating against his chest as he kissed her. Her lips were firm, yet soft. He gave her a deep, slow kiss. He knew she'd never been kissed like that before, and he wondered if she felt the same electric jolt of pleasure flow through her body that he did. She gasped and pulled away."

"What do you mean by that?" she said.

"Mean? I didn't mean anything," he said.

"That's what I thought!" she said.

"Why are you angry?" he asked.

"You're always saying, 'What if things were different.' Well, they're not. Things are what they are. I think that's just an excuse," she said.

"An excuse? An excuse for what?" he asked.

"Don't be stupid! You know what I mean. Our parents want us to get married, but you always have a reason to say 'not now,'" she said.

Otto smiled at her. He thought that her angry little face was the most beautiful one he'd ever seen. "I thought you weren't interested in getting married."

"Well, I'm not . . . I mean, I wasn't . . . Not if you aren't," she stammered.

He laughed, and she blushed. He held out his hand. She hesitated a moment, and then took a step toward him and took his hand.

"I'm ready," he said. "It's not the right time, but we can make it work. Shall I talk to your dad?"

Jana nodded.

Suddenly, Max walked in. "Oh, there you are," he said to Otto. He looked from Otto to Jana and back again, unasked questions in his gaze. Jana dropped Otto's hand and stepped back from him.

"Jana was just bandaging my shoulder," Otto said. "Thanks, Jana. You'd better get back to the house now. They'll be looking for you."

She gathered up her dropped supplies and left.

After the funeral, Albert hurried back to his apartment. He turned on the radio and listened to the news while he grabbed his suitcase and threw clothes into it. There wasn't an announcement of a curfew being imposed, yet.

The gunfire coming from the direction of the university had terrified him, and he was still scared. He felt slightly sick to his stomach and had to wipe sweat from his brow, even though he felt cold.

After his bag was packed, he sat down at the table, lit a cigarette, and took a drag, hoping it would calm him. It seemed quiet in the hallway; he opened the door, looked both ways, and then walked down to the pay phone hanging on the wall at the end of the hall.

He'd decided to phone his dad to see if the paperwork was in order so he could leave the country. Every nerve taut, he listened for footsteps, inserted the coins into the phone with trembling fingers, and then dialed the number. The conversation was brief. His dad kept his voice low and his answers short. Albert knew that was because his mom was listening. “There’s a problem,” his dad said. “I’ll do everything I can. Call again tomorrow.”

He went back to his apartment and noticed the radio on the table. That was another bonehead move, leaving it out in plain sight. *If I’m caught with an illegal radio, that will be the end for me*, he thought. He grabbed it, unplugged it, and threw it into a paper bag. *But what can I do with it? If I just throw it in the incinerator, it could still be found, and then suspicion would be cast on everyone in the building.*

He threw on a jacket, grabbed the bag, and ran down to the street. He looked around, trying to figure out where to dump it in a hurry. He couldn’t just leave it in an alley, or in front of an apartment building—that would just shift the suspicion to other people. He thought of the tram tracks. If he left it by the tracks, there would be no connection to anyone. He ran down to the nearest track and dumped his package.

Albert got little sleep that night and spent the next day pacing, and smoking. As it was getting close to the time for him to call his dad again, he was startled by the sound of footsteps in the hall, followed by a knock on his door. His knees shook as he walked to the door and cautiously opened it. It was Otto.

“Boy, am I glad to see you!” he said. He opened the door wide and waved him in.

Jana had a hard time falling asleep after her conversation with Otto, but she was wide awake early the next morning. She hummed to herself as she got ready for work. She had hoped she would see Otto before she left, but, as usual, only Aunt Marie and Max were up.

“Was Otto still sleeping, or had he gone out already?” she wondered as she rode beside Max on her way to work. Finally, her curiosity got the better of her, and she asked, trying to sound casual, “Have you talked to Otto this morning?”

"Not since last night. Why?" Max said.

"I just wondered. I didn't see him this morning," she said.

Max studied her, and then asked, "What were you two talking about last night?"

"Didn't Otto tell you?" she asked.

"No. Tell me what?" he asked.

"Never mind," she said.

They sat together, quietly, for a few minutes, listening to the *clip-clop* of the horse's hoofs. Jana wondered if she should say anything about their marriage plans, or wait for Otto to say something first. For all she knew, he might have changed his mind.

Max sat quietly for a while, semingly lost in thought, and then said, "He went out last night—just after I saw the two of you together. He said he was going to see Albert."

As they approached the castle, they saw extra German guards at every entrance, and there was a new guard at the service entrance, where they normally entered. He motioned for them to stop. Max jumped down from the cart after handing the reins to Jana and went to talk to him. Max pulled out his ID. The guard checked it, looked at a list, and then shook his head no. Max turned around and walked back to the cart.

"What's going on?" she asked.

"They won't let us in. He said that only authorized personnel are allowed in, just those who are on his list, and we're not on it."

"What about my job?" she asked.

"It looks like you no longer have a job," he said. He turned the horses around, and they headed back home.

They waited until after dark—it was a moonless night—and then Jana's father, Josef, finished packing up his family's caravans, padded the horse's hooves, and oiled the wheel axles so they could move as quietly as possible. He and his brothers had carefully planned a route out of town, following back roads and walking paths along the river, where they were unlikely to be seen.

They had been talking about leaving for some time since they had been warned that it would soon be against the law for Gypsies to travel. They'd managed to purchase a few horses from farmers willing to sell illegally, for an exorbitant price. After hearing what had happened at the castle that morning, they decided that it was time to leave. They would try to make it into Slovakia, where they would spend the rest of the winter.

Jana hung back until everyone else was in the wagons and ready to go. She hoped that Otto would come home so she could say goodbye. Finally, she had to go, and hugged Aunt Marie one last time, trying not to cry.

"Thank you so much for everything," she said.

"You're very welcome, child." Marie gave her a big hug. "I'm sure we will see you again soon. Here, take this," she said, giving Jana a small envelope. "Don't look at it now—just put it in your pocket. You'd better go now. Your father is waiting."

Jana slipped the envelope into her pocket, gave Marie one last hug, went outside, and clambered up into the caravan.

"It's about time. Where have you been?" said her sister, Lili.

As their caravans slipped through the dark, Jana lay awake thinking about everything that had happened during the past year, until the familiar, gentle swaying of the wagon and the clinking of the horse harnesses lulled her to sleep.

The next morning, they stopped in a small clearing to water and feed the horses and have a cold breakfast. For safety's sake, no fires were built. As soon as Jana had a chance, she wandered a few yards down a wooded path and stood next to a frozen stream. The wind rushed through the pine trees, causing them to sway and bow, and sending a shiver through her. The sharp odor of pine filled her nostrils as she pulled the envelope that Marie had given her out of her pocket and opened it. Inside she found a photograph of Otto. He was younger, just a gangly teenager, standing in his backyard and squinting into the sun. She held the photo to her breast and let the tears flow that she'd been holding inside since learning that they were leaving Prague.

The cold wind blew through Albert's thin shirt, which was damp from perspiration. After a sleepless night, he was almost numb to the shouting as he was kicked and prodded into a straight line along with the other students who had been dragged from their dormitories and homes last night.

After being arrested, they had been herded onto city buses and taken first to Gestapo headquarters and then to the military barracks in Ruzyne, on the outskirts of Prague. This morning they had been awakened before dawn with more shouts and kicks, and now stood on the parade grounds. Every muscle in his body ached, and he shivered in the gray light of dawn.

After he had taken his place, he noticed a line of nine people standing a short distance away, facing them. With a shock, he recognized the students. They were the Student Union officers! Only a few weeks ago, he'd heard one of them speaking about how there should be Czech-German understanding. *Why are they here?* he wondered.

He looked around for Otto. They'd been arrested together, last night, but they'd been separated when they got to Gestapo headquarters, and he hadn't seen him since.

"Eyes forward"—a shout in German, and a sharp blow from a rifle butt to the side of his head stunned him. He could taste blood in his mouth. His tongue tested a loose tooth.

A line of riflemen took up positions in front of the larger group of students, facing the nine of them. A German SS officer stood to the left side of the riflemen and read a statement accusing the Student Union officers of being ringleaders in recent disturbances, and saying that they were going to be shot as an example for the others, showing what would happen to them if they failed to cooperate.

He talked on, but Albert stopped listening. His head was ringing from the blow of the rifle butt. He stared at the young men in front of him—some were softly crying, others stared stoically ahead. Suddenly there was a volley of gunfire, and the nine young men crumpled to the ground.

As the rest of the students were herded back into their dormitories, Albert realized that the fear that had been his constant companion over the past several months, ever since his first arrest, was gone. In its place was a wave of cold anger, and a determination to do whatever he could to avenge the murders he had just witnessed, or to die trying.

Later the students were lined up and interviewed, to determine if they were under age twenty, foreign, or if there was any other reason that they should be released. When it was Otto's turn, they determined that he was not a student and, after checking his name against the names of registered students, he was given a pass that would allow him to leave.

"What about my friend—Albert Bretfeld? Is he going to be released?" Otto asked.

The SS man who had questioned him stared at him for a moment, incredulous that he dared to ask a question, and then shouted,

"Perhaps you would prefer to go to the concentration camp with your friend?" Then he turned, without waiting for an answer, and shouted, "Next!"

After his release, Otto headed to Albert's parents' house, making sure he wasn't followed, to inform his father, Karel, what had happened.

After listening to the whole story, Karel asked, "Where is Albert now?"

"We were held at the military barracks in Ruzyne, but they might have already moved him. I heard that they were going to be taken to a concentration camp near Berlin," Otto said, then after a pause continued, "I'm sorry that I left Albert behind."

"No, you did the right thing," Karel said. "At least now I know what happened to him. Don't worry, I'll work with my contacts and see if I can get him released."

After that, Otto went home. It was after dark when he arrived. Rather than going directly into the house, he went to the barn to find Max and told him everything that had happened, but asked him to keep it to himself because he didn't want their parents to worry. Max told him that Jana and her family had left.

"What? When did this happen?" Otto asked.

"Just last night. Her father decided it was safer for them to try to make it through the winter in their caravans in the mountains of Slovakia. She left a letter for you," Max said. He dug in his pocket and handed him a small white envelope; then he left, to give Otto privacy while he read the letter.

Otto sat down heavily on a wooden chair and stared at the envelope with his name printed on it. Suddenly he felt very tired. He stared into the fire in the stove for a moment before he carefully opened the envelope, removed the folded lined paper that was inside, and smoothed it out against his leg. It was also carefully printed, with several erasures where Jana had corrected her spelling. It said:

Dear Otto,

By the time you read this letter, we will be gone. My father decided it will be safer for us if we leave Prague, for the time being. I would rather stay with you and your family, but I know my stepmother can't get along without me with two little ones to watch. Without my help, my dad and the other kids would suffer. Soon my sister, Lili, will be old enough to help, and the baby will not need constant care, but for now, my family needs me.

I know that you are also needed by your family, your friends, and your country. I won't say my country, not yet, but I know how important it is to you. For me, home is with the people I love, and when you read this, my heart and my home will be in two places. I hope that soon we can be together again.

Love always, Jana

Otto read the letter twice and then, with tears in his eyes, he carefully refolded the letter, placed it back into the envelope, and put the envelope in the inside pocket of his jacket, close to his heart.

HISTORICAL NOTES

Caravans in the Dark is a work of fiction set in WWII Czechoslovakia. A great deal of information is available on WWII, but there are gaps. One of the gaps, which is only slowly beginning to fill in, is the victimization of the Roma people. Here is a brief summary of how the war started and its effect on the Roma.

World War II is often cited as beginning in September of 1939 when Germany invaded Poland. However, it began a year earlier than that for the people of Czechoslovakia. In a desperate attempt to prevent a Second World War, the Munich Agreement was signed in September of 1938, by Germany, Italy, France, and Great Britain. This agreement awarded large swaths of the border area of Czechoslovakia to Germany, effectively rendering the country defenseless. This was, of course, Hitler's aim. In March of 1939, he marched in and occupied the rest of what is now the Czech Republic, which Germany renamed the Protectorate of Bohemia and Moravia. Meanwhile, Slovakia broke away and became a Nazi puppet state.

One of the aims of the fascist state was to remake Czechoslovakia into a German land. Long-term goals included driving out, killing, or enslaving the Czech people. First steps in this plan included preventing Czechs from attaining an education by closing all Czech colleges and universities, and eliminating people they considered undesirable, including the Jewish and Roma people.

While the Jewish holocaust is well documented, the holocaust of the Roma is not. Almost nine out of ten Czech Romani people perished during the occupation, according to *The Historical Dictionary of the Gypsies (Romanies)*, pp. 43–44. In the section about Czechoslovakia, Kenrick says, "A count of Gypsies on August 2, 1942, registered 5,830. . . . Only some 600 . . . survived the Nazi occupation of the Czech lands."

If you are interested in learning more, here are a few books that will get you started.

Fonseca, Isabel. *Bury Me Standing: The Gypsies and Their Journey.* New York: Random House, 1995.

Kenrick, Donald. *Historical Dictionary of the Gypsies (Romanies).* Lanham, MD: The Scarecrow Press, Inc., 1998.

Kenrick, Donald, and Grattan Puxon. *Gypsies Under the Swastika.* Hertfordshire, UK: University of Hertfordshire Press, 1995.

Lewy, Guenter. *Nazi Persecution of the Gypsies.* Oxford: Oxford University Press, 2000.

Luza, Radomir, and Christina Vella. *The Hitler Kiss: A Memoir of the Czech Resistance.* Baton Rouge: Louisiana State University Press, 2002.

Mastny, Vojtech. *The Czechs Under Nazi Rule: The Failure of National Resistance, 1939–1942.* New York: Columbia University Press, 1971.

Novacek, Charles. *Border Crossings: A Memoir.* Detroit: Ten21 Press, 2012.

Unfortunately, discrimination against the Roma is far from a thing of the past. My thanks to Dr. Habiba Hadziavdic for pointing me to the work of Markus End, one of the leading voices against

Roma oppression and continued discrimination in Europe. Go to metropolitanstudies.academia.edu/MarkusEnd for his recent publications and other research in the field.

ACKNOWLEDGMENTS

I would like to thank several people who contributed to the development of this novel. Peter Gelfan, author and book editor, helped me with editing and story development. Dr. Habiba Hadziavdic, PhD, with an expertise in Romani Studies, provided valuable insights. Peter Geye is an author, editor, and teacher. Taking his yearlong Novel-Writing Project class, at the Loft Literary Center, increased my confidence as a writer. He also helped with some edits and suggested improvements to this work.

I would also like to thank the staff of She Writes Press for cover design, final edits, and everything else that goes into the publication of a novel.

I especially want to thank my first reader and husband, Randy Oldre. His enthusiastic requests for the next chapters kept me busily writing, and his positive feedback encouraged me to forge on.

ABOUT THE AUTHOR

photo credit: Lisa Buck

B. K. Oldre is a former librarian with a BA in English literature and an MLIS degree. She studied writing at the University of Minnesota and The Loft Literary Center, where she completed the year-long class The Novel Writing Project, taught by best-selling author Peter Geye. She writes short stories, historical fiction, and historical mysteries. She and her husband live in Minneapolis, Minnesota.

SELECTED TITLES FROM SHE WRITES PRESS

She Writes Press is an independent publishing company founded to serve women writers everywhere. Visit us at www.shewritespress.com.

A Ritchie Boy by Linda Kass. $16.95, 978-1-63152-739-5
The true, inspiring World War II tale of Eli Stoff, a Jewish Austrian immigrant who triumphs over adversity and becomes a US Army intelligence officer, told as a cohesive linked collection of stories narrated by a variety of characters.

All the Light There Was by Nancy Kricorian. $16.95, 978-1-63152-905-4
A lyrical, finely wrought tale of loyalty, love, and the many faces of resistance, told from the perspective of an Armenian girl living in Paris during the Nazi occupation of the 1940s.

An Address in Amsterdam by Mary Dingee Fillmore
$16.95, 978-1-63152-133-1
After facing relentless danger and escalating raids for 18 months, Rachel Klein—a well-behaved young Jewish woman who transformed herself into a courier for the underground when the Nazis invaded her country—persuades her parents to hide with her in a dank basement, where much is revealed.

Expect Deception by JoAnn Ainsworth. $16.95, 978-1-63152-060-0
When the US government recruits Livvy Delacourt and a team of fellow psychics to find Nazi spies on the East Coast during WWII, she must sharpen her skills quickly—or risk dying.

Portrait of a Woman in White by Susan Winkler. $16.95, 978-1-93831-483-4
When the Nazis steal a Matisse portrait from the eccentric, art-loving Rosenswigs, the Parisian family is thrust into the tumult of war and separation, their fates intertwined with that of their beloved portrait.

The Sweetness by Sande Boritz Berger. $16.95, 978-1-63152-907-8
A compelling and powerful story of two girls—cousins living on separate continents—whose strikingly different lives are forever changed when the Nazis invade Vilna, Lithuania.